VAMP AWAKENED

SILVER DAGGER SISTERHOOD

KB ANNE

Published by Gripping Tales, LLC, Pennsylvania.

Cover Design by Anika Willmans, Ravenborn Covers

Editorial Services by Laura Parnum, Laura Parnum Books

SUMMARY OF VAMP REVEALED

In case you forgot, a little refresher.

AT THE END of August in the early morning, Cynda was a mortal on her way to attend West University for microbiology. Her boyfriend dumped her the night before, and her parents were more than happy to shove her out the door and return to their regularly scheduled lives.

Perfectly ordinary. Perfectly mundane.

Until a gorgeous woman with black hair and purple eyes showed up, claiming to be her sister. The introduction included a flash of fangs and Cynda blacking out. When she came to, she found herself in the passenger seat of her Prius with the maniac woman named Dez at the wheel. Before she could plan her escape, a mysterious car smashed into them, sending the Prius and the two sisters careening off a cliff and straight into a tree.

Thus began Cynda's new life as a Sempiternal, a pure

blood vampire, aka the Elvis Presleys of the supernatural world.

After surviving the Vampire Change at Silverwood Prison and her initiation into Silverwood Academy, Cyn begins her supernatural life with her overbearing and slutty sister, Dez, as her roommate. Her class schedule includes Demonology, Magickal Creature Riding Lessons, Elemental History, Yoga & Meditation, and Weapons Training, which, not going to lie, is as terrifying as it sounds, but as long as Cyn follows the three rules of Silverwood Academy she should live to see another day.

Well, until she meets sunshiny and gorgeous Canyon in a dark hallway. The call of bloodlust overpowers her senses, and she bites him without his permission. The ability to compel others is a beautiful thing. If only she could compel her sister away. Someday she plans to test the third rule of Silverwood Academy. Consequences be damned.

Dez Wickershim grew up as a supernatural hunter's daughter. She knew exactly what her future life entailed: going through the Change, attending Silverwood Academy, then joining Silver Dagger Sisterhood, but she didn't know what happened to her baby sister, and she was determined to find her. While in Silverwood Prison, a tip on her long-lost sister's whereabouts sends her racing to Kentucky to find little sis before the Children of the Sun do.

She thought that after forcing the Change on Cynda, the two of them would get along brilliantly. Oh, how wrong she was. Little Sis needs a full-time babysitter to keep her out of trouble.

When Dez isn't in class or keeping an eye on Cynda, she prowls the halls of Silverwood Academy, seeking schmexual satisfaction but she always falls short until she meets her hot yoga professor. She prefers one-night stands, but with Jace, she'd make an exception. When he rebukes her advances, it only makes her want him more. And what Dez wants, Dez gets.

Attending classes, mastering the Elements, and training for the Sisterhood should be all Dez and Cyn need to worry about. But forces outside of the goddesses and gods' realm of power threaten the very existence of the supernatural world. It's impossible to tell who's on their side and who wants to kill them, but trusting the goddesses and learning to command the elements is exactly what they need to do if they want to make it out of Silverwood Academy alive.

Time to take a bite out of Vamp Awakened.

SILVERWOOD ACADEMY RULES

Silverwood Academy has three rules:

Don't use magick on someone without their permission.

Don't bite anyone's neck, for nourishment or otherwise, without their expressed verbal consent.

Don't stab another classmate in the back. (Even if it's your own sister.)

CHAPTER
ONE

yn

Life had become easier as a vampire. Walking. Seeing. Eating. Even showering. I still hadn't completely embraced my life as a Sempiternal, but it made certain aspects of it easier. A lot easier. The sting of a lifetime of disregard from my adoptive parents no longer informed my life choices. I was no longer worried that my every action would lead to disappointment. Of course, I still worried about a lot of other things. Becoming a Sempiternal didn't eliminate my anxiety, but now I acknowledged it and didn't let it rule me. Well, mostly. At least I had a sister who cared about me and a mother who, as difficult as it was to come to terms with, refused to let me out of her sight.

"Caw, caw!"

"Caw, caw!"

"Caw, caw!"

Or out of the sight of her three ravens. Or one of her sisters, since my birth mother and her sisters were actual goddesses. Together they had created Silverwood Academy, a school for recently turned supernaturals who demonstrated the aptitude to perhaps one day join Silver Dagger Sisterhood or Silver Cloak Brotherhood. If they could make it through the Academy alive, that is, which some days was much harder than others.

A sharp jab to my gut drew me out of my head.

Today was one of those days.

"Pay attention," my sparring partner, a wolf shifter named Peeta, growled.

"You'll pay for that."

"Promises, promises. It's not my fault when you drift into another world without fear of repercussions."

"I'm Air." I pointed to the air symbol on my tank top. "Lilith is my goddess. What did you expect?"

He shook his head. "Just because your element is Air doesn't mean you have to spend all your time in it. Another partner wouldn't have given you a gentle warning shot."

I rubbed my ribs, which were already knitting back together. "You call that gentle?"

He twirled his wooden sword like a baton. "I could have knocked you on your ass. An enemy rogue would kill you dead."

Sometimes people just didn't know when to shut up. I rolled back my shoulders and sank into a crouch, narrowing my eyes at him. I shut out the beauty of the Wildwood Preserves grove where Bladecroft liked to train her class. I ignored the gorgeous blue sky that begged me to stare at it. I closed off my senses until all I saw and smelled was him.

"Now you've done it." I kicked my legs into his gut.

He flew across the grove, hitting an oak tree before crumpling to the forest floor.

He pushed up on his elbows and shook his head. "Where did that come from?"

I shrugged my shoulders. "I've got a few tricks up my sleeve."

The private training sessions my sister and I had with Professor Lara Bladecroft, renowned assassin of Silver Dagger Sisterhood and our Weapons Training instructor, had paid off. Dez served as a much more worthy opponent than most of my classmates, though I'd never admit that to her. Her head was big enough.

Peeta smiled at me, his eyes brightening to a lovely shade of gold—the sign of his wolf, as well as his potential future status as alpha. "Evidently. Please forgive the oversight. Want to grab a bite to eat after class?"

A knot formed in my stomach. The person I really wanted to grab a bite with—and not just from his neck—Canyon Goldwell, was the one person I was supposed to stay away from. I could immediately feel my resolve weakening at the mere thought of him and the way he made me feel: cherished, loved, adored . . .

"Is that smile a yes?" Peeta asked, eagerly appearing in front of me.

Crap. Slipped off into my head again.

Do it. Do it, I imagined Dez chanting in my ear. She wanted me to date other people. Might as well start with a gorgeous, muscular wolf shifter. The sacrifices we must make.

"Okay."

His face lit up. "Okay, I'll pick you up at your room."

"I thought we were grabbing a bite to eat after class."

"We are. Figured you'd want to shower after I kick your ass," he said, crouching into a fighting position.

"I believe I was the one who just kicked your ass across the courtyard."

"Is that so?" a voice behind me said. Professor Bladecroft stepped up beside me.

Crap. I was supposed to hide my abilities, and here I was showing off.

Goddess, Dez really was a bad influence. She was the show-off. I was always the student who had no problem letting my friends be at the top. My ex always took the top. He'd get what he wanted and leave me, feeling soiled and unsatisfied, wondering what all the fuss about sex was about. Based on Dez's graphic descriptions, I was missing a lot.

Peeta rushed to my aid. "I had it coming to me. I took a cheap shot when she wasn't paying attention."

Professor Bladecroft tilted her head as she studied me with those piercing silvery-blue eyes of hers. I swallowed the saliva pooling in my mouth, anticipating what was coming next. As a tactile telepathic, she could lay a single finger on me and speak to me in my head, as well as read my mind. In the beginning she had discussed things with me she didn't want my classmates or anyone else to overhear. These last few days, as my abilities broke free of their constraints, she had often used her gift to remind me to hide my blossoming skills and growing strength from my classmates.

"Is that right?" she pressed further, trying to unnerve me—her attempt at getting to the truth.

But Peeta had set up the lie so neatly, all I had to do was agree with it. I nodded, worried my voice would betray me.

"Peeta, in class, be mindful of your sparring partners. Especially those with their heads in the clouds."

He bowed. "Yes, ma'am. My apologies, Cynda."

Students around us began breaking off from their partners, grabbing their belongings, and heading toward the portal to take us back inside. I backed away from Professor Bladecroft and Peeta, wanting to let the two of them engage in conversation and leave me out of it for once.

Bladecroft's hand shot out like a viper strike and wrapped around my wrist. "Not so fast. Peeta, would you mind if I shared a few words with Cynda before she leaves?"

"Nope. Not at all." He spun on his heel and hurried away, then, remembering he'd asked me out, he turned around. "Cynda, I'll see you in your room in a half hour."

No, you won't. You and I have plans. Make an excuse.

"Sorry, Peeta, I just remembered I told Dez we'd study this afternoon."

You are a terrible liar.

I really was. My sister, on the other hand, delivered lies like a fine wine—brilliant and smooth without a bitter aftertaste.

Peeta's face fell. "Oh, okay. Maybe some other time?" he asked hopefully.

"Maybe."

"See you later, Cynda. Bye, Professor Bladecroft."

"Bye," we said together.

He smiled as he turned back around and disappeared into the portal.

When he was gone, Bladecroft tugged me along with her. "Now, let's have that chat."

"Can't wait." Since turning into a Sempiternal, my sarcastic nature had blossomed. Hanging around with Dez,

Alyze, and Red hadn't helped either. Brilliant and beautiful, the three of them delivered witty retorts as easily as a sword thrust.

"You might not like what I have to say, but your sister will love it."

I swallowed hard. If Dez would like it, weapons, blood, or sex were involved. And if it combined all three, even better.

TWO

ez

A MISSION. My first one since arriving at Silverwood Academy. Of course, I had spent my teen years tagging along with Dad on many of his. He'd discovered quickly that I tended to get into less trouble fighting rogue supes than if I stayed home. Throw one rager with Satan's daughter and labels like "bad influence" and "juvenile delinquent" get tossed around by the Devil himself. (He wasn't the wild child everyone assumed him to be, and apparently he didn't want his daughter filling that role either.)

Sigh.

But tonight, Cyn and I would take our next step toward one day carrying on the family business—hunting monsters and kissing things. (Well, I added that last part. My dad didn't kiss and tell, although he had slept with a goddess, so who really knows.) I glanced over at my sister in the seat next to me in the giant SUV. The manner in which she was clutching that staff like her life depended on it gave me pause. Staffs were useful tools for a hunter who regularly trained with them, especially if one wanted to disable rather than kill. (I opted for killing, myself.) Bladecroft had made us spar with them during several of our training sessions, so Cyn should at least have a clue how to use it. And the fact that Bladecroft had equipped her with one suggested our mission target was an easy mark. But in case that wasn't the case, or the mission took a horrible turn, the silver daggers in the sheaths tied to her back and her belt of wooden and silver stakes would keep her safe. Along with me stabbing anyone who came within range of her.

Cyn looked at me, her forehead pinching. "What are you smiling about?"

I tapped her knee. She'd adopted the black leather pants as part of her uniform after trying on a pair of mine. "The question is, why aren't you?"

Bladecroft laughed from the front passenger seat. "See, Cynda. I told you Dez would love it."

Cyn rolled her green eyes at me. "That you did. My sister thrives on adrenaline."

I straightened, acting as if I was taken aback by her comment, which I kinda was since the sister part was still growing on me—but mostly because I enjoyed messing with said sister. "Sister, you don't even know me well enough to make the judgement."

She raised her eyebrow, calling my bluff. "Well, aren't you?"

I slapped her knee hard, causing her to jump. "Yes, I am. You'll see what a rush it is staking a misdirected vampire or decapitating a siren or stabbing a mermaid with her own trident."

"You don't even know what the mission is," she muttered.

"I don't need to. If Professor Bladecroft wants us to come, I'm in. She's the kick-assiest of the kick-assiest."

"I appreciate the endorsement, Dez, but most of the missions I've been on I didn't complete alone. A team helped me. My teammates deserve as much of the praise as I do."

Professor Lippincott glanced at us in the rearview mirror. "Don't listen to her. I've been her teammate longer than you two have been alive, and she deserves *all* the glory."

Bladecroft nailed Lippincott's shoulder with a tight fist. "Quit dodging credit. If it wasn't for your driving skills and . . . ," she turned and winked at us, "your ability to command and control any beast that can be ridden, I would have died a thousand deaths."

"That guardian angel hardly counts," Lippincott said, catching on to Bladecroft's slick innuendo, which was further proof they worked together a lot.

But it was what Lippincott had said that truly fascinated me. I leaned forward. "You've had a guardian angel? I didn't think they did that."

Lippincott threw back her head and barked before replying, "Oh, they do that. Several times, actually."

Cyn gasped in shock and tried to cover it with a fake coughing fit.

I settled back into my seat. "I probably should have tried harder with Scrumptious at Silverwood Prison."

Cyn snorted, ready to jump into the conversation now that I'd made it personal. "You tried hard all right, but nothing you did made him hard. He turned you down every single time."

I groaned, gripping my boobs at the memory of pressing them between the bars of our cell at Silverwood Prison. Scrumptious hadn't acknowledged them or me. "Don't remind me."

Bladecroft punched Lippincott's arm again. "That's because he's in love with this one."

Lippincott massaged her abused arm with her left hand.

Cyn's fingers twitched on her staff. "Shouldn't you have at least one hand on the wheel, just in case a deer or something jumps out at us?"

"That's what my knee is for."

Cyn took a sharp intake of breath. "Your knee?"

Lippincott turned her head to look at my sister. "I am very talented at riding things," she said with a straight face before she and Bladecroft dissolved into cackles.

I freaking loved my professors and future Silver Dagger Sisters.

I glanced over at Cynda. Her face was pale. "You okay over there?"

She blinked a few times before looking over at me. "Yeah, yeah, I'm fine."

But I could tell what she was really thinking. The professors she would have had if she had gone to a regular college were nothing like the firecrackers in the front seat. Full of piss and vinegar—just the way I liked them. Cyn needed to learn to embrace this aspect of a warrior woman's nature, or she wouldn't make it through Silverwood Academy.

"To become one of the F.A.T.A.L., you've got to have a sense of humor."

Bladecroft punched my thigh. "You got that right, Dez."

"Yes, you do," Lippincott added as I rubbed my bruised muscle. Bladecroft really packed a punch. Holy Mother of Goddesses. Cyn had better reevaluate my acts of violence. Mine were child's play compared to Bladecroft's.

Cyn swallowed several times, probably trying to decide how to proceed with the conversation. She eventually just stared out the window instead.

I glanced out the window too and realized the scenery had changed significantly. We were no longer in the quaint, lush forests of Northeast Pennsylvania but dashing across the barren highways of the high desert.

"When did we drive through the portal? I didn't even notice."

"When you were busy gushing about the mission," Lippincott replied. "You clearly forgot the lesson I emphasize in every class. Always be aware of your surroundings."

But rather than feel the sting of the scolding, I took it in stride. You didn't get into the Sisterhood by being passive and cowardly or hiding from the truth. "Sorta forgot in my excitement. Guess I was a tad starstruck going on a mission with the two of you. What is the mission anyway?"

Bladecroft and Lippincott glanced at each other out of the corners of their eyes, an exchange I didn't miss. Especially after getting reprimanded for not always being aware of my surroundings.

"Dish."

Bladecroft turned around to study us. "First rule: What happens on this mission stays between the four of us."

"Of course," I quickly answered.

Bladecroft pinned my sister in place with her stare when she failed to answer. "Do we understand each other?

We tell no one." The stern warning in her voice left no doubt that she would not divulge any further information until this point was settled.

Cyn slowly nodded. "Yes. What happens on the mission stays between us."

"Good. Second: Nothing is mentioned to any of the goddesses about the mission."

This struck me as an odd request, but it kinda already went along with her first point.

"What happens on the mission stays with us," I replied like the obedient woman I was. Well, one who was determined to go on a mission no matter what the cost.

Cyn templed her fingers together. "We can't tell any of the goddesses? Not even Lilith?"

"Especially not Lilith," Lippincott said.

The hair rose on the back of my neck. Lilith meant everything to Cyn and me. Lilith had chosen us to join her. I traced the Air pattern on my palm. "Won't she know? Won't they all know? They're goddesses."

Bladecroft's lips pressed into a tight line. Her nostrils flared as she breathed in and out. "They are not all-knowing. They each possess faults and weaknesses."

"That's blasphemy," Cyn squealed, her religious upbringing rearing its ugly head.

"It's not blasphemy. It's the truth, and not one of the goddesses, Lilith, Brigit, Rhiannon, Maeve, or Morrigan, would disagree with that statement. They don't pretend to be perfect. Not even Mother Earth is perfect."

Cyn gasped and clutched her throat, probably wishing she had her fake mom's pearls to clutch in this self-righteous exhibition.

Unfazed by my sister's reaction, Bladecroft continued. "Even Mother Earth and Father Sky make mistakes. That's why Silver Dagger Sisterhood exists—to right their wrongs. Their experiments that went bad."

Cyn clenched her jaw, keeping her mouth shut. She didn't like the whole "right their wrongs" bit, but she knew part of the Sisterhood's purpose was to protect humans from rogue supernaturals and that those beings were created by Mother Earth and Father Sky.

I clapped my hands together, excitement building in me. "So, we're hunting a faulty experiment? What are we talking here? Big, muscular green guy?"

"You and your gargoyle fetish," Cyn muttered, knowing full well Gage wasn't green but equating him to the Hulk anyway. Hey, he was definitely Hulk-like. Every part of him was.

"Don't knock 'em till you try 'em."

"Do you agree not to discuss this mission with any of the goddesses, including Mother Earth?"

"Yes," we answered together, finally agreeing on something.

Bladecroft clasped her palms together, her eyes shining bright. "Fantastic. And no, we won't be fighting any muscular green guys. Though I do agree with Dez about the gargoyles. But I prefer the females."

Never in all my years would I have guessed that I'd be talking about sex with my professors, let alone during a mission briefing, but I was in for all of it, hook, line, and sword.

"We're hunting Lamashtu. Mother Earth created her as a protector of woman, but when she entered Earth's atmosphere, her brain chemistry got corrupted."

"Probably a chemical reaction to oxygen and carbon dioxide," Cyn mumbled, falling into a science-nerd-brain session.

I frowned at Bladecroft, having a difficult time believing what she told us. "Protector of woman? Like Lilith?"

Bladecroft nodded. "Exactly like Lilith. Lamashtu was Lilith's predecessor, but rather than protecting women, she preyed upon pregnant mothers and their unborn babies, causing miscarriages or actions much, much worse. She feeds on newborns. She became a mistress of demons—the really bad ones—using their power to build onto hers."

I settled back into my seat. I had hunted all sorts of supernatural beings, but I'd never hunted a goddess. Well, a former goddess, but still, never a being so powerful.

Cyn stared at me. "Why are you white as a ghost?"

I latched on to her question, diverting her own concern. "Common misconception. Most ghosts are not white. They're ethereal and generally wear the clothing they died in. They're more gray or fog-like."

She rolled her eyes. "Fine. Why did all the color drain out of your face?"

"Lamashtu was a goddess."

She raised her hand. "Yeah?"

"Would you want to fight any of the goddesses you've met so far?"

"No . . ." She tucked her chin in as if I'd slapped her. "Oh, that's what you're worried about. Shit. I didn't think that through."

"Whoa, whoa," Lippincott yelled. "Before you two spiral, remember, Lamashtu is a failed experiment. She's nowhere near as powerful as any of the goddesses."

"Right," Bladecroft added. "Tiana and I have handled former goddesses before. Gods too. While they should never be underestimated, it's not as bad as you think, Dez."

"What I think is that the two of you have lost touch with reality, because one of you is the legendary Lara

Bladecroft and the other is the legendary Tiana Lippincott, and neither of you have any idea what it's like to be nonlegendary Dez Wickershim and even-lesser-known Cynda Wickershim."

"Gee thanks, Sis," Cyn said under her breath.

"It's true. You've never even been in an actual fight before, let alone on a mission."

"I fought you."

"And I kicked your ass multiple times. And don't forget what happened at Silverwood Prison with the shifters. If Gage and I hadn't shown up, you would have become doggy kibble. And don't even get me started on—"

"Dez!" Bladecroft shouted, her voice somehow silencing me.

I tried to move and couldn't. Bitch froze me too.

When my tangent was cut short, Cyn looked over at me, soon realizing something was up. She waved her hand in front of my face. I couldn't even blink. She punched my thigh in the same spot Bladecroft had, adding further insult to injury. My fingers itched to react, but I was completely paralyzed. My sister leaned closer, studying me. I wanted to punch her so bad.

"What did you do to her?"

Bladecroft revealed a small vial. "I immobilized her. She was spiraling, and I didn't want to have to fight her inside a moving vehicle. I've done it plenty of times, but it's messy, and I'd rather not destroy our sole mode of transportation. If the SUV gets trashed, we'd have to hoof it back to the Academy, and I'd like to make it back in time for class tomorrow."

"Same," Lippincott said.

Cyn's forehead bunched as she watched me. "Can she hear us?"

"Yes, she can. I want her to hear this without arguing."

"And what is that?" Cyn asked cautiously.

"No one—no goddess, no god—is without weakness, and when fighting the enemy, a warrior exploits every resource available to her."

"And what is Lamashtu's weakness?"

"A newborn baby."

"You'd put a baby at risk? No mother would ever agree to that!" Cyn shrieked.

If I could, I'd concur with her. Well, after I kicked Bladecroft's ass for tossing magick at me like confetti.

Bladecroft's lips curled into a mischievous smile, her eyes flashing with amusement. A sense of dread came over me. I wasn't going to like her answer. Not one bit.

"No babies will be harmed in the making of this mission," she said, and she cracked a vial.

THREE

 yn

THE AIR around Dez twisted and spun. Sparks exploded off her and around her. I winced while trying to keep an eye on her, but everything was too bright, too blinding. Horrible, stinky smoke filled the SUV, sending me into a coughing fit, but the stench was fleeting. The sourness disappeared, replaced by the fresh scent of baby powder.

I waved my hands to clear the air. Where my sister once sat was now a tiny, naked baby.

Motherly instincts took over. I quickly unbuckled the baby's seatbelt and cradled her to my chest. When she was safe in my arms, I directed my outrage at the two women who deserved it. "You turned my sister into a baby?"

Bladecroft revealed a large vial. Black smoke billowed from its opening until she capped it with a piece of cork.

"It's only temporary." She waved her free hand as she

tucked the vial into a pocket inside her vest. She was acting like it was no big deal. What was wrong with her?

"But she's a baby. A defenseless baby."

At that perceived insult, Baby Dez's purple eyes morphed into red ones, and bright laser beams blinded me. I jerked my face away from her and closed my eyes. As if dissatisfied with my reaction, she unleashed the most terrible scream I'd ever heard from that little mouth of hers. My eardrums pounded, threatening to shatter if the terrible screaming continued. I quickly laid the baby on my lap and covered my ears. Her screams got louder, more terrible, more piercing. I didn't know what to do—try to soothe the baby or protect my hearing. I couldn't hunt if I couldn't hear, but if Dez got hurt in baby form, would it be permanent? A dozen more questions sprang to my mind. Freaking out was kinda my thing.

Three loud claps broke through the screaming. The car went silent.

"Still think she's defenseless?"

My eardrums burned as echoes of Dez's screams rang through them.

"Definitely not defenseless," I shouted.

Bladecroft screwed her finger in her ear. "No need to shout. I'm right here."

"Sorry," I yelled. Then registering what she'd just said, I lowered my voice. "Sorry."

"Much better."

"So you turned her into a baby?"

"I did. But Baby Dez is equipped with several powerful tools, as we've just witnessed."

"Will she change back?"

"Within twenty-four hours. Give or take."

"Twenty-four hours?" I squealed, imagining myself

responsible for a baby for an entire day. Should I buy diapers? Feed her? Burp her?

Dez squirmed in my arms as if thinking, *Oh hells no.*

"Or until one of us drops one of these on her." Bladecroft leaned back and tucked a small glass vial in the front pocket of my vest. She handed another one to Lippincott. "But don't use it until the right time."

Dez bucked and flung her body, trying to either force the spell out of her or bite me—I couldn't tell which—but as I clutched her freaky little naked baby body to my chest, I made sure to keep her sharp fangs away from my skin.

"When will that be?"

"You'll know." Bladecroft patted my knee in support as Baby Dez's little fangs snapped at the air, wanting to chomp anyone who came within range. "You've got good, natural instincts."

"No one is going to believe that's a real baby, Lara. Look at how she's moving. Worse than a Chucky doll," Lippincott said.

We all shuddered at the comparison.

Bladecroft withdrew another vial, popped the cork, and flicked the glittery contents over Baby Dez, one, two, three times. Baby Dez instantly went still.

"That should hold her until Lamashtu grabs her."

"Then what?"

Bladecroft's lips lifted into a smile. "Freaky Baby goes psycho killer on Goddess Gone Bad."

"*Psycho killer, qu'est-ce que c'est? Fa-fa-fa-fa, fa-fa-fa-fa-fa-fa,*" Lippincott sang, banging her hand on the steering wheel.

"The punk phase is over, Tiana. Get past it."

Lippincott slapped Bladecroft's thigh. "It will never end. Punk rock will never die."

Bladecroft rubbed her face. "Oh goddess, save me now. Maybe I should carry Freaky Baby instead of Cyn so I can get the hell out of this car before you start singing again."

"You're too recognizable. Besides, Cyn will handle Lamashtu and Freaky Baby like a true Sister."

A rush of warmth ran through me at her words because I knew she meant it as a future member of Silver Dagger Sisterhood as opposed to a biological sister. I gripped Freaky Baby close to my chest. I would do anything to protect her.

"So, what's the plan? What do I do?"

Lippincott pulled the SUV over to the side of the road and turned to face me. She shivered as her eyes fell on Freaky Baby then shook off her reaction.

"Up ahead there's a famous crossroads on Route 66. A place of hundreds if not thousands of disappearances."

Fear gripped me, but I pushed the approaching panic aside, trying to act much braver than I actually felt. "And they're all connected to Lamashtu?"

She shook her head. "No."

"No?!" I squealed again. Goddess, I sounded like a big wussy.

"There are at least a half dozen demons and phantoms who frequent this crossroads," she explained.

A lump lodged in my throat. Normally this was where Dez would pepper them with questions, but she was in Freaky-Baby mode. It was up to me to interrogate. I swallowed hard. "How do you know Lamashtu will come instead of someone else? Or something else?"

Bladecroft caressed Freaky Baby's forehead. "That's why you have *her*. A newborn baby will ensure Lamashtu rears her ugly head."

"Why this crossroads? She's got to visit different ones

across the country." I had learned about ley lines and crossroads in Professor Salzbury's Elemental History class.

"Oh, she does, but this one is the most remote, and demons love the heat. A few feet from the crossroads is a gate to one of the hells."

Of course there was.

"And do I get to know where the gate is, or are you going to keep that a secret?"

I could imagine my sister slapping my knee, shouting, *Spicy, I like it.*

Bladecroft waved her hands in front of her. "You don't need to worry about the gate. You can't pass through it unless you're part demon. It's one of the reasons we selected you and Dez. As pureblood Sempiternals, there's little chance you can get through."

Except that we were wolf shapeshifters too, and something else—though I didn't know what. However, I couldn't reveal those secrets to anyone. Dez and I had sworn secrecy to our mom and the other goddesses. No one could know about our other natures. But since I was a terrible liar, I decided not to even respond to Bladecroft's comment for fear of giving myself away.

Lippincott slid out of the SUV, walked around, and opened my door for me. "Let's get this mission over with."

I climbed out with Freaky Baby in my arms. Bladecroft joined us outside.

"When will you two show up? Or do we fight Lamashtu all by ourselves?"

That would be especially concerning since I'd left my staff in the SUV in order to hold Freaky Baby. Plus, with her in my arms, I couldn't grab my daggers or stakes.

Bladecroft snorted. "You're not really going to fight her. She *is* a goddess."

"But you said—"

She threw up her hand. "Did I mini-me the wrong sister?"

I snapped my lips shut.

"Tiana and I laid a trap for her. You just have to set it."

Bladecroft and Lippincott might be respected Sisters and professors at Silverwood Academy, but they frustrated me to no end.

"Do I get to know where the trap is?"

"Just walk to the middle of crossroads, drop this spell over Freaky Baby," Bladecroft said, handing me another vial, "and we'll take care of the rest."

"That's it? That's all the briefing we get?"

"That's all the briefing you need. The rest you're better off not knowing in case we have to improvise."

"I'm not a fan of improvising."

Lippincott put her hand on my back, but instead of calming my reservations, she shoved me forward. "Welcome to your first mission. Walk straight and you won't miss it. We'll be there soon."

"Thanks, and love you too," I shouted over my shoulder. My goddess, I really was hanging out with my sister too much.

"And remember not to ask for assistance from the goddesses. Or the elements, in case it gets back to the goddesses. We're on our own with this mission."

"Yup, I remember," I said under my breath.

I stepped into the darkness with Freaky Baby, my eyes barely making out the faint outline of the road. The sound of my boots crunching across the gravel echoed in the stillness of the night. I glanced down at my feet. No need for stealth on this mission. At least not for me. The more noise I made, the better the chance of Lamashtu finding me since Freaky Baby was under the silencing spell. But still, it felt wrong. It took everything in me not to cast my own silencing spell on myself.

I cleared my throat loudly and hummed a tune as I walked. Large, dark shapes lined the gravel road. I inhaled deeply. The sweet smell of sagebrush still warm from the hot Arizona day assured me that the herbaceous vegetation wasn't actually monsters lying in wait. That, at least, was something. I'd just pretend I was out for a leisurely stroll in the desert in the middle of nowhere in the middle of the night, taking in all the delicious scents the desert had to offer with my Freaky Baby in my arms. Nothing suspicious about any of that at all.

There was no hint of civilization for as far as I could see. Not a light, not a town, not even a car for miles in any direction. The fact that this crossroads served as the most notorious of them all made me curious. Perhaps a paranormal beacon? A former alien landing strip? We were in the middle of nowhere, and no person, lost or otherwise, would willingly travel down this stretch of Route 66 unless they wanted to die. Or wanted to capture a science experiment gone bad.

I could imagine my sister's snarky response. *Don't knock it till you try it.*

I rolled my eyes, not paying attention to my location until a voice whispered in the darkness, "Well, well, well. What do we have here?"

I stopped and looked around, trying to place which direction the voice came from. Heavy darkness coiled around me, making it difficult to see more than a few feet away. I glanced down at the ground, realizing I had already reached the middle of the crossroads. Sempiternals walked fast. Even without vamp speed, I could outpace a human by a mile. Maybe I should join an Olympic speed-walking team or something. I'd kick ass without breaking a sweat—my favorite kind of ass kicking. Unfortunately, Bladecroft and Lippincott had other plans for this evening.

I peered into the black night, trying to pick out a shadow or shape in the darkness, but I couldn't see anything.

"Wh-who's there?" I called out, sounding afraid without even trying to.

"Just Grandma Lamashtu here to take care of you," the voice said, chilling my very bones.

I clutched Dez tighter to my chest as a giant being took form in front of me.

"I-I don't need any help."

Damn it. Why did I have to sound so scared?

I breathed in and out of my nose, trying to calm my racing heart. When I felt more together, I continued. "I'm good. I'm just out for a late stroll with my new baby."

"New baby, you say? I love new babies." She cackled.

I bet you do, you psycho baby killer.

Long blood-stained fingers stretched out toward Freaky Baby. I yanked Dez away from her. Everything about Lamashtu screamed predator.

"Don't be frightened," she cooed, sounding closer.

I could feel the power of her words thrum through me, as if she was casting a spell over me. I blinked, fighting the magick.

"Interesting," she whispered.

"What is?"

"I can smell you're not human, yet you hold a human baby. An ally perhaps?"

An ally in her baby-killing scheme? I don't think so.

"I'm human and just delivered my baby this morning."

"Liar."

I cursed. Bladecroft should have turned me into Freaky Baby instead of Dez. I was no better than Pinocchio.

"I'm not lying. How dare you call me a liar."

That's it. Piss off the psycho baby killer.

"I don't believe you." Suddenly, gravel shifted as bird feet appeared ahead of me followed by a lion's head.

I screamed, almost throwing Freaky Baby at Lamashtu and running in the opposite direction. I wasn't ready for this mission or any missions. I had lived a human life for almost two decades. Monsters didn't exist.

"Oh yes, they do," Lamashtu answered.

Guess, I voiced that out loud.

An almost-human face peered at me beneath the lion's head, and by "almost human" I meant not human at all. Instead of human teeth or fangs, her teeth reminded me of a donkey's—too large for her mouth, white, and squared off. But what was really disturbing was her hairy naked body with enormous breasts. And let's not forget the creepy yellow eyes with pupils undulating like a cobra.

"There's no reason to be frightened," she whispered, the power of her words falling on my ears again. But the spell no longer took root.

"Says every monster ever!" I yelled. Freaky Baby started to buck in my arms. The quieting spell must have been wearing off. Where in the hells were Bladecroft and Lippincott? And where was the no-fail trap they'd talked about?

"Let me have your baby," she murmured in a quiet yet powerful voice, which was all the more bizarre coming out of a mouth with donkey teeth.

Goddess experiment gone wrong, all right.

I warred with myself. I couldn't fight her with Baby Dez

in my arms, and I knew once she held Freaky Baby, I could use the vial to lift the quieting spell completely, and Freaky Baby could disable her with her teeth and her scream, but everything in my body warred against it. This mission might want me to give Lamashtu the fake baby, but my mission in life insisted I protect the innocent. All the innocent. And the only crime Freaky Baby had committed was questioning our professors and their half-cocked mission.

Her long, bony fingers wrapped around Freaky Baby. "That's it," she cooed. "Just let me have her."

And I did, whipping out the small vial and shaking it on Freaky Baby, who released a bloodcurdling scream. I slammed my palms over my ears and murmured a spell I'd read the other day. Miraculously, the screaming stopped. At least in *my* ears. Freaky Baby's mouth was wide open, sucking all the oxygen out of the air as she belted out her ferocity. That was until she bit down on Lamashtu's exposed breast.

The former goddess howled.

I circled around the psycho baby killer, keeping an eye on my sister, whose body was thrashing and bucking beneath Lamashtu's sharp nails. Blood erupted from fresh wounds.

Anger surged through me. This bitch was going pay for all the innocent babies she'd killed. All the poor mothers who'd lost their babies in miscarriage or childbirth. All the unborn babies who never had a chance because their mothers were ruthlessly slaughtered by this psycho killer.

I reached my arms behind my back and withdrew two sharp silver daggers.

Yes, Lamashtu would pay for her crimes.

CHAPTER

FOUR

ez

I WAS PISSED OFF. Furious. This bitch was going to die, and then I was going to kick the asses of two legendary members of Silver Dagger Sisterhood for turning me into a baby.

Sharp nails bit into my body, trying to rip me off her breast, but I refused to let go. I'd chomp her fucking nipple off for all the torture and pain she put little innocent babies through. And the mothers? Those poor souls losing their babies? Most probably not even knowing what had happened to them. They certainly had no idea that a horrible science experiment gone bad was the cause of it.

My eyes burned into Lamashtu's hairy chin. I had always wanted red lasers shooting out of my eyeballs, so of course I was taking advantage of the opportunity. Her howls of pain stung my ears, but I also found them very satisfying. Once I rid the world of her nipple, I'd unleash my own terrible scream, and Lamashtu would never forget who she was dealing with.

Two pale arms wrapped around her neck, and her chin disappeared completely as my little sister unleashed her own inner beast on the psycho baby killer.

A mound of flesh dropped into my mouth, followed by a fountain of blood. My stomach churned. I wanted to permanently maim Lamashtu. Well, until I killed her. But Sempiternal or not, I didn't want her blood or her nipple in my mouth. I twisted my head and spat out the nasty appendage. It hit her bird claws unceremoniously before landing in the gravel.

I unhinged my jaw and screamed like the scariest, loudest bean sídhe the world had ever heard.

Cyn paused her strangulation efforts as if my scream affected her too, but then she was back at it. I spun my head wildly around, searching for this trap our fearless leaders had set. Where were they anyway?

My vocal cords thrummed with the scream. I suspected I'd feel the effects long after we rid the world of Lamashtu, but my morphed state left me with limited maiming opportunities. I bucked and flapped around wildly. Lamashtu's grip loosened as my blood-soaked baby body slipped in her grasp. Suddenly, she dropped me. Gravel rushed toward my naked little body. I wasn't afraid of a little road rash—I had my fair share of scars from years of fighting monsters—but my little baby body didn't seem quite so durable. If I broke my spine or cracked my baby head open, would I die? Lippincott and Bladecroft hadn't gotten into the particulars of what could happen while I was in baby form, and I didn't want to find out.

I called upon every ounce of magick in my body and

pushed with all of it, expelling the baby spell Bladecroft had hit me with. Just as my infant body smashed at Lamashtu's feet, my arms, legs, and body exploded out of the breakable baby form and back into my svelte, fully dressed adult one. Gravel dug into my leather-covered ass, but at least my skull didn't split open. I threw my arms over my head as I arched and flung my legs up, springing into a standing position.

Cyn whirled and twirled around Lamashtu like the fierce female I knew her to be. Silver blades whipped through the air, jabbing and stabbing as she unleashed vengeance on the psycho baby killer. I allowed myself one quick smile before joining in on kicking the former goddess's ass. I delivered a throat-punch with dead-on accuracy. Lamashtu gasped, reaching for her neck. Taking advantage of her weakened state, I roundhouse-kicked her in the gut. Groaning, she folded over, her lion headpiece slipping off and crumpling at her freaky bird claw feet in an unremarkable heap. I dropped into my Black Widow signature lunge with one hand touching the gravel as I swung my right leg, knocking Lamashtu's legs out from under her. She crashed sideways, hitting the hard gravel road with a mighty "Oooof." Cyn expertly pinned the psycho baby killer as she hit the ground.

Her bird claws thrashed, trying to knock Cyn away. The former goddess was strong and dangerous. We'd overpowered her for the time being, but rogue supernaturals were cagey and often waited to unleash hidden talents when their life was at risk. If we could spring that trap, we could end this.

Where in the hells were Bladecroft and Lippincott?

Careful not to take my complete attention off Cyn and Lamashtu, I glanced around in the darkness, searching for our mentors or their trap. What I found curdled the contents of my stomach. It wasn't just two sisters fighting a former goddess or two Silver Dagger Sisters angling for attack. No, Lamashtu had brought friends.

Red eyes flashed as dozens of demons emerged from the shadows. I spit on the ground, anger rushing through me. I'd fought demons before but never this number of them or without any weapons.

Fuck. My claws came out, but the trouble was, demons had claws too, and their skin was tougher than my pretty Sempiternal skin.

"A little help over here!" Cyn shouted, trying to keep Lamashtu under control.

"She must be feeding off the demons' energy," I muttered.

"She can do that?" Cyn squeaked.

My sister needed to work on her poker face. Or, in this case, voice. Adversaries exploited any weakness. Panic, fear, frustration . . . she had to learn how to hide them all if she fostered any hope of surviving in this new world.

Then again, I hadn't expected our first mission to turn sideways or that we'd be fighting a fallen goddess.

Where was fucking backup?

"Hey, Dez," a voice whispered, edging closer. "Long time no bite."

I crouched into a fighting stance. My lips curled down at the sight of the cocky son of a bitch who'd harassed a trio of human women along with his wing demon when I worked at Femme Fatale, a bar owned by a retired member of the Sisterhood who liked to keep in the know and who didn't mind if I showed up to work or disappeared on a mission. This bastard would meet the tip of my sword. Well, if I had one. My fist would have to do.

"Little Dicky, I see your sense of humor has returned. How's your friend? Oh, that's right. I killed him."

"Why you cunt!" He sprang at me, exposing his midsection.

So easy.

I threw my legs up, kicking him in the stomach and sending him flying backward, taking three other demons with him.

"You always were an easy target. Your sister was a much more worthy adversary. Too bad I killed her too."

"Less talking, Dez, and get over here!" Cyn shouted, her voice sounding strained.

"Can't. A little busy . . ."

Two demons approached from my left and right, trying to sneak up on me, only they sounded like a herd of stampeding elephants and smelled like rotten sewage. Don't ask how I knew that.

I breathed in and out, calming my pulse, savoring the moment before what came next. I lived for this shit. It had been months since I'd hunted.

"Holy mother fanger!" Cyn screamed. "This bitch bit me."

I spun around to see blood spurting out of Cyn's arm and Lamashtu's maniacal grin with red-stained teeth.

Crap. A magickal chomp from a former goddess couldn't be good. At least it was bleeding heavily. Most of the toxins should seep out. But she needed to tend to that wound before she lost too much blood.

I threw out my hands just as the demons sprang at me, naively believing I wasn't paying attention. It wasn't their fault. They weren't familiar with my reputation, and clearly Little Dicky hadn't filled them in. Not that I cared. They were going to get their asses kicked whether or not they'd heard about me.

I grabbed their noses and twisted.

Cyn's eyes widened. "Watch behind you!"

I flung my head back and headbutted my assailant, keeping my grip on the schnozzes of the other two.

Little Dicky reappeared on the other side of the crossroads, far from me but too close to my sister.

"You touch her, you die," I growled.

His red eyes brightened in the darkness. "Who's going to lose their friend this time?"

My stomach turned at the mere thought of losing Cyn, but it was fleeting, replaced by fiery rage. How dare he threaten to harm my sister. How dare he stalk her like the skulking bastard he was. How dare he . . .

But I didn't bother to finish the thought. Red lasers shot out of my eyes and burned two holes into Little Dicky's skull.

He screamed as black blood ran down his face from his forehead. His hands shot up to shield his head, but it didn't stop my red laser beams from burning into him.

I grinned, watching with fascination. Finally my dreams of shooting laser beams from my eyeballs had come true. I thought it was only a little extra boost from Bladecroft's freaky-baby spell, but this . . . this was fucking fantastic!

I swept my gaze down his body, and lo and behold, the red lasers burned through his hands, neck, and stomach. Let's see what I could do about his sexually harassing probing device. That bastard deserved a toasty roasting.

Little Dicky's hands flung to his burning member, and he collapsed to the ground. His body burned to ash.

I gasped, staggering to my knees as his remains disappeared in the evening breeze.

The high of the kill was soon extinguished along with my newfound ability. I sensed the energy signatures of dozens of demons swarming around me, but my strength was leaving me at a rapid speed.

This was not good.

Drip. Drip. Drip.

Drip. Drip. Drip.

Drip. Drip. Drip.

I jerked awake, my cheek scraping across hard, jagged stone.

"Where the hells am I?" I croaked, barely recognizing the sound of my own voice. My throat felt like I'd swallowed sandpaper after drinking an entire desert. I smacked my lips together, trying to gather moisture in my mouth.

"You mean, where the hells are *we*?" Cyn grunted from the darkness a few feet away.

I peered over at her, assessing her condition. The last thing I remembered was the hunk of flesh missing from her arm and blood spewing out of it.

"Are you . . . ," I cleared my throat and tried again. "Are you okay?"

"Do you mean aside from our current imprisonment in what appears to be some ancient dungeon or the raging burning sensation of Lamashtu's bite? You'll have to be more specific."

The hair rose on the back of my neck as I pushed myself to stand, but my head swam with wooziness. I folded back into a seated position, resting my head against the stone wall. I swallowed a couple times to steady myself before speaking again.

"You haven't healed yet?"

"Should I have?"

Her fear spiked, and the sourness of it entered my mouth, causing bile to rise up in my throat. I bent over to the side, my hands clenching the cold, wet, sticky stones as the contents of my stomach emptied across them with a disgusting splash. I spit out the remainder, wiped my mouth, and sat back up, using the wall for support again.

"Are *you* okay?" she asked, sounding concerned for my well-being. That was nice. I hadn't had anyone care about me during a mission for a long while. After Dad died, I'd chosen the solitary hunter life rather than forming attachments.

The stench of my puke rose to my nostrils. My stomach roiled again. I held my hand to my mouth, trying to keep whatever was left in my body inside of it. The wave of nausea passed quickly.

"Not so great. If you could try not to be afraid, that would be especially helpful."

"Excuse me?" Annoyance replaced her fear.

I smacked my lips together. "Much better."

"What are you talking about?"

"I'll explain later, once I figure out where we are. Never divulge secrets when you aren't familiar with your surroundings. You never know who could be listening."

She grunted. "Well, Sherlock, we're locked in a cell, and I'm pretty sure no one is listening down here."

Another wave of nausea rippled through me. I swallowed hard to keep it down. This crap wouldn't do. Not at all. I needed to feed to heal myself. Cyn needed to feed to heal herself. Both of us had gone too long without blood or energy. I had gotten lazy at Silverwood Academy—not feeding as often as I should. Maintenance was key. I knew better, and I'd teach Cyn when we got out of this shithole.

I glanced around the dark space. Three stone walls, a fourth made up of bars, damp stone floors, and—I peered up—a stone ceiling too. Indeed it was a cell. My fingers reached out, tracing the bars until they got pricked on hidden barbs. I closed my eyes and called on the elements. First Air, because I needed some oxygen to clear my nausea. The element answered with a rush of clean air, circling around me. I gulped in mouthfuls of it, filling and emptying my lungs until I felt more like myself.

"Better," I sighed.

"What are you doing?"

I held up my hand to quiet her, knowing she could see my raised palm in the semidarkness. "Just hold on."

I called on Earth and felt her vibration a story or two below us but also all around us. A multilevel below-ground dungeon. Difficult but not impossible.

My fingers touched the damp stone floors, careful to avoid my vomit. I called on Water and felt her droplets dance across the tops of my hands. My mouth filled with moisture. I sensed a spring nearby. I wanted to suck down mouthfuls of pure water, but that would have to wait.

I shivered from the dampness, wishing for some heat. I called on Fire, inviting it to build inside of me. Instead I felt it above us and below us, all around but not in us. Interesting.

I called on Spirit, asking for a vision of our location. An image of a gothic castle forged into a mountainside formed in my mind. I dug into the vision until a rough form of the dungeon appeared before me.

"Complicated, but not impossible," I said under my breath.

"What is?"

"Our situation."

"Not impossible? It feels pretty impossible to me." Her emotions escalated again. I needed to stave off her unease to keep the nausea away.

"Just relax. Come here and let's talk through this."

She crawled over and slumped against the wall next to me. "I thought we weren't supposed to talk about stuff when we don't know where we are," she said barely above a whisper.

I smiled to myself. "You're learning. I know where we are."

"You do?" she said, her voice squeaking. Then, remembering herself, she said again, "You do?"

"We're in a demon dungeon. They took us through the hells gate. It took us to the Demon Realm."

"What?!" Her fear spiked, but my stomach no longer reacted since I had grounded myself.

"Shhh . . ."

"Right. Right. I'm supposed to remain calm when we're locked in a demon dungeon." Her voice dripped with sarcasm.

"Not all demons are bad."

"Clearly the ones who kidnapped us are."

"Obviously Lamashtu's minions. She must be their mistress. They exchange blood during sex. That must be how Little Dicky and the rest of them showed up at the crossroads."

"What happened to the trap? Why didn't Bladecroft and Lippincott show up?"

That was what I wanted to know.

"No idea."

"Any idea how to get out of here?"

"One or two, but you aren't going to like them."

She groaned. "How did I know you were going to say that?"

"Because you have glaring trust issues."

"Can you blame me?"

She did make a point, but first, time for a prison break.

FIVE

 yn

I WOULD NEVER ADMIT it out loud, but with Dez here, our situation didn't seem quite so daunting. She sounded confident that we'd get out of here. I glanced around the dank, dingy cell and couldn't imagine how we'd escape, but I kinda believed her. She had grown up as a hunter's daughter and had even hunted on her own before entering the Change. Most likely she'd been captured before and had successfully escaped—proof that she knew what she was talking about. Of course, the trust-issues thing still ruled much of my emotions, but she was slowly gaining mine.

"What's the plan?"

"Well, let's see just how strong these bars are." She shifted, still keeping her back against the wall, but she grabbed hold of the bars and pulled.

"Careful!" I reminded her. Those barbs looked nasty. "You might cut yourself and get an infection."

She laughed as she pulled, wincing as the barbs dug into her palms. "Don't worry about me. I'm a big girl. Sempiternals heal quickly for the most part."

"I wouldn't be so sure. That's what everyone thinks until they catch something."

"Highly unlikely." She spun her feet and pressed against the lower section of the bars, with her hands pulling above.

I frowned at her position. "What good will that do?"

She glared at me. "Leverage. Now, help me."

I positioned myself next to her. "It's not going to do any good, but I'll humor you. Besides, there's not much else to do in this cell."

"Aside from catching a disease," she grunted as she pulled.

My fear spiked. "But you said . . ."

She stopped and looked at me. "I was joking. Sarcasm. Dry wit. Sparkling personality with a sense of humor to boot."

"You're not very funny," I grumbled, placing my hands and feet on the bars. The bars pricked my palms, but it was nothing unbearable. Not even that uncomfortable. More of a bark-was-worse-than-a-bite situation. But instead of pulling into the cell, I pulled out to the sides. Not sure why, more of a feeling. Intense heat surged through my palms, but it wasn't from the bars, and it didn't burn me. The heat came from inside of me. As I continued pulling, the bars moved with me.

Holy mother of demon dungeons!

I stopped, staring at the curved bars as they slowly straightened to their original position. I blinked, unable to believe my eyes. "Did you see that?"

"See what?" she grunted through clenched teeth, yanking on the bars as if she could pull down the entire cell wall from her seated position.

"Just stop and watch me."

She released the bars, which still hadn't budged despite her effort.

I grabbed the bars again and pulled out to the sides. They arced with me, the circle growing bigger and bigger the more I pulled.

"Whoa."

I stopped and grinned at her. "I know, right?"

"What happens when you let go?"

"This." I released the bars, and they returned to their straight, upright position.

"Let me try." She pulled out on the bars, but they didn't move. Didn't shudder. And definitely didn't curve. She finally gave up, scratching at the cuts on her palms.

I looked at my own hands. Blemish free. "Huh, that's weird. Why can I do that, but you can't?"

"I don't know, but you saw my eyes back at the crossroads, right? Can yours do that?"

I narrowed mine at the bars and focused, but nothing happened. "I wish. I would have loved to have been able to shoot laser beams at you after you forced the Change on me. Like Scarlet Witch but more badass and without the villainous alter ego."

"Let me handle the villainous-alter-ego part. For now, let's not focus on what each of us can't do and instead focus on what we can do, and that's getting out of here."

"I demand to see the prisoners now," a voice thundered from above, sounding far off yet shaking the dungeon floor, vibrating the stone walls of our cell, and sending my heart into panic mode.

Dez stiffened. I mirrored her behavior. If she was alarmed, I definitely was.

I leaned closer to her. "Who is that?"

"I don't know," she murmured.

"Should we be scared?" Because I was freaking out right now.

"Not yet."

A heavy stone door slammed open, shaking our cell. As solid as the dungeon appeared, it was no match for whoever wanted to see us. Demanded to see us.

"Should we be scared now?"

"Pretend you're unconscious," she ordered. She shimmied down the wall and lay on her side.

"Excuse me? Shouldn't we act brave? Unaffected by our surroundings? Say something sexual? Scandalous? Make fun of his penis? That's what you did in Silverwood Prison."

"This isn't Silverwood Prison," she hissed, yanking me down beside her. "We're doing reconnaissance. We need to assess this new threat, and the best way to do that is to feign weakness."

"That's the opposite of what you always tell me."

"True, but we must adapt to any given situation. That power thrumming through this cell, vibrating in my very core? That tells me we need to reevaluate our situation."

I was about to respond, but the ground beneath us vibrated as footsteps approached.

"King Asmoday, we were only doing what Lamashtu ordered us to do."

"I have not taken the title of King. It is still Prince Asmoday. And Lamashtu does not rule here. She is a guest. Your whore's insolence has gone on long enough. Rumblings about her murdering innocent babies again after she pledged reformation cannot be ignored. I will attend to her following my meeting the prisoners."

"But, King—"

"Silence!" Prince Asmoday roared, the cell bars rattling.

Dez's body quivered in response to his voice. I pressed my fingers into her back to calm her. Her energy levels were depleted. She had collapsed after killing that demon who'd threatened me at the crossroads. I felt weak too. I didn't really know how the whole Sempiternal thing worked, but I think we both needed to feed if we had any hopes of getting out of this dungeon.

The floor bounced as he got closer, as if his very presence called forth an earthquake, and for all I knew about demons, maybe it did. But Dez remained quiet and subdued, so I followed her lead.

The footsteps halted outside our cell. His disgust filled the air above us, weighing down upon us. I squeezed my eyes shut, forcing myself not to look at him for fear that my consciousness might further enrage him. I didn't grow up in this magickal world, but I knew when I was outmatched, and this guy would crush us with his fingers.

"Open the cell!"

"But, King— Prince—"

"Do it." His order offered no room for dispute. His tone demanded submission or severe consequences.

Dez's back trembled with trepidation. I pressed more energy into her. Who was this prince, and why did he frighten her? She wasn't afraid of anything.

"Awaken!" he demanded, snapping his fingers.

I froze. Was I supposed to obey him or act like I was still unconscious? I awaited Dez's reaction.

She moaned as she lazily stretched like a cat beside me before sitting up. It was then that I realized she wasn't nervous at all. Her body shook with sexual desire for this demon prince.

I peeked my eyes open and peered up at him. A gold mask hid most of his face, but from my position, I could see his nostrils flare in and out, catching Dez's scent.

"We meet again," she said in a low, husky voice.

Oh goddess. Time and place, Dez. Time and place.

His chest rumbled in reply.

She drew closer to him, a moth to a flame. So much for her great affections for Jace. She raised her hand as if to touch him. He moved back, avoiding her.

A demon stepped between them. "Don't you dare touch Prince Asmoday."

"Oh, I don't think he'd mind very much. Would you, Prince Asmoday?"

Her raw voice from earlier was replaced with lusty silkiness.

Prince Asmoday grabbed the demon's shoulder and shoved him out of the way. "I do not need protection from *her*," he snarled.

The way he said *her* gave me pause. Was it indeed as Dez hinted that the two shared history together and he could handle her, or was it that my sister posed no threat to him whatsoever? A mere fly he could squash at the slightest provocation. Of course, he'd have to catch her first, but she'd probably like that.

She giggled, not the least bit intimidated by the Demon Prince. "I wouldn't be so sure if I were you. Without the righteous judgement of the Council, we could have our way with each other right here."

So that was their common history. Dez had never gone into detail about what happened at her trial. Of course, bloodlust had ruled my entire existence at that time. But now that I had that under control, I was more than a little curious about the Council and its members and the goings-on of her trial.

His lips turned down in disgust, but still, he moved toward her, almost as if he wasn't even aware he was doing it, a power outside of his control. "With your sister present? You overestimate your abilities."

She laughed. "Perhaps." She edged closer to him, their chests almost touching. "Or you *under*estimate them, although I am a very hungry woman."

Prince Asmoday put space between them so subtly I didn't even notice him move away from her. "You are both welcome to leave. Jeevs will show you the way to the gate."

She put her hands on her hips, her chest flaring out. "That's it? No explanation why we were imprisoned in the first place? No 'Sorry about dragging you to the Demon Realm?' No 'Let's get between my silky sheets and find out what hot, Sempiternal-demon sex is like?'"

He growled, spinning on his heel and walking away from her. Soon his heavy footsteps climbed the stairs but not anywhere near as thunderously as before.

Dez glanced over her shoulder at me. Her purple eyes filled with mischief. "Was it something I said?"

I huffed, brushing past her on my way out of the cell. "Maybe that you offered yourself up like a harlot to the Demon Prince."

"Nah," she drawled. "That can't be it." She prowled out of the cell behind me. "He wanted me as much as I wanted him."

The dungeon door slammed shut behind us, and the ground rumbled beneath our feet. I put my hands out to keep my balance.

She chuckled. "Somebody needs to work through his repressed sexual desire."

I rolled my eyes. "Perhaps you can take a lesson in restraint."

"He needs a night of wild abandon to remove his restraints." She leaned toward me, the warmth of her voice tickling my ear.

I whipped my head around. We were talking quietly, but our demon guides, the prince's servants, would no doubt go running back to their kind. "Do you ever stop? What about Jace? Do you even miss him?"

She punched my shoulder blade. "Don't ever mention him to me again. What I feel or don't feel about him is none of your business."

I snorted. Prince Asmoday wasn't the only one with sexual repression issues. "So, you're hitting on a prince rather than facing your emotions."

"He's not just a prince. He's a member of the Council. He advocated for me at my hearing."

"Perhaps he fears he made a mistake."

"No. He wants me as much as I want him."

"His reaction would suggest otherwise."

"Bring the prisoners to me," Prince Asmoday roared from wherever he was above us.

"Yes, Master!" the demon who had stepped between Dez and the prince shouted.

"And ask them to refrain from speaking for the remainder of their stay."

"Yes, Master!" The demon whipped his head at us, his red eyes flashing in warning. "You heard Prince Asmoday. Silence."

"He heard us?" Dez whispered.

"YES, I DID! Now, please stop!"

She snorted. "At least you said please."

Something smashed against a wall above us. Debris showered down on our heads as we began climbing the stairs.

"Sexual repression issues," she said under her breath.

Another explosion from above shook the stairwell.

She snorted again but surprisingly kept quiet.

THE GUARD who led us from our cell and up the stairs stepped to the side and waited for us to cross over the threshold before quietly closing the giant dungeon door.

The other guard grabbed Dez's hands. She jerked back, but his hold was strong. I clamped my hand on his shoulder, letting my claws dig into him. "Let go of her."

"Wait!" he mouthed. His silent request gave me pause.

"What?" I mouthed back.

He glanced over at the other demon who was now looking down the ornate hallway as if watching for someone. He waved his hand in a circular motion. Magick circled around us, as he casted a silencing spell.

"Master has been away for long time," he said in an impressively quiet voice. "Please don't make him leave again." He stared at Dez.

Her eyes widened, realizing he was pleading with her. "Me?"

He nodded.

"This way," the other demon said loudly, signaling someone was coming.

The guard squeezed Dez's hands. "Please," he silently pleaded.

"Okay, okay," she mouthed back. "Not that I have any

say in the matter," she whispered under her breath as he released her.

His head whipped around.

Dez held up her hands. "Sorry, sorry."

"I'm waiting . . . ," Prince Asmoday thundered, sounding much closer. We rounded the corner to observe him at the end of the long corridor pacing back and forth in a tight circle. Several pedestals lining the hallway were askew. Many were missing busts, the remains of which were strewn across the black and white tile floor.

Everything about Prince Asmoday screamed power, and not just of the magickal kind. His gold, form-fitting uniform revealed a tall, muscular frame. His movements were graceful, yet I'd witnessed firsthand how the ground shook when he walked. His black hair was tied neatly back in a low ponytail. His tense jawline went on for miles. His tan skin, or at least the part I could see outside of his gold mask, hinted at time spent outdoors.

Our escorts rushed down the corridor, avoiding the fallen debris. I quickly followed, doing the same, until I stopped suddenly, sensing Dez's absence. I turned back to see her swaying her hips as she prowled down the hall, the hunter stalking her prey. The way Prince Asmoday stilled as she approached suggested he was caught in her trap.

"Took you long enough," he growled, trying to regain his authority.

"You didn't mind watching me," she purred, continuing her advance.

He raised his hands. "Stop."

An invisible force made her halt. She jutted out her hip. "You can play hard to get all you want, but I know what's already hard on you." Her gaze fell right to his manhood, and indeed there was a bulge. A giant freaking bulge. I looked quickly away, my cheeks heating.

"Why don't you get rid of that mask and let's see what lies behind it?"

I was surprised she stopped at just the removal of his mask, but perhaps she did possess some sense of self-preservation.

"I doubt very much you'd like what you saw."

She held a single finger to her lips as she shook her head. "I'm not particularly judgmental."

"Or very discriminating," he snapped.

She stretched her arms up in the air, revealing her muscular abs. "Oh, I don't know about that. I tend to have a very . . . enormous appetite." Her attention trailed back to his bulge. "You appear to fit that description."

"You will never know how well I fit."

She dropped her hands below her chest and pushed up, drawing his gaze to her bulging boobs. "Oh, I'm sure I will."

Prince Asmoday growled—or purred. I couldn't quite tell which. I shifted my feet, uncomfortable with a conversation I'd rather not be privy to.

The guard who'd begged Dez not to make the Demon Prince leave cleared his throat. Prince Asmoday blinked, remembering others were present.

"Shall I return the prisoners to the gate, Master? We have but a small window before the next opportunity."

Prince Asmoday's gold eyes fell on Dez. "Right you are. Take them. Get them out of my sight."

Dez turned and began walking toward me, her hips swaying back and forth. Prince Asmoday watched, riveted by her body.

"Remember me in your dreams, Prince," she called out over her shoulder.

"Concentrate on your prayers," he murmured.

Her eyes narrowed in suspicion. She spun around, but the prince was gone.

I touched her back. "What is it?"

She bit her lip. "I'm not sure."

"Seems to be the theme of this mission."

Her purple eyes fell on me. A storm of emotions swirled around them. "More than you know."

SIX

ez

I paced back and forth in our room as Cyn took her sweet old time in the shower.

Bang! Bang! Bang! I smashed my fist against the bathroom door.

"What?"

"What's taking so long?"

"Washing off the blood and guts of Lamashtu. It's like black sludge. And don't even get me started on the filth and stench of the dungeon. There were probably all sorts of plagues and diseases down there that haven't seen the light of day in centuries. I won't be responsible for causing the next pandemic."

Oh goddess, my sister had brought her human paranoia with her.

"We can't catch any of that crap!"

"How do you know that? There could have been some special strain down there that could take down Sempiternals with one cough."

I groaned. There was no point arguing with her. She was stubborn, neurotic, and OCD—a dangerous combination for a future hunter. But with more training some therapy, and a shit-ton of luck, she'd get over it, or at least learn how to control it. Mainly she needed some good sex. Hells, I needed some good sex. I'd settle for mediocre sex because I feared that, after Jace, everyone else would fall short, including demon princes.

A quickie might do me good, but I refused to leave the room until I checked Cyn's arm wound. It still hadn't healed by the time we got back to the Academy. I had wanted to head straight to the infirmary to get it looked at, but Cyn insisted on showering before going anywhere— even to the cafeteria to eat, which she desperately needed to do.

I didn't possess Cyn's human neuroses. Ramone, a more-than-willing dragon shifter I'd had sex with a few times to try to rid myself of the sexual frustration I felt when Jace refused my initial advances, let me drink from his vein whenever I wanted. Of course, I never did that either during or immediately following sex. That was one rule I had made for myself, and I would never break it. There were too many rumors about Sempiternals becoming bound to another, and I refused to be bound to any man, or woman, for that matter. My marking with Jace was bad enough.

I continued pacing the room. My meeting with Prince Asmoday unnerved me. I had no idea the man behind the gold mask at the Council meeting was Prince of the Demons. I mean, I harbored no prejudice against demons, but I never realized one sat on the Council. And there was something about the prince that triggered something in me. A memory. A feeling. Maybe even a past life. I really couldn't tell. The prospect of seeing him again both thrilled and scared me.

Knock. Knock. Knock.

I swung our bedroom door open and came face-to-face with Bladecroft and Lippincott. Their shredded clothes, bloodied and bruised bodies, and their pissed off expressions suggested they'd been in a fight, but not the one Cyn and I were at.

Bladecroft placed her hands on her hips. "We need to talk."

"Feeling remorse? Abandonment issues? Yeah, well, join the club," I snapped and slammed the door in their faces.

But Bladecroft was ready for it. The sly warrior. She had wedged her boot into the doorjamb and caught the door. She pushed it open and strolled in. "May we?"

I rolled my eyes. "Do I have a choice?"

"No."

"Well, then, you can both stand there and watch me pace around the room, waiting for my sister to remove potential contaminants from her body."

"But supernaturals can't—"

I threw up my hand, stopping Lippincott. "Believe me, I told her. But she's insistent."

"Okay . . . ," Lippincott said with a healthy dose of reservation.

"How are you?" Bladecroft asked.

I whirled around to face them. "How am I? Where were you?"

The bathroom door swung open, and Cyn walked into the room with a towel wrapped around her. "Yes, where were you?" she demanded. Water droplets still dotted her arms and legs. That disgusting bite wound from Lamashtu looked clean but still gross.

Bladecroft put her hands back on her hips. "We were going to ask you the same thing."

"What's that supposed to mean? We fought Lamashtu at the crossroads. Then, as we waited for you to spring your 'trap,' hordes of demons showed up and kicked our asses before taking us to some disgusting demon dungeon. If it hadn't been for Prince Asmoday, we'd still be trapped there, most likely dying from one of the diseases Cyn is so worried about."

Cyn's mouth dropped open at that last bit, her pale green eyes with purple flecks watching me. I had left out some vital pieces of information about our mission, including the red laser beams shooting out of my eyeballs along with Cyn's ability to bend the dungeon bars. The point was, Bladecroft and Lippincott had never shown up. I felt betrayed. Not for me, but for Cyn.

Thankfully Little Sis kept her mouth shut. Her smart brain processed that it was wise to keep our new abilities hidden. Each one of our professors had instructed us on that very thing. Suspecting they trained two extremely gifted students was one thing. Actually seeing those powers in action was quite another.

"We couldn't get anywhere near the crossroads," Lippincott said. "A thick fog-like shadow drifted in, and we couldn't get through it. A fucking demon army showed up ready to rumble. We fought them off but just barely. Neither one of us expected an ambush of that magnitude. When the sun began to rise, the demons disappeared, the fog lifted, and you two were gone."

Bladecroft kept her lips pressed together and her arms

crossed as Lippincott recounted their evening.

I matched Bladecroft's stance and let Cyn ask the questions.

"What do you mean you couldn't get in? I thought you had already laid the trap and all you had to do was spring it."

Lippincott threw her hands up in the air and sank down on Cyn's bed. "We did. It was all set. Lara tiptoed over to one side, and I sneaked over to the other, but when we tried to release it, the fog drifted in and . . ."

"We. Got. Ambushed," Bladecroft ground out. "I don't know how those demon minions knew we were coming, but they did, and they were ready for us."

"How? Cyn and I didn't know what the mission was until the last minute. That leaves the two of you and . . . ?" I side-eyed Bladecroft with suspicion before glaring at Lippincott.

"No one," they said together.

Bladecroft ticked off her fingers. "Not one goddess. Not one professor. No one."

Lippincott straightened. "There was someone. Goldwell. She saw me driving the SUV around to the back entrance."

I pretended to hit a bell. "Ding. Ding. Ding. We have a winner!"

Bladecroft frowned at me. "Goldwell? She's a professor here."

I shook my head. "You of all people should know that professors and students aren't always what they seem."

Her nostrils flared in and out. "What are you suggesting?"

Jace had told me not to trust anyone and to stay away from Goldwell, but I didn't want to reveal my source.

"Someone told me that Cyn and I should stay away from Goldwell. That she might be a spy for the Children of the Sun."

"Goldwell?" Lippincott scratched her head. "She's intense, but I figured that was a turned-vampire thing. Turned vamps tend to retain much of their human neuroses."

My eyes slid over to Cyn, but she didn't notice. She was too busy studying the cuts on her arms for imagined plagues. Was Cyn so neurotic because she was turned rather than changed? I shuddered to think of the potential ramifications.

I shook my head. Nope. Not going there. Not now. Not ever.

I returned to the problem at hand. "The only thing is, that if that's true, then Goldwell spies for the Children of the Sun not for Lamashtu and her demon lovers. So, again, who set up the ambush?"

Bladecroft slumped onto my bed.

"Make yourself comfortable, why don't you?" I snapped.

"Thanks, I will." She propped up my pillows for back support.

She suddenly seemed tired. Sure, she was like two hundred years old, give or take, but she never acted like her age affected her. She had roundhouse-kicked my ass in more than one training session without breaking a sweat, but now, it appeared the years had caught up to her. She rubbed her face as the three of us watched her. She rested her hands on her knees and released an enormous sigh.

Lippincott rushed over to her. "What is it?"

Bladecroft breathed in and out of her nose several times, grounding herself. "I think I know the reason why the Children of the Sun's power grows exponentially every year."

Cyn came over to stand beside me. "Why?"

"They've aligned with demons."

The hair rose on the back of my neck. "But not all demons are bad."

"No, they're not, but there are a few extremely powerful ones who are."

"Like who?"

"King Asmoday, for one."

"But the prince let us go."

"He did, but his dad is cruel and unyielding."

The need to defend the Asmoday name came over me. I couldn't understand the source of it, but I went with it all the same. "But King Asmoday has been missing for years. He's presumed dead."

Bladecroft's eyes pinned me in place. "Presumed, not proven."

Lippincott dragged her fingers through her hair. "The ramifications of this . . ."

"Could be devasting? Yeah, I know."

Cyn's head whipped back and forth between the three of us. "Shouldn't we let the goddesses know what's going on?"

I wasn't a quarter as old as Bladecroft, but Mama Morrigan's words weighed heavily on me. "I think the goddesses already know. At least some of them do."

Her forehead pinched. "They do?"

"Forces outside of their realm of influence?"

Her eyes closed. "Right. That."

Lippincott stood up. The room filled with her power as she took charge of the situation. "It's time to inform the Sisters."

Cyn's eyes widened. "As in Silver Dagger Sisterhood?"

"As in Silver Dagger Sisterhood, along with all the goddess sisters. Everyone needs to know what's going on. It's time we all start working from the same playbook."

I clamped my hands. Finally the action was starting. "Great! When do we meet?"

Bladecroft rose from my bed. "Nuh-uh. The two of you will put your heads down and get through Silverwood Academy as fast as possible."

I glared at her. "You can't be serious. We've got to fight. Hit them when they're down."

She gestured to her ravaged clothing. "Does it look like they're down? If I got this banged up with all my experience, what do you think would happen to you?"

I raised my chest. "I'm very advanced. I fought several demons today, and I don't look half as bad as you."

Cyn grabbed my arm. "Dez!"

But Bladecroft laughed, shaking her head. "I was cocky once too. I felt invincible, but I've learned that one can't do it alone, and one can't go in half-cocked."

"I normally take the cock whole."

Cyn gasped, but this tangent was mine.

"You forget, I lived a hunter's life before I even entered the Change. I've got tons of experience fighting rogue supernaturals."

Bladecroft strode up to me, stopping inches away. "I know you do, but does your sister? Are you willing to risk her life for your own ego?"

My stomach soured. I pressed my lips together to prevent dragon shifter blood from splattering all over our floor.

"That's what I thought. Now, go to classes, study hard,

train harder, and when it's time, you will join the ranks of F.A.T.A.L."

She spun on her heels and marched to the door.

"Until then you expect us to do nothing? To just sit back and wait?"

She turned back to me. "That's exactly what I want you to do."

"But you asked Cyn and me to go on the mission to get rid of Lamashtu."

She raised her eyebrows. "How'd that turn out?"

"We were overtaken by demons."

"And if it hadn't been for Prince Asmoday, the two of you would be rotting in a demon dungeon."

I opened my mouth to argue that we had been well on our way to escaping on our own, but Cyn dug her nails into my shoulder.

Quiet. Not a word.

My eyes met hers. Tactile telepaths were rare, and evidently, my sister was one. I pressed my lips together. I hated being told what to do, but my sister was right.

Lippincott studied us, sensing that we were communicating without speaking.

"Tiana, are you coming?" Bladecroft growled from the hallway.

Lippincott tapped a finger against her lips, nodding at us before closing our bedroom door behind her.

"She won't tell anyone about me being a telepath" Cyn said confidently beside me.

"I sure hope not. The number of people we can trust keeps dwindling."

Cyn stepped up to me and held my hands. "We've got each other."

I smiled at her. "That we do, Sis. That we do."

CHAPTER

SEVEN

C^{yn}

THE LAST TWENTY-FOUR hours were a whirlwind. An absolute and utter whirlwind. I had barely caught my breath after Bladecroft and Lippincott left before Dez yanked me out of our room and led me out into the courtyard.

"Don't move," she ordered after forcing me to sit at one of the tables. "I'll be right back."

"Where are you going?"

"Back in two seconds." She winked before disappearing back inside.

She reappeared moments later with Gage, her gargoyle "friend" from Silverwood Prison. Now, face-to-face with him in a civilian setting—well, a setting that wasn't a prison—he did remind me of the Hulk, at least in size and stature, but he wasn't green. No part of him was. Not even his eyes which were an ice blue, made even more striking against his ebony skin.

No longer dressed in an orange jumpsuit, his button-down white shirt and jeans strained against his muscles, making him seem all the more massive. His short dreads were gone, replaced with a buzz cut.

Goddess, he was gorgeous. A specimen of perfection if ever there was one.

Dez forced him to sit beside me. Well, even she can't force a gargoyle to sit down, but Gage obliged her. He cared about her. I could tell by the way he looked at her before he tore his attention from her and turned to me.

"Hey, Cyn. How's it going?" he asked, his voice deep but also kind.

"It's going."

Dez pushed me toward him. "Eat," she ordered.

My sister was strong and stubborn and driven, but still, I wasn't about to give in to her. "Excuse me?"

"Eat. You need to eat."

My stomach rumbled in agreement. My eyes met Gage's, and a blush crept up my cheeks. I wanted to die from absolute mortification. I dropped my head and stared at his giant knees. Was there no end to my sister's outrageous behavior?

He lifted my chin. "Cynda, I know you're uncomfortable, but let me help you. You can take your fill of energy and blood, and it won't affect me whatsoever."

My fangs descended at his invitation. They had a mind of their own sometimes. I pulled them back inside my mouth and pressed my lips together.

"It's really not a big deal."

It felt like a big deal. A hulking ginormous deal.

"Just eat," Dez growled.

Gage frowned at her. "Listen, could you give us a few minutes alone without hovering over your sister like the overbearing woman you are?"

I straightened. No one got away with talking to Dez like that without getting punched in the face or the balls.

"Fine," she snapped, "but if she doesn't eat in the next five minutes, I'm not introducing you to Libby."

He snorted. "I'm not helping your sister in order to meet another woman."

"She's a hot gargoyle."

He looked at me and rolled his eyes. "I can get all the hot gargoyles and any other supernatural I want, thanks."

His tone wasn't cocky, just matter-of-fact.

"Whatever," she snapped and stomped away.

His eyes met mine. "Sorry about that. Your sister . . ." He trailed off, not wanting to insult her in front of me.

"Is a pain in the ass?" I offered.

"That's one way to put it. I really care about her."

"Is that why you're helping me?"

He shook his head. "No, I'm helping you because I'm a good person, and I like to help people."

"Are you a student here now?"

He laughed. "I already attended Silverwood Academy, just didn't advance into the Brotherhood. It's fantastic and all, but gargoyles can't really go undercover. Even the best disguises don't work."

He *did* make a point. "Gotcha. So, what are you doing here?"

"Professor Logan asked me to visit and be a guest speaker for some of his classes."

I pulled my hand to my chest. "I'm one of his students."

He tilted his head. "Well then, I guess I'll be seeing you." He glanced behind me and sighed.

I looked over my shoulder but couldn't see anything. "What is it?"

"Your sister is lurking in the shadows behind that giant tree. I don't want to force you to feed from me, but you're weak. Blood bags will only tame a Sempiternal's thirst, never satisfy it. And that's if your energy stores weren't emptied. If you're half as powerful as your sister is, you need more sustenance. That's where I come in." He tapped the side of his neck.

My mouth watered at the gesture, and my fangs descended again.

"Now, you can feed from my neck because it is the best way to get both energy and blood, or you can feed from here," he said, revealing his wrist. "You'll get both from my wrist too, but it takes longer."

The wrist seemed far less intimate than his neck. I felt safe around him but still wasn't sure how to ask.

He rolled up his sleeve and offered his wrist to me. "I'll make the decision for you, if that's okay?"

I pulled my lips in, nodding. Hunger ruled me.

He lifted his wrist to me. "Go ahead."

And I bit into the soft skin of his wrist. Blood and energy poured into my mouth and down my throat, racing to quench my raging hunger. I could feel my skin stitching Lamashtu's wound back together and energetically sealing it.

Wow. Of course I'd bitten Canyon twice, but I had never pulled his energy and blood at the same time. And I didn't need to worry about draining Gage. He wasn't fragile like a human. I also trusted him to stop me if I drank too much.

"That's it," he murmured. "Just keep drinking. You need this."

And you know what? I did.

POWER THRUMMED through me as I walked back to my room. Gage and Dez were right. Blood bags paled in comparison to a living being. They also didn't fill my energy stores like an actual person could. Of course, I had drawn from Canyon, nearly draining him of every last drop of blood, but I'd been too high on it (and too horrified) to acknowledge how it made me feel. But now . . . I was ready to take on the world, fight a thousand of Lamashtu's demons, and break out of a prince's dungeon.

After my feeding session, Gage had left to meet up with Professor Logan, and Dez had disappeared as soon as I began feeding on Gage. Initially I wondered if she was jealous about me feeding on her sometime gargoyle lover, but I immediately dismissed the thought. She wouldn't have brought him to me if she didn't want me to eat.

Gage cared about Dez. Anyone could see that. Plus, he had said as much. Dez trusted him—and from what I'd come to know about my sister, she didn't trust easily. She cared for Gage but not in the same way he cared for her. She liked to have sex with him, but that didn't equate to love. She liked having sex with lots of people—though after her confrontation with the prince, she'd seemed a tad unhinged. Well, more unhinged than normal.

An arm hooked around me and tugged me close, red hair swinging into my vision.

"How's one of my favorite Sempiternals?" Red sang in my ear.

"Keeping it together as best as can be expected."

"What happened?" She clenched my arm. "Wait, there's something different about you. What is it? What happened?

Tell me everything. Details. I need details. I live and breathe through details."

Bladecroft and Lippincott had sworn Dez and me to secrecy about the mission. I didn't want to betray their trust, but I also didn't want to lie to one of my only friends either. So I embraced my inner Dez to use a half-truth to distract and befuddle.

"I had a gargoyle."

Her green eyes widened. "What? Who? When? How?" She grabbed my hand. "Are they as good a lover as they're rumored to be?"

Worked like a charm.

I raised a hand to stop her. "First, I didn't sleep with Gage. I probably should have rephrased that statement. I meant I drew energy and blood from him."

Her enthusiasm faded, and I worried I might lose her and have to start all over again with new misdirection.

"But"—I squeezed her hand—"if he's half as good as his energy blood was, he could satisfy the most desperate of souls."

She closed her eyes as if falling into a dreamlike state. "I knew it."

Mission accomplished.

"Wait—" Her attention snapped back to mine. "You said his name was Gage?"

"Yeah."

"Professor Logan's guest this week?"

"That's the one."

She leaned closer, her face inches from me. "How do you know him? You're new to this world. You didn't even know it existed until a couple months ago, and now you fed from a gargoyle?" She looked over both her shoulders to make sure we were alone. "I didn't think you'd fed off an actual person since Canyon that first day," she whispered.

Embarrassment warmed my cheeks. There was also that second time, when I'd almost left him for dead, but no need to relive all my dirty details. "Dez. And I was in really bad shape."

She slapped her thigh. "I knew it. Of course she's had a gargoyle. Your sister has all the luck."

"I wouldn't necessarily call it luck, but she does like sex."

"Hey, Cynda," a deep voice called out.

We both turned in its direction.

Gage strolled toward us, taking up the entire width of the hallway with his stature. A few people walking toward him changed direction and slipped past us rather than try to get around him. He slid his hands into his pockets, his shoulders rounding, as if trying to make himself small and maybe less intimidating.

"How you feeling?"

I smiled up at him. I had never found him scary at all. He had a kind aura around him that invited people in. He was probably one of the nicest people I'd ever met.

"I'm good. How's it going for you?"

Red cleared her throat. Her excitement to meet Gage wafted off her along with a slight hint of . . . I breathed in. The blush of my cheeks deepened as I realized what she smelled like.

Gage's attention shifted to her, and he winked. Did a gargoyle have as sensitive a nose as a Sempiternal? Or was my enhanced sense of smell from the shifter part of me? In any event, could he smell her too?

He offered her his giant hand. I studied his wrist. My teeth marks were completely gone. I let loose a sigh of relief. Now that I knew I hadn't permanently marked him, I would be much less hesitant about feeding off him or other supernaturals in the future. I'd keep away from humans—ephemerals as Dez called them. They were far more breakable.

Red threw her hair over her shoulder as she took his hand. I had missed their initial exchange while I was in my own head, but apparently, whatever had transpired included Red getting more horny. I wondered if there was a potion, or whether I could create one, that blocked my sense of smell. I'd have to visit the potion's lab later to see what I could find.

"I can't wait for your presentation," Red gushed. "I'm sure you'll be amazing. Cyn said as much already."

He smiled, his white teeth flashing brightly against his dark skin. "Oh, I don't know about that. I just hope I don't bore everyone."

She tapped his arm playfully. "There's nothing boring about you," she all but purred.

Oh goddess, get me out of here.

"Well, I better get going. I'm meeting Professor Logan for dinner. Hey, Cyn, have you seen your sister? She's not in her room."

"No. We don't have any classes together today. She does run at the track a lot."

"I'll try there. Anastasia, it was really nice to meet you. We'll have to hang out sometime."

Her body vibrated with excitement. "Yes, yes, definitely."

He winked at me. "See you both tomorrow."

I smiled. "See you later."

Red waved enthusiastically beside me. "Bye, Gage. See you!"

When he disappeared around the corner, she sighed, then moaned. "Did you see his fucking ass? I wonder what the rest of him looks like."

"Should I give you a minute alone?"

"Oh, honey, I need more than a minute. And he wants to hang out with me!" Her eyes shot to mine. "Wait, oh no. Are you interested in him too?"

I shook my head. "I am not interested in him that way. I'm taking a no-relationship stance for the remainder of the semester."

"If I was your sister, I would remind you that you don't need to be in a relationship to have sex. Actually, I'm not your sister, and you don't need a relationship to have sex. You can sleep around. In fact, I encourage it."

I continued down the hall. "I know, but I've got enough complications. No reason to add to them."

"Do you think he was looking for Dez because he wanted to have sex with her?"

"I can't say for certain, but I don't think so. He's one of the only people Dez trusts. She's had sex with him plenty of times,"—I shuddered at the memory of him fingering Dez in front of me at Silverwood Prison—"but it's more of a convenience thing than an actual desire to have sex with each other. Well, at least for Dez, if that makes sense."

"Strangely it does, but I'll be honest with you. I've got a strong desire to have sex with Gage."

"Oh, I can tell."

EIGHT

ez

I RACED around the track for the twentieth time, but as much as I tried to escape them, a bazillion thoughts kept storming around in my head. My encounter with the Demon Prince left me unsettled and unsure, and it wasn't just because my energy stores had been depleted at the time. It was because of something else. Something I couldn't quite put my finger on.

After ensuring Cyn ate, I considered returning to Ramone's room and fucking his brains out under the guise that I wanted to demonstrate my appreciation to him for always letting me feed off of him, but really it was because I wanted to hide from this feeling inside of me that I'd had since meeting Prince Asmoday. I couldn't bring myself to have sex with Ramone or anyone else for that matter. Well, other than the one person I swore to keep my distance from.

Sweat poured off me. My leg muscles burned. My heart pounded against my chest. But still I ran. My arms swung forward and back, keeping in line with my body. Intense physical exertion often brought me clarity, and I desperately needed it. The gold-masked man at the Council meeting was a prince and a demon. A powerful one too. His demon power wrapped around me, electrifying me, inviting me for a taste, igniting fire in me.

Then there was that thread pulling me toward Jace's studio. I cursed, ignoring the impulse, and pushed my body faster. If I wanted any chance of surviving at Silverwood Academy, if I harbored any hope of joining the Sisterhood, if I desired finding my father's killer, I needed to break that marking bond between us. My connection to Jace made me weak. I was a hunter, and I couldn't properly hunt if I kept thinking about those damn gold eyes or the mind-blowing sex. I should have Gage fuck me senseless, but truthfully, the thought of sleeping with someone else made me want to vomit.

I pushed my muscles to run faster. A frenzy of motion. Tearing down the track. The buildings nothing but a blur. Even with the wolf asleep inside me—thanks to dear old Mommy Morrigan—my Sempiternal abilities increased every day. I far surpassed the other Sempiternals at Silverwood. The woman who had replaced my father on the Council would be amazed at my progress. If I continued advancing at my current rate, I'd be able to beat her in a race before I graduated.

Caught up in my fantasy, I failed to process the obstacle standing in the middle of the track. The obstacle I was supposed to avoid. The obstacle that drew me to him. His arms wrapped around me as I slammed into his chest, and we sailed through the air. Me moving forward. Jace flying backward. Pressed together airborne for entirely too long before hitting the track, cracking the ground beneath us. Dazed, I lay there not fully aware of what had transpired. My body pressed against his, thrumming with want and need. My chest rumbled, betraying my desire.

"Aw fuck," I grunted, trying to push myself off him. His arms tightened around me, and his gold eyes bored into mine. His raven-black hair splayed out, creating a halo around his head.

"Hello, darling," he purred. "I would love nothing more than to fuck you right now, but that's not the reason I'm here."

At his mere use of the word, my folds pooled with wetness.

Damn him and his vocabulary.

I shoved my arms between us. My fingers pressed against his hard, muscled chest as I tried to get away from him. "Let me go."

He released me before the Academy's spell of consent and protection could be invoked. Free from him, I leapt out of the crater we'd created, fully intending to sprint away from him.

His hand snapped out and grabbed my arm as if sensing my intention. He moved much quicker than I remembered, his long black hair swinging back and forth from the motion.

"Not so fast."

"Let. Go. Of. Me. Jace," I gritted out through clenched teeth.

His face softened, observing my anger. "Just allow me one minute before you run away again."

My cheeks burned. "I wasn't going to run away." (I had planned to sprint.)

"You've been avoiding me for weeks."

Two, actually, but who was counting?

I tried pulling away from him, but he held firm. "I don't know what you're talking about. You're imagining things."

He tilted his head, watching me. "You skip my classes. You put up a wall of protection around yourself when you're outside so I can't see you, though I can sense you. You take the long way to your other classes that are in my wing rather than pass by my studio."

He'd forgotten a few, but I didn't want to give away all my secrets.

I turned my lips down and snorted. "Sounds like someone's obsessed."

His eyes burned into mine. "I'm not obsessed, and I am not imagining things. There's something between us, and you know it."

"I feel nothing for you," I snapped.

He inhaled deeply, and a cocky smile appeared on those sexy-ass lips. "That's not what it smells like to me."

I yanked away from him. "Don't flatter yourself. When I crashed into you, I was thinking about fucking someone else."

His jaw feathered as he straightened.

Knowing I'd struck a nerve, I kept going. "He's sexy as hell, and the electricity between us is undeniable. I don't think I could ever go back to sex with"—my gaze fell on him—"anyone else. He's ruined me."

"Who?" The hard lines of his jaw reminded me of the tight planes of his abs.

I placed my hands on my hips, my chest lifting triumphantly. "Jealous?" I teased.

"Who is it?"

I grinned at him as I lifted a hand to the side of my mouth and leaned toward him conspiratorially. "A lady never tells."

His nostrils flared in and out, but this time it wasn't from scenting my desire. His gold eyes shifted to red, and his chest rose and fell as he tried to calm himself through one of his mindfulness exercises. Time to poke the beast.

"Lucky for you, I'm not a lady."

"Who. Is. It?" he stamped out, his hands clenched in two tight balls.

"A member of the Council. Very powerful. Very well endowed, if you know what I mean."

But rather than losing his mind and stomping off in a fit of rage and dejection, his shoulders softened and he folded his hands behind his back, his luscious dimple appearing on his cheek. "A Council member?"

Not the reaction I was hoping for.

"And . . . a prince."

He cocked his head to the side. "Huh. Really? And the two of you slept together?"

"Rutted like animals."

His eyes sparkled with amusement. "And when did this happen?"

Anger rose in me. "You don't believe me?"

He snorted. "No. I think it's a pathetic attempt to get a rise out of me."

"Pathetic?" Fire ignited inside me. "A few minutes ago, you wanted to fuck me senseless, and now I'm pathetic."

He shook his head slowly. "I never said senseless. We're two consenting adults who enjoy each other's company, but if you're involved with a prince . . . ," he spread his hands out wide in front of him, "I guess I don't stand a chance."

"He *is* a prince and a Council member."

He put his hand over his mouth, hiding his smile. "You mentioned that already."

"You're not mad? I would think you'd be furious after all your stalking."

He shrugged and turned to walk away, his snug T-shirt revealing his muscular back muscles and his yoga pants accentuating his tight ass.

"But we marked each other!" I cried out. This conversation had turned sideways real fast.

He glanced over his shoulder and winked. "Guess I can't compete with this well-endowed sex god."

Dampness bloomed between my legs. My goddess, I wanted him.

"Jace, wait." I hurried to catch up. He dashed into the Wildwoods. I growled, vamp-speeding after him. That bastard was ignoring me. He'd called me pathetic. He was the one who was pathetic, creeping around Silverwood Academy, keeping tabs on me.

I caught sight of his muscular back in the distance before he disappeared behind a tall oak tree. Adrenaline coursed through me at the chase. The Sempiternal side ruled me. The inner predator kicked into hyper vamp speed.

I rounded the tree. His sexy earthy scent filled my senses. He was close. Two arms shot out and wrapped around my waist, drawing me to him.

"Yes?" he whispered in my ear.

Rather than being angry that I was caught, shivers ran down my spine.

I spun around, still in his grasp. Our chests pressed

against each other, rising and falling from the thrill of the chase.

"Why did you leave?"

"Our conversation ended."

"You called me pathetic," I murmured, jutting out my lower lip.

A rumble rose from his chest as he gently pinched my pouting lip with his skilled fingers. "Is that why you chased me? You wanted me to apologize for insulting you? Why don't you ask *your prince*?"

His other hand trailed down my back, finding skin as it wound its way to my ass. I gasped, forgetting how electrifying his touch was.

"I might have overplayed my hand."

"Oh, I don't know. You acted as if you had a real connection with this well-endowed prince," he teased as he pushed me against the tree, pressing his long, hard cock against my stomach. "How could I possibly compete?" He slid his knee between my thighs, shifting closer. A moan escaped my lips.

His eyebrows rose in wicked delight. "And he's a member of the Council." He cupped my ass, his fingers wrapping around it, taking possession of it. His other hand slipped into the front of my shorts. My leg curled around him, allowing him better access. "I'm just a yoga instructor. How could I possibly make you as wet as a prince?" He slid two fingers into me. "Although, you seem pretty wet to me."

A tiny voice inside my head reminded me I was supposed to keep away from Jace. That he couldn't be trusted. I thought about stopping him. I really did, but then, his fingers pulsed in and out of me, and my core tightened around him.

"Oh my," he teased. "Whatever would the prince say?"

I groaned. One of his fingers found my clit.

"Does he know how to stroke you?" His fingers rubbed against me. "Can he make you come with a few caresses?"

"Yes," I gritted out, already losing myself to his touch. That's what Jace did to me.

His hands disappeared. "Yes? Or do you mean, no? He doesn't know how to send you over the cliff with some well-placed movements."

"Please," I begged.

"Please what?"

"Stroke me. Fill me."

His nose trailed along my neck. "But what about your prince?" His finger returned to dancing along my clit.

"Fuck the prince."

His finger stopped moving. "Oh, I don't think you did. I think you just said that to make me jealous. Did you want to make me jealous?" His fingers thrummed alive in me, triggering a mini orgasm.

"Yes!"

"Does the prince make you come like I do?"

"I never. We never . . . ," I panted, his fingers winding my core into a frenzied peak.

"So you lied about the prince?"

"Yes."

"You wanted to make me jealous?"

"Yes."

"You promise not to hide from me anymore?"

"Yes!"

Almost there. So close.

"You promise to go to class?"

"Yes!"

"Do you want me?" He stroked right where I needed him to be.

"Yes. Yes! YES!"

So fucking close.

"Come for me, Dez," he demanded.

And I did, clenching his fingers, unraveling completely.

CHAPTER

NINE

C^{yn}

I WATCHED myself in the bathroom mirror as I dabbed ointment under my nose. I wanted to make sure I gave myself ample coverage because Red and I always sat together in class, and Gage was presenting today, so Demonology would serve as my first field test. After many hours last night in the potions lab (and a lot of failed experiments), I finally concocted the right mixture to block sex smells, specifically pheromones, but still allow other scents to come through. Initially I planned to block my sense of smell completely, but then Canyon stopped by the lab, looking for me. He didn't see me—my Circle of Protection worked like a charm—but his appearance reminded me that eliminating one of my senses entirely was dangerous, especially since in the field, one can't predict what senses might become disabled when a mission turns sideways. (Thanks, Bladecroft and Lippincott, for that lesson.) Starting off with all senses intact allows room for the unexpected.

For instance, say I didn't hear Canyon come in or I hadn't cast a Circle of Protection, at least I would have caught his mint and cedarwood scent before I wound up on his lap, sucking him dry.

A strong sense of smell was also vital for potion making. Sometimes potions soured, becoming volatile, and I didn't want to blow up the potions lab, or Silverwood Academy for that matter.

Dez appeared behind me, watching my reflection in the bathroom mirror. "What are you putting on under your nose?"

"I bought a special salve to block pheromones."

Still no reason for her to know where I spent most of my free time. She wouldn't approve, and I didn't like fighting with her all the time.

"Why?"

I studied her in the mirror. From her raven-black hair to her purple eyes to her toned body, my sister was gorgeous. She reminded me of our mom, but I'd never tell her that. She'd probably dye her hair and gouge out her eyes.

"Can you smell when someone is . . . ," heat rushed up my neck, "horny?"

"Yes. When I was just a Sempiternal, I caught notes of it, but now, with this wolf inside me, I can smell everything. It's very inconvenient."

She didn't go into further details, nor did I want her to. I had smelled Red's horniness more than enough yesterday.

"It blocks pheromones but not a person's signature scent. So Red smells like roses, which I'll still be able to smell, but if she starts thinking about sex, I won't smell that."

She gave me a mischievous smirk. "She wants to have sex with Gage, doesn't she?"

"How'd you know?"

"Gage found me outside after I . . ." she cleared her throat, "after my run yesterday." She arched her back, her chest rising in front of her. "He asked me about Red and if I thought she would go out with him."

"What did you say?"

"The truth."

"Which was?"

"He'd have to ask her himself because she's a grown-ass woman with a mind and opinions of her own, and she's horny as fuck."

My eyes widened. "You didn't."

She barked out a laugh. "No, but you should have seen your face." She thrust her hand out to me. "Can I use some of that?"

I raised an eyebrow, offering it to her. "You want to block pheromones? You're the one who's horny as fuck."

She swiped her finger across the top of the jar and began applying it under her nose. "And that's why I need to block my nose."

"It doesn't block everything. Only pheromones." I carefully closed the jar and shoved it in my front pocket.

She sighed, her eyes taking on a faraway look. "That should be enough. It has to be."

"Who'd you have sex with?"

Ignoring my question, she spun and prowled out of the bathroom.

"Who'd you have sex with?" I shouted.

When she still didn't answer, I hurried out of the bathroom, just as the door slammed shut.

"I just hope it wasn't Jace," I said to the empty room. "Or the Demon Prince," I added as I grabbed my bag and stepped out into the hall. I took a deep breath before heading to class. Time to test if the salve worked like it was supposed to. I probably should have mentioned that to Dez before she left. No way would she actually put herself in the line of pheromones to test it, right?

I sighed. That's exactly what she would do.

CONCERN for my sister's sexual well-being faded as I entered the crowded auditorium.

"Man, looks like everyone wants to watch Gage in action," Red murmured, sounding unsure and hesitant—a stark contrast to the confident witch I'd walked down the stairs with.

"Don't worry. I have it on good authority that Gage asked about you."

She sighed. "I hope so. I kept dreaming about our meeting last night."

Time to test out my salve. "Is that *all* you dreamed about?"

"Yes. Believe it or not, I kept replaying how we shook hands and the way his voice rumbled when he spoke to me, and the look of concern he had for you when he wanted to make sure you felt okay after your feeding. He's so compassionate." She sighed.

I inhaled but didn't catch the hint of pheromones. I really wanted to test this mixture with a controlled pheromone blast.

"I bet he's a compassionate lover too."

I groaned inwardly. What a terrible sexual innuendo. If Dez were here, she'd punch me for that lame line. I could do better.

"I bet he's hung like a fucking horse."

Ewww. I couldn't believe I'd just compared a gargoyle's penis to a horse's, but maybe it would work.

"Oh yeah," she growled. "I bet he is, and I know exactly where he can put it."

I inhaled deeply and smelled . . . nothing. Absolutely nothing aside from her rose scent.

Well, that worked better than expected. Maybe I should start marketing my stuff. Create a pop-up apothecary or something.

Red squeezed my bicep. "Look, there he is. Let's get closer. I want to study his muscular body up close."

I inhaled again. Still nothing. Not a hint of desperation or hormones. I closed my eyes and smiled. The salve worked like a charm.

We wound our way through our classmates. Red threw elbows, shoving women out of the way. Men too. Threats of spells and beatings followed us to the front row, but my witchy friend remained unfazed. The rules of Silverwood Academy prevented acts of violence against other students or faculty while on campus. Of course, it never stopped Red from using her magick on others without their permission, but she attached good intention to it, and usually it was to heal one of us.

Gage waved at us from his seat. "Hi, Cynda! Hi, Anastasia! Glad you could make it."

"Hi, Gage. Wouldn't miss it," she called out as she skillfully slid into the first available seat before the guy in front of her did.

He scowled at her, his bright blue eyes flashing.

"Sorry," she said, not sounding sorry at all.

"That was my seat."

"Not anymore." She pointed at the row behind us. "You can sit there."

But instead of moving, he placed his hands on his hips. "No, that was my seat. Now move."

I recognized stubbornness when I saw it and decided, for the safety of everyone involved, to deescalate the situation. "Hey," I said, placing my hand on his shoulder.

He jumped, his claws extending. I couldn't tell if they were vamp claws, shifter claws, or faerie claws, but they were claws, and they were sharp.

I stared at him. I wasn't completely sure how to compel people, and technically it violated Silverwood Academy rules because it removed free will, but I figured one little request wouldn't get me in trouble. "Why don't you sit in the row behind us?"

"Why don't you? And don't try any of your Sempiternal crap on me. I despise your kind," he snarled, revealing fangs.

So faerie then, because shifters tended to like me, and Azalea and her harem did not.

"Why don't you tell me how you really feel?"

"Is there a problem here?" Two giant hands wrapped around the angry faerie.

All the color drained from his face as Gage held him in place, but he wasn't done arguing his point. "This redhead witch took my seat."

"Her name is Anastasia, and she's my guest, so I suggest you sit somewhere else."

"But—"

Gage's big fingers curled into his pointy shoulders.

"Okay, okay. I'm leaving."

Gage removed his hands. "Great. Enjoy the presentation."

The faerie scurried away up the aisle to the back of the auditorium. There he stopped to whisper to someone as he pointed at us. Azalea's eyes narrowed.

"Looks like you made a new friend."

I glanced over at Alyze, who had just climbed over the seat next to me from the row behind us.

"Guess we did. What are you doing here?"

She thrust her chin in Red's direction. Red was making googly eyes at Gage, who was returning them.

"Just taking in the show."

"You haven't seen anything yet," I said under my breath, but it wouldn't have mattered if I'd shouted it. Gage and Red were spellbound with each other. "Don't you have Demonology tomorrow with Dez?"

"Yeah, I do, but Ghostbusting was cancelled, so I came here. What's that shiny stuff below your nose?"

I withdrew the jar from my pocket and unscrewed the lid. "You're gonna want some of this, trust me. It blocks pheromone scent." I gestured toward Gage and Red, who were still staring at each other.

"Sirens don't have a strong sense of smell. Water puts a damper on that ability."

"Oh, right. Well, Sempiternals do, so"—I added some more under my nose—"I need to safeguard my sanity."

"Good afternoon," Professor Logan said. Gage broke away from Red and quickly climbed up the stairs to join Professor Logan. "I'd like to introduce you to our special guest, Gage Ramsford."

The entire auditorium gasped.

"He's a Ramsford?" Red squealed.

I leaned over to Alyze. "Is that a name I should be familiar with?"

"The Ramsfords are one of the original gargoyle families. They're the most well-known and highly regarded Guardians of our world."

Red clutched her chest as if trying to keep her heart inside her body. "Oh goddess, oh goddess, and a Ramsford just asked me to dinner." She breathed out, sounding like she was a having a quiet orgasm.

"Bet you're glad you reapplied that potion," Alyze whispered.

"Yeah, definitely."

Gage stood next to Professor Logan with his unmoving chest flared out and his chin raised as if the audience's reaction didn't affect him in the least. That was how it would appear to anyone who didn't know him, but I could tell he was nervous. His hands thrummed against his legs inside his front pockets. He kept straightening his shoulders because they kept curling in, as if the enormity of the audience's expectation weighed heavily on him. When his eyes met mine, I mouthed, "You got this. Just breathe."

He gave me a small smile. His nostrils flared as he breathed in and out in a slow, steady rhythm. His chest rose and fell as he found his breath.

"Many scholars consider gargoyles the ideal specimen of perfection."

Red nodded vigorously next to me.

"But not for the reasons you assume." Professor Logan turned to Gage and smiled—which he didn't do often—as if he, too, sensed my gargoyle friend's nervousness. "Gage, would you mind stepping forward?"

"Sure."

Gage's immense frame dwarfed Professor Logan's short

height. His arm, leg, and chest muscles bulged against his snug black clothing. In the dim lights of the auditorium, the whites of his deep blue eyes served as bright beacons in stark contrast to his dark skin and clothing. If he closed his eyes, he'd disappear, and that was probably exactly what he wanted to do in front of this spellbound audience.

"In hand-to-hand combat, few other species could match a gargoyle's raw strength, but his greatest power lies in the ability to closely observe his opponent and render him or her powerless with the least amount of physical exertion and contact possible." Professor Logan circled in front of Gage and stopped directly in front of him. "Can I have a volunteer?"

Red's hand shot into the air, bouncing up and down. "I volunteer. I volunteer."

"Hope it's not like the Hunger Games or this won't end well for her," I mumbled to Alyze.

Gage rose on his heels, his chin pitched forward as if searching the audience. "How about that person in the back row?"

I turned around, following his gaze, guessing exactly who he wanted to try his special ability on. The faerie tried ducking his head, but the empty seats around him made it impossible for him to hide.

He pulled his hand to his chest. "Me?"

"Most definitely." Gage's voice boomed through the auditorium. A twinge of guilt shot through me. The only reason the poor guy was picked was because Red had taken his seat. Then again, he didn't have to act like such an asshole about it or insult Sempiternals. That was rude.

Guess I didn't feel so bad after all.

I watched him skulk forward, his head moving from side to side as if waiting for someone else to volunteer as tribute, but the only person who might have was Red, and her hands were now folded on her lap.

"Thank you, Stewart," Professor Logan said as the faerie reluctantly climbed onto the stage. "Now, all I need for you to do is stand there. Gage will do the rest."

He stopped at the edge of the stage. "Like this?"

"Just like that," Gage said, turning to face him.

Stewart's Adam's apple bobbed nervously as he swallowed. He shifted from foot to foot, but to his credit, he stood his ground.

"Now, observe," Professor Logan said.

Gage didn't move. Not a muscle. Not a wrist flick. Not even a small chin lift, but suddenly, Stewart turned a pasty gray, and I remembered a few pasty-gray prisoners from when Dez and Gage had saved me after I attacked the pack of shifters at Silverwood Prison.

"A gargoyle's true power comes from their ability to immobilize any living being with their stare."

"Is he dead?" someone shrieked.

I glanced over my shoulder. Azalea watched the frozen Stewart.

"No, he's not," Gage replied. He snapped his fingers and Stewart reanimated. He collapsed on the stage, grasping his chest.

"Now, most of you do not possess a gargoyle's ability to immobilize, but you each have your own gift that allows you to stop your opponent with the least amount of power expenditure. It's not about size or might. It's about focus and protecting yourself. Break off into pairs and see what you can do."

I thought back to Dez's collapsed form after she'd fried the demon with her red laser beams. She probably could have dispatched him more quickly and with less energy expenditure if she'd vamp-sped over and shoved her dagger into his neck.

I cracked my fingers and turned to Alyze, figuring she'd partner with me, but she was gone, replaced with a very hot man giving me a very sly grin.

"Hi, Cynda."

Guess the salve didn't work as well as I thought it did. If it had, I wouldn't have missed the mint and cedarwood.

Crap. Back to the drawing board. Well, if I could survive this class.

TEN

ez

Fuck, I'd done it again.

I slammed my fist against the oak table.

Crack.

Jace's presence had overloaded my senses, making me forget the promise I'd made to Cyn that I'd keep my distance from him. I punched the table again, and the strong wood splintered down the length of it.

Gage slid into the seat across from me, taking in the damage.

In my disgust with myself, I'd forgotten to cast a Circle of Protection around myself when I got outside. I had tried meditating, but my lady bits kept recalling the orgasm Jace gave me yesterday, wanting to replay it again and again and . . .

"What did this table ever do to you?"

"Would you like me to pummel you instead? You're stronger than this flimsy piece of tree."

"As much as I would love to serve as your personal punching bag, I have plans."

"So what are you doing here?"

"I wanted to check in on you. Last night you seemed out of sorts."

"I'm not apologizing for being a bitch. It's part of my DNA." Which wasn't a lie. Morrigan adored strength and valor, which she sometimes rewarded with insults to spur her warriors to battle frenzy.

Not that I could even tell Gage who my mom was. I trusted him with my life, but I would never endanger him with that information. The Children of the Sun had spies everywhere, and they exploited weaknesses. Gage's affection for me was his biggest flaw.

Gage snorted. "Actually, the opposite. You were nicer than usual. Like a lioness content after gorging herself. Then Jace strolled in right behind you."

I slammed my fist again. "Don't mention his name."

"Sore subject. Noted. But he's a good guy. Misunderstood mostly. I went through Silverwood Academy and Guardian training with him."

My eyes narrowed, my red laser beams primed and ready. "I told you I don't want to talk about it."

"Just thought you should know some of his history."

My claws emerged from my fingers. "Gage," I growled in warning.

"Fine. Fine. I won't tell you how he tried to help me overcome my"—he glanced around to make sure we were alone—"death stare, but I was stubborn and arrogant. I relied too much on my family name when I should have been actually learning how to master my abilities including how to meditate. That's why I had to go through another round in Silverwood Prison even after graduating from the Academy and sailing through Guardian training—punishment by the Brotherhood for my unwillingness to control myself."

Memories of both our times together at Silverwood Prison sliced through my core. Maybe Gage could make me forget Jace.

"How did you learn to control it in a jail cell?"

"I spent twenty-one hours a day by myself. I meditated the entire time, only breaking to eat and sleep, finally embracing Jace's instruction."

"I told you not to say his name," I ground out through clenched teeth.

"There you are," Red shouted from the other side of the courtyard. She rushed over to us.

"Hi, Anastasia." Gage pushed himself up from the split table but froze when he saw her. "Wow," he paused, swallowing hard as he ran a hand over his head, "you look gorgeous."

And she did. Her tight green dress hugged her in all the right places, showing off her curves.

She smiled up at him. "Thank you. You don't look so bad yourself."

It was then I realized Gage wore a black tie with a white button down shirt and black dress pants.

"Ready for dinner?" He asked her.

She nodded vigorously. She was ready for dinner and whatever came after.

I looked up at him with a smirk. "Guess I know why you can't spar with me this evening." Or fuck me silly, I mentally added.

He slid his hands into his pockets. "You're not upset, are

you?"

"Gage, you deserve someone far better than me, and I adore Red."

She squeezed my shoulders. "Aw, I adore you too, Dez, even if you broke my favorite table out here." She released her hold from me and placed one hand on the crack. "Lucky for you—and the table—I can fix it."

She closed her eyes and chanted a spell. Magick whirled in the air around us, tickling my nose before drifting down and encircling the table. She opened her eyes and snapped her fingers. "That should do it."

And lo and behold, the crack sealed back together, and the table was back to pre-Dez destruction.

She pointed a finger at me. "Now, be nice to it. This table never did anything to you." She hooked her arm around Gage. "You ready?"

He tilted his head, looking down at her. "I thought you were only a first year."

"I am."

"That's a really powerful spell."

She looked up at him. "I *am* a really powerful witch."

"Blessed by Brigit herself," I added.

Silence stretched between them as they stared at each other, her looking up at him and him looking down at her. Their size difference was not that shocking. The air around them clouded, and I caught the distinct scent of want and need. Not sex, per se, Cyn's ointment blocked that, but something deeper. Roots twining together into something more. I didn't feel the least bit jealous, even though moments ago I had wanted Gage to pound the images of Jace from my mind. Our days of feasting on each other in riotous sexcapades were over. My only regret was that Gage was the only one who even came close to making me feel the way Jace made me feel.

My fist curled, and I stared at the newly repaired table, Red's warning the only thing keeping me from smashing it to toothpicks.

ALYZE AND CYN found me in the courtyard soon after Red and Gage left. They filled me in on Gage's performance in Demonology. He'd blown their minds with his ability to immobilize someone without any movement. I recalled Gage mentioning that Jace had helped him learn to meditate. Had Jace given him prayer beads too?

Concentrate on your prayers.

I can't believe I didn't think of that earlier. Cursing, I leapt from the table and stormed back into the building. Alyze and Cyn were hot on my trail, calling out for me to wait, sensing I needed company, but the type of company I needed, they couldn't give me.

I headed straight to Ramone's room. A little dragon shifter blood was exactly what would get my mind off Jace. The second I knocked, Ramone opened the door and gave me a knowing wink as I entered. He closed the door behind me and lifted his chin, offering me his neck without me even asking. I took what I wanted, ignoring his hands trailing up and down my body, until I'd had my fill. When I broke away, he pushed me up against the wall, cupping my ass. The movement reminded me exactly of Jace shoving me up against the tree in the Wildwoods yesterday but with nowhere near the hot sexual tension. A wave of nausea swept over me. I slapped my hand over my mouth, broke away from him, and dashed out of his room. He called after me, asking if I was okay. I ignored him and sprinted to my room before I went somewhere I might regret—like Jace's studio.

Hours later, Cyn found me curled up in a fetal position in my bed. I'd never felt so miserable before, so twisted up inside about feeding off someone, so confused about my own mind. Without a word, she gave me a sleeping draught, and for the first time, I slept through the night without dreaming of Jace or his powerful, muscular body and the things he did to mine or the fact that I had to keep a distance from him.

The morning brought new perspective and renewed determination. I strolled down the hallway to the very room I had avoided the night before. In the throes of passion, I'd made a promise to Jace that I would attend his class. I cursed myself for agreeing to it. Desperation made otherwise sane people agree to things they normally wouldn't, and the truth of it was, I wasn't sane to begin with. Of course, I could skip, and the thought had crossed my mind more than once on my way to the studio, but that was the coward's way, and I'd already taken that route the past few weeks. It was time to face the Meditation instructor on his home turf.

Embracing my inner bitch, which thankfully was never far off, I shoved open the studio door. It slammed against the inside wall with a satisfying bang. With my chin lifted and Cyn's pheromone-blocking salve under my nose, I was ready for whatever torture my Meditation instructor had in store for me.

"Dez, it's really not necessary to take your sexu—" Gage paused, knowing a classroom full of witnesses was listening to his every word, "*frustration* out on an innocent slab of wood."

KB ANNE

I shrugged as I strolled over to my section of the floor. Xan, the merman I had hooked up with at the beginning of the year, had taken up residence in my spot. I embraced the anger rising up in me, welcoming it like an old friend. "Move."

"S-sorry," he sputtered, pulling his yoga mat out of the way. I threw mine down in a violent flick of my wrists.

Gage stood with his hands on his hips. His eyes narrowed.

"Yes?" I snapped.

He cleared his throat. "Whenever you're ready."

It was only then that I realized he was wearing yoga pants and a T-shirt, along with bare feet.

"You're our instructor today?"

"Would you rather *Jace*, your regular instructor?" He quirked his head to the side with a raised eyebrow. A challenge if I ever saw one. Any other time, I'd rise to it, but I refused to take the bait during class.

"No, just wondering why you're here instead. Any hope you'll be replacing him for good?"

He raised a single finger. "Excellent question, and no, I will not be your full-time instructor. Just filling in for *Jace* for the next few classes."

I scowled at him, wondering how my red laser beams would fare against his immobilizing stare one-on-one. Maybe we'd find out this morning if he kept tossing that name around.

He met my glare in challenge. Daring me to say something. Then, as if remembering we weren't alone, he took in the rest of the class.

"Please forgive me. I cannot allow rude behavior to pass. Anyway, I'm Gage Ramsford, and I'll be guiding you through your next few meditations. I'm sure Jace shared with you the importance of meditation in order to harness your emotions and guide your abilities. Jace and his meditation methods saved my life. Many of you were at the assembly yesterday, or you heard about it since news travels fast at Silverwood Academy." Murmurs of agreement rose from the other students. "If I hadn't embraced meditation and recognized it as a tool, I would have died just as easily as any of you could with a silver dagger to the heart, because my stare can not only freeze someone, but it can also kill, and before I learned how to meditate, I killed more than I should have."

Gasps of surprise rippled through the classroom. Gage captured this class just as he did the full auditorium yesterday. I had figured I'd get to watch him in action during Demonology with Professor Logan this afternoon, but evidently I'd get to witness his meditation skills this morning.

At least I wouldn't have to listen to Jace's voice. I glanced over at his bedroom door. I breathed in and out, calming my racing heart and trying not to think about what Jace and I had done in that room or out in the yoga studio or against the oak tree in the Wildwoods.

"Let's begin." Gage's voice glided over us. "You're walking along a worn path in the forest. In the distance . . ."

I WAITED after class to speak with Gage. A few starstruck students stayed behind, including Xan, fawning over the handsome gargoyle who happened to come from the famous Ramsford line. Two years ago, I didn't know what Gage's last name was when he ambled into Femme Fatale. All I knew was that he drank top-shelf whiskey and tipped well. He and I immediately hit it off. After a night of indulging in too many shots, I spilled my guts about my dead parents and my long-lost sister. He confessed his family heritage along with a laundry list of intimate secrets I would take to my grave. The two of us pinky swore an allegiance of lasting friendship and secrecy, and to date, neither one of us has gone back on those promises. The friends-with-benefits thing came much later. Prison life makes one horny.

He turned to me when the last of his adoring fans departed and gave me a sheepish grin, shoving his hands into his pockets.

"I know. I know. It's hard to be famous."

He blushed. "I really despise it."

"Fake it till you make it, right?" I punched him in the arm. "Great class, by the way. You should take it over."

He crossed his arms over his chest, giving me a knowing look. "Dez, it's okay to care about Jace."

And pop goes the fucking bubble.

"I don't. I'm only here because he made me promise to attend class."

His serious expression vanished as he broke down in a fit of laughter, clutching his stomach, tears streaming from his eyes.

I walloped him in the arm. "What's so funny?"

He swiped some errant tears. "No one makes you do anything you don't want to do."

"I promised, and you of all people know I don't break my promises."

He immediately sobered up. "You're right. You don't."

"Where is he anyway? Not that I care or anything. I just want to know when the stalker is returning to campus."

He rubbed his palms together. "Okay, deflecting emotions by calling him a stalker."

"He does stalk me. He marked me, Gage."

His forehead bunched, all signs of joking gone. "What?"

"He marked me without my permission."

He shook his head, crossing his arms over his massive chest. "No, that's not possible. He's always in control of his actions. He can never lose control or . . ."

The hair on the back of my neck stood up. "Or what, Gage? What happens if he loses control?"

He turned away. "Nothing."

I grabbed his bicep. Well, part of it. "Or what, Gage?"

He froze in place, but not because I was stronger than him. It was because he knew I wouldn't let the subject drop until I found out what I wanted.

"It's not my story to tell," he finally offered.

"What about his marking me?"

He pressed his lips together, watching me. "That *is* concerning."

Finally he was agreeing with me. I threw my hands out. "I'll say."

"But it does explain his recent actions and why he left suddenly."

I leaned toward him, Jace's location suddenly of utmost interest to me.

Gage inhaled sharply, catching my scent, his nostrils flaring in and out and his eyes widening. "Did you, by chance, mark him too?"

I bit my lip, looking away from him. I could never lie to Gage, but I refused to answer him.

"Even more interesting."

I decided to turn my silent acknowledgment to my advantage. I grabbed ahold of his arm and squeezed, calling on Lilith to boost my compellation powers. My purple eyes pulsed as I stared into his ice blue ones. "Where did he go?"

"To take care of a former goddess."

"Oh, did he?" I growled, my anger causing me to lift my compellation before I could wipe his memory.

He cursed. "Damn it, Dez. Don't force an answer out of me."

"Sorry." I waved at him as I vamp-sped out of the room. "I've got a psycho baby killer to take care of."

"Dez, don't," he called out, his voice echoing down the hall.

Of course, I ignored him. Lamashtu was mine, and no one would take that kill from me, least of all Jace.

ELEVEN

 yn

I WALKED INTO MY ROOM, somewhat expecting to find my sister curled up in her bed again, only to find the room empty. This was both a relief and slightly concerning given her uncharacteristic behavior last night, but I was too tired to go searching for her. After a long day of classes, including a particularly grueling Weapons Training class with Bladecroft, all I wanted to do was collapse on my bed and fall asleep. Ever since the failed Lamashtu mission, Bladecroft, Lippincott, and several other professors, including Logan and Salzbury, had amped up their instructional techniques. Of course, no one complained about the increased intensity. They all held dreams of joining Silver Dagger Sisterhood or Silver Cloak Brotherhood. More training meant they'd be better equipped to handle the initiation trials. They didn't know the cause, but Dez and I did. The Children of the Sun had partnered with a powerful force, and we needed to be ready for battle.

I flopped onto my bed and reached inside my pocket, withdrawing the piece of fluorite Canyon had given me yesterday. Last night I had slept with it under my pillow, and tonight I fully intended to do the same. The crystal made me feel safe, protected, cared about. I lifted it to my desk light.

When Canyon and I first met, he told me my eyes reminded him of fluorite, which apparently often came in a super-light, almost clear shade of green, and which sometimes had purple strewn through it. He promised he'd give me a piece once he found one that reminded him of my eyes.

I had avoided him since the "blood draining incident," but that didn't mean I hadn't seen him. I spent hours in the potion's lab each evening, so I saw him plenty. He just didn't see me. That was, until yesterday. The pheromone-blocking salve I created was supposed to allow other scents to filter through, and it had seemed to work. I could smell Red's rose scent but not her horniness. But then Canyon had slipped into the seat next to me after Alyze ditched me for a hot faerie. When he asked me to pair with him, I couldn't say no. He handed me the purple organza bag with the small piece of fluorite with the biggest smile on his face. I'd do anything to see him smile like that again.

The bedroom door flew open, slamming into my dresser. I bobbled the crystal and dropped it on my comforter. I quickly snatched the fluorite and shoved it in my pocket before Dez could smash it to pieces. But I didn't need to worry about Dez seeing the crystal because she stormed over to her closet, ripped off her tank top, tugged on a plain black one without an Air emblem, and slipped her dagger holster around her shoulders in a whirlwind of movement. As she yanked on her leather jacket, she turned to me.

"Get changed. Grab your sword and your daggers, and let's go."

"Where are we going? We don't have another training session with Bladecroft scheduled yet."

She hooked more knife sheaths to her belt, then flung daggers into the air, catching them at the handle and shoving them in. "To finish our mission. We're going to kill Lamashtu."

Something didn't add up. My sister's frenzied movements raised my suspicions. That and the fact that Bladecroft and Lippincott had sidelined us from the mission and any subsequent mission for the foreseeable future, ordering us to complete our studies at the Academy.

"On whose orders?"

She cracked her knuckles. "Don't worry about it. Just get ready."

"I don't think so."

She stomped over, stopping inches from me. "Get. Ready."

"No."

She raised a tight fist in front of her chest.

I raised both of mine and dropped into a fighting stance. "You plan to beat me into submission? It won't work."

"As much as I would love to beat your cocky insubordinate ass, I've got a goddess to kill."

The air in the room shifted, electrifying with energy. Wind began blowing around, soon picking up into hurricane speeds. It sounded like a freight train was going to smash into us. I squeezed my hands to my ears, but it didn't do any good. The noise overpowered everything. Second only to the punishing hurricane winds.

"What did you do?" I screamed.

"Me?" she yelled back. "I didn't do anything."

As quickly as the wind picked up, it vanished, and before us stood Lilith in a black leather jacket, a black tank top with the Air element emblem showing underneath, black leather pants, and her scuffed Doc Martens. Her outfit's resemblance to Dez's was uncanny.

"Oh, but you did, Deziree Wickershim."

My sister winced at Lilith's use of her full name. She adjusted her belt sheath, which had slipped sideways in the hurricane winds. "I did nothing of the sort."

Lilith stalked over to her. Dez's purple eyes flashed in uncertainty, but she held her ground. Lilith pointed at her. "You called on me for extra power. You didn't expect me to show up?"

"No, actually. I know how much you goddesses don't like to intermingle with the students here. I just needed a little boost. Figured it was the least you could do, since you've kept so many secrets from Cyn and me."

My sister needed to work on her goddess etiquette. She was going to get her ass kicked by Lilith, and I had a front-row seat. If only I had popcorn.

Lilith placed her hands on her hips and shook her head. "You won't distract me with pathetic insults. You might be Morrigan's daughter and possess extraordinary abilities, but I won't be thrown into a battle frenzy because you've angered me. Your mother and I are sisters. We've trained together, studied together, fought together. Her taunts, her verbal assaults, her insults don't affect me. You see, we sisters have all mastered our own abilities and know exactly how to handle one another's talents. You haven't begun to discover what you're capable of."

Dez softened her stance. "You're right. I apologize for telling the truth. Thank you for aiding me with your power. Now, if you don't mind"—she stepped away from her— "my sister and I have someplace we need to be."

Lilith smiled as she crossed her arms. "Do you want to finish off Lamashtu because you want the glory or because you don't want Jace to have it?"

My eyes shot to my sister's. "How is Jace involved?"

Dez whirled around to face Lilith again. "That kill is mine," she snarled.

Lilith threw back her head and laughed. "I do love your brazen attitude, but you can't lie to me. I can smell him all over you. Out of curiosity, is that how you planned to find Lamashtu? Follow the tie that binds you?"

Dez's jaw feathered, but it was the only reaction she gave. "I don't know what you're talking about."

"You most definitely do. You marked each other. You're linked."

"You're linked?" I knew that Dez and Jace had marked each other, but I still wasn't exactly sure what that meant. I watched my sister closely. She refused to look at me or Lilith, pretending to be occupied with the contents of her backpack. She cursed, ripping the zipper. I went over and took the backpack from her. "Dez, are you?"

She dropped her head. "I don't know. I didn't even know I had marked him. I specifically didn't bite him or drink from him to avoid any chance of a Sempiternal blood bond, so I don't know how or why it happened."

Lilith hopped on my bed. "You know, that's exactly what Jace said when I confronted him about it."

Dez spun around, her eyes flashing red. "You knew, and

you're just discussing it with me now? It happened weeks ago."

Lilith studied her fingernails. "I've been busy with other matters."

"I'll bet. Pressing matter no doubt. Can you break it?"

Lilith put her hands behind her head and leaned back against the pillow. "As you know, we don't like to interfere with mundane matters."

Dez rushed over to her and yanked her off the bed. "Get. Out."

In a blur of movement, Lilith had Dez pinned against the wall.

"Careful, demigoddess. You test my patience, and that won't end well for you."

"Demigoddess?" Dez murmured.

Lilith released her. "You're daughters of Morrigan. Of course you are demigoddesses."

Dez scratched behind her ear. "I never thought about it that way."

"Well, you need to. You both need to. There are very few who wield as much power as the two of you. You need to learn how to control your emotions. Even during sex, as Dez can tell you."

"He marked me too," Dez said, trying to defend herself, but she didn't put much effort into it.

"He did, and I've already spoken to him about that. Unfortunately, those cards have been cast, and you must deal with them, but not through reckless abandon, nor through revenge."

Concern filled me about my actions with Canyon all those weeks ago. Had he and I formed some sort of blood bond when I drank from him? It would explain how he always found me, or at least sensed me. And was it permanent like Dez and Jace's marking, or did it fade if I stopped drinking from him? "Lilith?"

"Yes, Cyn. You, too, must deal with your actions," she said, answering me without me even having spoken the question aloud.

Dez studied me as if trying to read my mind too, but she didn't possess that ability. Not yet anyway. Goddess only knew what powers each of us might gain in the future.

"Neither one of you is going anywhere tonight."

Dez opened her mouth to protest.

Lilith flicked her fingers at my sister, and her lips snapped shut. "Actually, neither one of you can leave campus until I decide you can."

I frowned. I spent my human life being told what to do. I refused to live like that as a Sempiternal. "You can't do that. It's in direct violation of Silverwood Academy rules."

"Watch me." She grinned and snapped her fingers. Magick swept through and around us, creating a new magickal hurricane. When the wind finally died down, Lilith was gone.

"Bitch," Dez hissed.

For once, I agreed with her.

CHAPTER

TWELVE

 yn

ELEMENTAL TRAINING WAS FAST BECOMING my least favorite class. I didn't like to sweat. I didn't like feeling like a total newbie to the supernatural world because, even though my classmates had all recently gone through their own Change, they had at least grown up with a working knowledge about magick, the elements, and other supernaturals. I also didn't like pretending I had my bloodlust completely under control, because sometimes the cravings were so bad, I wanted to chomp down on the nearest supe's neck and suck them dry. Of course, I didn't tell anyone about any of this, because even in a world of freaky supernaturals with strange rules and questionable behavior, there were just some things a person shouldn't voice aloud.

Professor Salzbury, who taught the Water lessons in

Elemental Training, stood at the front of a large grove, as unimpressed with Northeast Pennsylvania's gorgeous fall foliage as he was with our commandment of Water. Recently, far too many people had stood in the same position in front of me, telling me what I could and couldn't do and how I should act, behave, and feel, and it was really starting to piss me off. I wanted to break something, and that something might be Salzbury's face if he didn't watch himself.

"Again," he ordered, his voice dripping with disdain at our performance.

My teeth ground together as I concentrated on calling forth a storm cloud to soak Alyze, who stood grinning at me like a maniac.

"Come on, you got this."

"Easy for you to say," I hissed, glaring at her in her blue clothing with the Water element emblem. "You're a Siren. Morrigan is your goddess. You were born in water for goddess's sake."

"True, but you witnessed me last class working with Earth. Not so impressive on that front. And Professor Logan didn't think so either."

She'd dumped a pile of manure on herself rather than moving it to the compost pile. The manure had stained her blond hair for two days until Red took pity on her and lifted the color.

"You're just trying to make me feel better."

"Is it working?"

"Not really."

"Ladies, focus," Professor Salzbury said sternly. "Focus on water droplets. What do they look like? What do they feel like? What do they smell like?"

Alyze closed her eyes and lifted her lips into a devilish

grin as she sighed. "Droplets of heaven."

I could guess exactly where her mind had gone, especially since she and Dez spent most of their time talking about sex.

"Gross," I said.

She opened her blue eyes, which twinkled with mischief, and winked at me. "Your sister's rubbing off on you."

"Don't remind me."

"And I was referring to what the air smells like when it rains."

"Oh, that makes more sense. Let me try that . . ."

I breathed in and out, imagining the smell of rain. Fresh. Pure. Light. Joy.

Soft raindrops landed on my forehead, kissing my cheeks.

I focused more intently on what rain smelled like. When I was seven, my parents gave me a puppy for Christmas, most likely to bribe me since they were leaving the next day for an all-inclusive vacation to the Bahamas without me. But I didn't care. I loved Duffy and all his playful antics from the very first time he licked my face. Duffy spent his puppy years listening to my complaints about my absentee parents. He also got excited along with me when something good happened instead of shushing me or scolding me or delivering some back-handed remark in the form of a compliment. My favorite scent? When Duffy came in from a cold, snowy day.

Of course, my parents had always complained about the wet-dog smell, but to me, nothing smelled better or was more comforting than Duffy's fur in the winter.

"Uh, Cyn, we're supposed to make it rain," Alyze said, her teeth chattering.

I opened my eyes to heavy snowflakes. I tilted my head to the sky as I inhaled deeply. The snowflakes smelled just like Duffy.

"Snow!" Professor Salzbury held out his palms to catch the flakes. "That'll work, and quite impressive for your first foray into working with Water, especially since it isn't your top element. Morrigan would be very impressed."

Yes, she is. Well done, Cynda. Memories with powerful emotions can help trigger our gifts, especially when first working with that ability.

I pressed my lips together, annoyed that Mom Morrigan had interrupted the beautiful memory of my best friend and what that golden retriever meant to me.

The snow changed to rain, and not just a light sprinkle. A deluge. And it wasn't just over my head, it was over the entire class.

"Shut it down," Professor Salzbury yelled. "Control your elemental power or it will control you."

It was controlling me, all right. A torrent of emotion whipped around inside me. Frustration. Annoyance. Worry. Fear.

"Make it stop!" he ordered, sounding strained, as if he was trying unsuccessfully to end the storm himself.

I tried to stop it. I really did. The wind picked up instead, reminiscent of Lilith's windstorm, only with water added, and the raindrops felt like marbles pelting our faces.

Alyze pushed her way through the storm, shielding her face with her arms until she stood next to me. "Cynda, we're going to wash away any minute," she shouted.

Anger combined with fear and panic, escalating my emotions into total chaos.

"I don't know what to do!"

"Focus on the memory that first called the snow and

reverse engineer it."

Duffy's white-speckled furry face came to mind. When he got older, he hated going out in the rain, preferring to snuggle with me under the blankets all day long instead. He made me feel warm and safe and loved and . . .

"You did it!" Alyze slapped my back. "You did it!"

I opened my eyes to a cloudless blue sky. The hail/sleet/blizzard/torrential rain was a distant memory—well, except for our soaking wet clothing and hair.

"I guess I did."

"Yes, you did." Professor Salzbury sloshed over to us, wringing out his tie. "In the future, try using a simpler memory that isn't saddled with the baggage of other emotions. That's why Air combined with Water and created Hurricane Cynda."

"Hurricane Cynda. I like it," Alyze whispered in my ear. "Dez will be so envious."

I rolled my eyes, because I knew she was right.

But Professor Salzbury's instruction worried me. If a simple memory of Duffy could get all jumbled up by just a compliment from Mom, how in the hells was I supposed to call forth any element? I needed to have a talk with Mommy Morrigan to make sure Hurricane Cynda didn't happen again.

A pain shot up my spine, dropping me to my knees. I clawed at my back as the pain evolved into an intense burning sensation.

"Ouch!"

"Oh my goddess! Cynda, look." Alyze's hand traced down my back.

"What is it? Did I get bit by something?"

"No, you just received the Water element mark."

"Excuse me?"

"Your Water element tattoo."

I threw up my palm, showing my Air element brand. "I already got one of those. I'm good."

"It means you've mastered Water and can call on it anytime you need it. The appearance of a second element means you're one step closer to entering the Sisterhood. It's a gift."

I pressed my lips together, not wanting to argue with her, because, to me, it felt like a curse. And if Alyze or Professor Salzbury believed I could command Water now, they were sadly mistaken. I had no better control of Water than I had over my own actions. I stormed away before I caused another hurricane.

"CYNDA! WAIT UP!" Red yelled, waving frantically.

She ran down her hallway, the Fire wing, toward me standing at the center of the star. When we'd first arrived at Silverwood Academy, the center of the star had transformed into the location of the Elemental Challenges, which had tested each of the initiates in ways I still couldn't believe I got through. But today, like most days, the center served as the dining hall and courtyard with a gorgeous dusk sky overhead. Magick fascinated me. I couldn't imagine ever getting bored with it.

Frustrated, definitely.

Annoyed, absolutely.

But bored? Never.

Red looped her arm through mine. "Congratulations on receiving your Water element!"

"Thanks," I snapped, still feeling the sting of the tattoo and the method by which I had received it. I hated getting branded like cattle. First on the hand, now on the back. Every time I mastered an element, I'd get another one, though apparently no one else had a problem with it.

"Ouch," she winced, rubbing the side of her face as if I'd slapped her. "That had some bite to it. Why so bitter? You mastered Water. You should be proud."

"What?" someone snarled.

We whirled around, both of us sensing a potential back-stabbing encounter—a direct violation of rule number three—and considering the pixie glaring at us with magickal energy swirling around her hands, not entirely unlikely.

"Well, well, well," Red said. "Long time no speak."

Azalea's face darkened. "I never had a problem with you, Anastasia, until you aligned with her kind. Then I lost all respect for you."

Red raised her hands, palms up, and if her stance was any indication, fireballs were at the ready. "Her kind? What's that supposed to mean?"

"A bloodsucker. A Sempiternal. Vampire. The lowest of all supernaturals."

My hands formed tight fists at the insult and my fangs elongated. Why that little . . .

Red patted my arm, sensing my rage along with my insatiable desire to chomp into Azalea's scrawny neck. A wave of calming energy coursed through me at Red's touch.

"According to your closed-minded pixie ways," she said. "Thankfully, the rest of the Faerie Realm doesn't feel that way. Other pixies don't either. Your hate is just your character flaw."

"That's not true. You chose the wrong side." Azalea stomped her foot, and vines exploded across the floor, heading in our direction at a rapid rate.

Red flicked her fingers out. The vines reversed direction and spiraled up Azalea's legs before she even knew what was happening.

"And as for the 'her side,' and I can only assume 'our side,' we attend Silverwood Academy. There are no sides. We all are on the right one."

"There are always sides," Azalea screamed, twisting and jerking as the vines wrapped around the bottom half of her body. They increased in speed as they wound up around her arms, instantly binding them to her body.

Alyze appeared next to us. "Maeve's got a lot of work to do with that one."

"Yes, she does," I muttered, watching with morbid fascination as the vines encircled Azalea's torso and shoulders. I appreciated Red coming to my aid and preventing me from doing something impulsive like draining the pixie, but I didn't want her to get in trouble because of an obnoxious, stupid faerie. "Red, think you should stop it?"

"Yeah, probably." She snapped her fingers, and the vines halted their advance just before they covered Azalea's mouth.

Red rehooked her arm through mine, grabbed Alyze, spun us around, and started walking toward the salad bar entrance.

Alyze tilted her head toward Red. "Are you just going to leave her there?"

Red laughed. "Make her squirm a bit."

Alyze laughed along with her. "You know, I'm not sure why Azalea hates vampires so much, especially Sempiternals, but you're definitely not helping her stance on witches."

Their amusement at the situation helped ease my

nerves. I no longer wanted to break Azalea and make her suffer, so at least that was the positive side to Red's aggressive actions.

"I thought the witch's motto was Do no harm?"

"It is. All I did was reverse her magick. They only grew that fast because of her spell, not mine."

"Do you think she wanted to strangle me with them?"

"What is the meaning of this?" a loud voice bellowed across the courtyard. I glanced over my shoulder in time to see Professor Goldwell rush over to the new garden accessory, realizing it wasn't a vine-covered gnome statue. "Who did this to you?"

"Th-them," Azalea sobbed.

Goldwell stared at us. "Is that so? We'll see about that." She vamp-sped toward us.

"You're leaving me like this?" Azalea yelled.

Goldwell skidded to a stop, growling as she realized her oversight. Her eyes narrowed as she watched us disappear into the dining hall. "I will be in touch."

"I look forward to it," I said under my breath, knowing the vampire could hear me.

Alyze slapped my back. "Spicy! I like it. And by the way, Cyn."

"Yeah?"

"That Water element looks good on you."

"I agree," Red added. "We're going to be four kick-ass members of the Sisterhood someday, and I can't wait!"

I wished I could agree with my witchy friend.

Red grabbed a plate and handed me one. "I'll come over and help you get ready for the Silver Crescent Moon Festival tonight."

"That's tonight? I completely forgot about it. I'll pass."

I wasn't a fan of parties or get-togethers, and I had too

much on my mind. Plus, there was the whole avoiding-Canyon thing.

Alyze piled her plate with food. The siren could eat more than Gage. "You and your sister are complete opposites when it comes to social gatherings."

"No kidding." Red shook her head, adding tomatoes to her plate.

"Thanks. I'll take that as a compliment."

"It wasn't a compliment, and the festival is required, so you can't get out of it."

"Required?"

"They want us to enjoy the wild side of our nature too."

"Dez is already in close contact with her wild side."

"That she is. That she is." Alyze chuckled. "Oh, hey, I made those necklaces you asked for during Metalwork today." She withdrew two silver twist chains from her pocket and dangled them in front of me. There was a large silver-with-copper-wire pendant hanging from the bottom of one, and the other was longer but with no pendant.

"They're beautiful," I sighed.

She handed them to me. "They're yours. The pendant is magickally enhanced, so you can attach any crystal or object you'd like."

"Thank you." I placed them around my neck. The naked chain hung low on my chest, perfect for hanging spells or charms hidden under my shirt where no one would know I came packing. The pendant on the other chain rested on my chest about three inches below my neck. The perfect length. I knew just the crystal I wanted to wear tonight. The one in my front pocket. The one Dez would smash if she found out who gave it to me. But what my sister didn't know wouldn't hurt her.

CHAPTER
THIRTEEN

ez

NEWS of what transpired with Azalea quickly traveled to me via the supernatural gossip mill. That and Alyze filled me in. Lilith had worked out the Goldwell situation, so Red, Cyn, and Alyze didn't need to fear punishment for the vine incident. I'm guessing it was Lilith's way of smoothing things over between her and Cyn and me after our fight the other day, but also because the goddess jumped at any opportunity to keep Goldwell in line. I didn't understand why they just didn't fire the vampire professor, but then, all the goddesses seemed to enjoy spinning intricate webs and toying with their food.

And speaking of food, my sister looked positively scrumptious. Men and women alike would fight for a chance to be with her tonight. She'd finally discover what it meant to be a Sempiternal and feast on their energy with their absolute blessing.

Cyn fidgeted in front of the bathroom mirror, trying to hide her lovely cleavage, but the sexy silver number she had on wouldn't cooperate. The three of us—she, Red, and I— wore the same dress, as would every woman at the Academy tonight for the Silver Crescent Moon Festival.

"You need to shake what your mama gave you," Red sang. She piled Cyn's hair on top of her head, revealing my sister's new Water element symbol at the base of her neck. "You also need to show off your new tattoo. It proves you're on your way to joining the Sisterhood."

Cyn's light green eyes met my reflection. When she'd returned from Elemental Training, she hadn't been able to stop shaking from anger and frustration. She refused to go into details, but she'd angled her back to show me. I congratulated her on mastering Water, but she kept muttering "She took it from me," over and over.

When Cyn wouldn't expand on who "she" was, I figured Mama Morrigan had shown up at my sister's lesson and interfered. Not that she'd given Cyn the tattoo without Cyn earning it, but our mother had pushed Cyn in a way she didn't appreciate, and that pissed me off. No one messed with my little sister. I was the only one who held that right.

I stretched toward the ceiling, my own silver dress skimming the tops of my thighs.

"Don't do that in front of everyone when you dance," Cyn squealed.

"Why not?"

"Your ass cheeks will stick out. And while you don't have a problem with public nudity, there is a certain level of decorum we should strive for at any Silverwood Academy event."

Red dropped Cyn's hair, clutching her stomach as she bent over in hysterics. When she finally gathered herself, she straightened, shook her head, and returned to Cyn's hair. "You obviously have never been to a pagan dance."

Cyn's eyes flashed. "And you have? This is your first dance at Silverwood too."

"It is, but I've heard plenty about the Silver Crescent Moon Festival. The crescent moon after the Fall Equinox brings out the wildness in all of us."

I prowled toward them, swinging my hips. "That's why it's held in Wildwood Preserves. They want us to release our inner beast."

Cyn swallowed hard. "I thought we were supposed to keep that shit locked up."

Our inner wolves were indeed locked up by Mommy Dearest. And our physical beings were tied to the campus, unable to leave until Lilith released us, but that wasn't going to stop me from partying, and it shouldn't stop my sister either.

"Doesn't mean we can't have a good time." I pointed at her in the mirror, deciding to mess with her because it delighted me. "Don't forget to get verbal consent if you feed off of someone's energy tonight. They'll be watching closely to make sure no one breaks one of the rules."

"Says the person who always breaks the rules," Red teased.

"I try not to. And the key is not getting caught. But once rules are invoked, they are unbreakable. I learned that lesson the hard way."

Weeks ago Jace had revoked his consent, and I couldn't

enter his protective bubble. Then I had to do the same to him when my She-Beasty wanted his He-Beasty.

I shook myself of the memory. I refused to think of Jace and the things we'd done to each other. Especially after he sent me to multiple climaxes in the Wildwoods with the mere brush of his fingers. I intended to find out if I could sever the marking bond between us by having sex with someone else, and I planned to find out tonight. First, I'd get drunk on faerie wine, then I'd grab the nearest person and have my way with them. Unfortunately Gage wasn't available. And even if he was, he wouldn't go anywhere near me with this damn marking. With any luck, my Academy mates, especially the first years, won't know anything about it and would be all too eager to help me clear my head of Jace, especially if they drank too much faerie wine as well.

I smiled at the back of the woman who'd won my best gargoyle's heart.

"Gage picking you up?"

"He's picking all of us up. Like any minute."

Cyn's eyes met mine. She knew the things Gage and I had done with each other while at Silverwood Prison, but she didn't know the half of it.

"Isn't that kinda weird?"

Red snorted, glancing at me over her shoulder, her green eyes sparkling as they met mine. "That Dez fucked the hell out of him? No. Ancient history."

"Not that ancient," Cyn muttered.

Red finished pinning up Cyn's hair. "He told me everything."

I raised an eyebrow, putting my hand on my hip. "You sure about that?"

"Oh yeah. Very sure. He told me a little about your friendship history."

I shifted my feet, not liking the level of intimacy this conversation veered into. I raised my chin and thrust out my chest into my shield of bitchiness. "Did he?"

She laughed. "You don't like your small friend group talking about you, do you?"

I narrowed my gaze, red laser beams at the ready. "You're about to be removed from that short list."

She spun faster than I could blink and wrapped her arms around me in a giant hug. "It's okay to care about people. It doesn't make you weak."

My nose itched at the sudden onslaught of emotion she attacked me with. I inhaled sharply, trying to steel myself. The loss of my dad had made me weak for a long time, and I vowed never to allow that to happen again, with the exception of my sister.

"What does it do then?"

"It makes you strong," she whispered in my ear, suddenly releasing me and causing me to sway back and forth. My arms flailed until she caught my hand and balanced me.

"Anyone home?" a voice called out from the bedroom.

"We're in the bathroom, Gage. Be out in a second." She leaned toward me. "You are a fierce warrior who cares deeply about those in her inner circle, and I will remain there, whether or not you'll admit it."

She spun, her energy surging with excitement, and bounced out of the bathroom.

I swayed again from her absence. Damn seer.

Cyn caught my hand, grounding me again. She dipped her head toward me. "You okay?" she mouthed.

I ripped my hand away from her and scrubbed at my nose. "As okay as I'll ever be."

She winked at me. "That's my sister."

I stared at myself in the mirror. A tsunami of emotions surged through me. How the fuck did I get myself mixed up with all these people? I had planned to act as a lone Sempiternal, and here I was unhinged by some witch.

"Coming, Dez?" the said witch sang out.

"Coming," I called, shoving my hands under my boobs to expose extra cleavage. I reached down and tore the seam of my dress, further exposing my thigh. Make every supernatural eat their heart out tonight. I would feed off all of them, whether or not they gave me consent. I was the bad guy.

TWINKLE LIGHTS HUNG from trees in the clearing ahead of us as we wound our way along the path into Wildwood Preserves. The smell of soft moss and humid pine filled my nostrils. Memories of my recent encounter with Jace in the Wildwoods rushed through me. The feel of his hands around me and in me. The roughness of the bark against my skin. The orgasms that shook me to the core when he commanded me to come. I cleared my throat, shaking my head of the memory.

Nope, not going there. Breaking the marking tonight. Freeing myself of his tie to me. The crowd of men dressed in snug silver button-down shirts with ass-flattering black pants along with women clad in tight silver dresses with ample breast exposure would prove fertile hunting ground. Faerie music pulsed all around us, calling to our more base desires. A bonfire roared at the center. I chugged a glass of faerie wine from the table, then grabbed two more, handing one to my sister before looping my arm through hers and tugging her into the fray. Her eyes widened as she took in the dirty dancing that had already begun. Her shoulders tensed as she spotted the man and woman in front of us already getting after it.

The Silver Crescent Moon Festival was my first Academy event too, but I'd been to plenty of pagan celebrations before, and with this much faerie wine flowing, it was bound to get more wild.

"Take a sip. It'll help you relax."

She did as I suggested, which proved just how freaked out she was. When the wine took hold of her, her entire body loosened up.

"That's it," I encouraged her. "Now, go slow with the wine. It's powerful shit."

Of course, my second glass was almost empty, but before I got a third, it was time to show my sister just what it meant to be a gorgeous Sempiternal. We prowled around the bonfire, our very presence an offering of tribute to the night, to the fire, to the gods and goddesses. Our scantily clad bodies inspired lust and want. I inhaled, devouring the desire-filled air. A blast of heat burst from the fire, accepting our offering.

Cyn whimpered as the air around us thickened with desire and lust, but we were only getting started.

"Why are you doing this? Can't we just blend in instead of parading around like we're famous?" Cyn whispered softly, her anxiety burning through the faerie wine.

My exposed right thigh caught the light of the crescent moon. Hormones surged through the air.

Cyn gasped when she realized what was causing the onslaught. "How did that happen?"

I laughed wickedly. "I ripped it before I left the bathroom." I inhaled deeply. "You can thank me later."

She broke away from me, her body shaking. "We're not supposed to. It's breaking the rules."

I shrugged, the strap of my dress falling off my shoulder, allowing a better view of my cleavage. "Gray area. I was messing with you earlier. No one cares what we do tonight."

"No," she backed away from me. "I won't allow it."

I cocked my head at her. "You can deny your true nature all you want, but I plan to gorge myself."

She fled from me, disappearing into the crowd. I spread my arms wide above my head, the hem of my dress skirting my ass cheeks, doing the exact thing Cyn had warned me not to do.

Envy, desire, and something else—I inhaled deeply —*rage*, mingled with the lusty thoughts that filled the air.

I circled slowly, my hands still fanned out above me, feeding off the rising levels of desire as I searched the crowd for the source of the rage. Two gold eyes rimmed with red met mine, familiar, but not attached to the yummy chiseled jaw and raven-black hair of Jace. No, the gold mask and hooded silver cloak proved a much more exciting conquest. Perhaps the one who could break the marking bond.

But the sudden feeling of hair standing on the back of my neck warned me that danger was close. Something wasn't right. My heartbeat spiked the moment the Demon Prince started stalking in my direction. I dropped my arms, recognizing that this opponent outmatched me. I turned to escape.

Combative energy filled the air around me. I lunged for Ramone in a frenzied attempt to disappear with him among the swarms of bodies. My arms stretched for his back, desperate for the safety of the unaware shifter. My fingers skimmed his silver shirt just as powerful hands curled around my biceps and yanked me backward, dragging me like a rag doll instead of the fierce predator I was.

No one reacted to his presence. Not one person stopped him. Not one person even moved. I narrowed my eyes, searching for someone, anyone, to help me, but everyone was frozen in place. I caught a glimpse of Gage over the heads of the rest of the partygoers. His eyes met mine. A shot of certainty raced through me. Surely he would stop the Demon Prince. All he had to do was stare at my adversary and the Demon Prince would be frozen in place. But the only action he made was a slight shake of his head.

What type of sorcery was this?

The lust energy I had fed off of the crowd moments ago filled my veins, making me strong. I twisted, kicked, swiped at the prince, but my efforts were no match for him. He was determined to remove me from the festival without anyone's interference. Without anyone even aware of what was happening.

"Let me go," I growled, jerking my body away from him.

My demand fell on deaf ears. Panic gripped me. I'd never been in a situation I couldn't get out of, and it scared me. As he dragged me into the Wildwoods, the revelers suddenly returned to their evening completely unaware of what was happening to me, as if someone had hit play.

I soon found myself pressed against a tree with the Demon Prince tight against me, his red-rimmed eyes glaring at me, his muscles coiled tight as if he wanted to tear me apart. Fear spiked in me, and I lost sense of who I was and my power.

Some demons possessed the ability to feed off

someone's fear much like a Sempiternal. An incubus—that was the male version. I closed my eyes, determined not to lose myself to him, determined to fight him.

"Get off me," I grunted through clenched teeth.

"Are you frightened?" he jeered.

I pressed my lips together, refusing to answer. *Never admit weakness.* That was what Dad had taught me. *Befuddle. Confuse. Distract. Until you regain your power.*

His fingers tightened around my arms and his claws slowly extended. Ten sharp points dug into my skin, but the pain wasn't unbearable. I had survived worse. I revealed my fangs, demonstrating that I, too, was a predator.

"Should I grab your sister? Perhaps that would strike the right amount of terror in you."

Fire ignited inside of me, racing through my veins and up my arms. "Don't you dare."

He hissed, lifting his hands off me, shocked at the intense burst of heat. I sprang to action. Flames shot through my clenched fist as it connected with his chin. He gasped and pulled his body away from mine to extinguish the fire with his hand. Taking advantage of the movement, I thrust my knee into his manhood and punched his chest with flame fist. I called up another fireball in my free hand and pulled it back in preparation to light up the Demon Prince. Crippling pain shot up my spine and seared into the nape of my neck. I dropped to my knees and clawed at it. The agony was worse than anything I'd felt before. Like fire burning me from the inside out. What evil magick was this?

He grabbed a fistful of my hair and wrenched me backward, flipping my body like I weighed nothing and throwing me to the ground. The air got knocked out of me at the shock of it all. He straddled my waist, his hands pinning my shoulders against the earth.

"Fire won't work on a Fire Demon."

An idea quickly formed. I called upon the Water element to assist me, pulling moisture from the air, the soil, my own body, to add strength to the wave I was readying to unleash.

"Thanks for the intel. Wonder what this does to you then?"

And I hit him with a freaking tsunami.

FOURTEEN

yn

THE LUST RISING from the crowd had filled me with a high I'd never felt before. More than when I got drunk the night of my high school graduation. More than the rush of feeding off Canyon in my room. More than drinking energetic blood from Gage.

It had been too much. Too overwhelming. Too overstimulating. I didn't trust myself. Couldn't trust myself. My fangs had descended unbidden. My fingertips had itched as my claws protruded from them. Dozens of heartrates quickened, their jugulars pulsing as my sister paraded us around as though we were the festival's special feature, she and I devouring the desire-filled air, thirsting for more. So much more.

Bare shoulders danced under the twinkle lights. Tight silver shirts showed off muscles for miles. I swallowed hard. Their testosterone called to me like a siren, inviting me to bite their necks whether or not they offered.

Bloodlust raced through me. I needed to get out of there before I did something I would regret. I broke free from my sister's hold and disappeared into the crowd. Euphoria exploded around me as I brushed past men and women. Hands swept over my shoulders. Calls of "Bite me" and "Use me" rose around me.

Red had warned me about pagan rituals, but I hadn't expected the level of debauchery to rise so quickly. Was it the faerie wine? Or the byproduct of our appearance? The guards at Silverwood Prison claimed Dez and I were the most dangerous inmates there. Did Sempiternals call to the primal urges of every supernatural like a fucking mating call?

"Hey, come dance with us," Gage called out over the din of desire, but I didn't trust myself with the gargoyle or Red. I couldn't lose myself in the festival any more than I already had.

"Cynda, dance with me." Peeta, the shifter who asked me out during Weapon's Training, reached out for me. I didn't want to dance with him or anyone else. A nice book and a cup of tea sounded like the perfect way to celebrate the Silver Crescent Moon. I skirted away from him, not paying attention to my surroundings.

Two hands wrapped around my waist, drawing me into a solid chest. Cedarwood and mint filled the air, along with the tangy musk of human blood. "Hey, yoooou," a low voice whispered in my ear. I whirled around, trying to back away from him, but Canyon didn't let go. "Where have you been? I've missed you." His green eyes sparkled with excitement. "Have you been avoiding me?" he accused, his lower lip jutting, begging me to bite it.

I didn't want to lie to him, but I didn't want to tell him the truth either. "Just busy."

He dipped his head toward me. His gorgeous jawline skimmed my lips as he whispered in my ear. "Somehow I don't believe you."

I inhaled sharply, the onslaught of Canyon's unique signature overloading my senses.

"It's true." I pulled my head away from his lips, arching backward, the byproduct of which thrust my boobs into his chest. His gaze dropped to the dress's neckline before slowly trailing back up to my face.

"I see you like the crystal I gave you."

I had added the fluorite crystal after leaving the bathroom. Luckily Dez had been too absorbed in her own plans to notice, and Red only had eyes for Gage. Most of the clothing supplied by Silverwood Academy was practical and loaded with pockets. The silver dress, however, was not, hence the reason I was wearing the crystal tonight, though I regretted that decision now.

He reached up to touch it, his fingers skimming across my skin. I gasped in shock as each fingertip sent a wave of current through me.

When Dez had asked him what he was, he'd never answered her, but two things were certain. He wasn't entirely human. And I wanted him.

Goddess, I wanted him.

As if sensing my change of heart, his lips rose into a smile. "There you are." His voice rumbled, his chest vibrating against mine. Without taking his attention from me, he returned the fluorite pendant to its resting place, his fingers lingering against my skin, traveling along my collarbone, charging me, filling me, tormenting me. "The chain's beautiful. The crystal fits it perfectly." He dipped his head closer. "Do you think of me when you wear it?"

I angled my lips toward his mouth. "Yes."

"Good," he whispered, his fingers slowly trailing up my chest toward my neck, sending explosive shivers down my spine and to everything that made me a woman. I bit my lip as I watched him. Canyon made me wonder if maybe I'd been wrong that sex was overrated. That maybe he knew how to make my body sing.

He curled his hand around the back of my head. His other pressed into my lower back. "You look radiant tonight," he whispered, his tone reverent.

Never had I felt so cherished. So desired. So turned on.

"Thank you."

"I want to kiss you, if that's all right."

Instead of answering, I pressed my lips against his. Our lips moved against each other's. Softly. Slowly. Seductively. Soon his tongue slipped into my mouth, dancing against mine. A titillating tango building in rhythm. My hands slipped around his neck, drawing him closer. An ember blazed to life inside me, building as his fingers traced up and down my arms, winding their way to an unknown destination at an excruciatingly slow pace.

More, a quiet voice begged inside my head.

Careful, another one whispered.

He's dangerous, I imagined Dez reminding me. But the thing was, she didn't know Canyon like I did. She didn't know what it was like to want something so badly it hurt. Everything came easy for her. I had to work hard to get where I was now . . . a turned Sempiternal barely in control of her bloodlust.

And she forgot—I was dangerous too.

My fingers tangled in his hair as his threaded through

mine. In his arms, I felt cherished. Never had I ever been kissed in such a profoundly reverent way. Part of me wanted to kiss him all night. But another part, the lusty Sempiternal part, wanted him here and now.

His lips broke away from me. Resting his forehead against mine, he sighed, "Cynda," reminding me of a prayer.

"Right here," I breathed into his neck, playfully nipping it.

"The things you do to me," he moaned, his fingers tracing along the straps of my dress, edging ever closer to my nipple.

Flames rose inside me as if his very confession breathed life into me. I slipped my hand into the front of his pants, wanting to feel him and his need for me. "There's more I'd like to do with you."

He sucked in a breath, his nostrils flaring in and out, as if warring with himself, a battle he wouldn't win.

I went for the kill. "Don't fight it. Let this happen."

His fingers wrapped around my dress strap, sliding it over my shoulder and down my bicep. He brought his lips down, kissing along my collarbone, darting his tongue in and out, leaving a trail of wetness and not just along my exposed skin. He broke away, returning the strap. "You're dangerous."

My chest rose and fell as I fought to catch my breath. The fire inside me sputtered. Did he mean because I was a monster? But he'd come to me. He had sought me out. I was tired playing the victim. I'd spent too much of my life trying to appease Derrick, my "parents," my friends. No more. No fucking more. I'd seen the way eyes had devoured Dez and me when we prowled around the bonfire. I didn't like it, but desire and lust had shot into the air from all those in attendance, feeding me, encouraging me, wanting me. Confidence rekindled the flames. If Canyon didn't want me, someone else would.

I lifted my chest, stepping away from him. "You're the one who's dangerous."

His eyes widened in surprise. His hands shot out, wrapping around my biceps faster than humanly possible. "I— I didn't mean it in that way."

He might not be completely human, but I was a Sempiternal. A tribrid of unknown origin. I was stronger, faster, more powerful than Canyon could ever be. I fantasized breaking his fingers one by one after I crushed him in the balls with my knee. The image caused my lips to curl. I jutted out my hip to the side, feeling saucy and powerful. His hold momentarily wobbled at my movement.

"What way did you mean?"

He stepped closer, watching me for any sign of violence.

Good. I frightened him. He ought to be terrified of my wrath.

"May I?" he asked, tilting his chin toward my ear, as if he wanted to speak privately.

"Sure."

His nose trailed along my jaw. I gasped in shock at the unexpected touch. His lips pressed against my ear, sending shivers down my spine as he spoke. "Because I want to take you right here, right now in this crowd of people, and I don't trust my own restraint."

"Oh."

His hands slipped around my waist, pressing me against his muscular chest. "I want to make you forget every person you've ever been with." His lips danced along my earlobe as he spoke. "I want you to scream my name."

He pulled away, angling his neck inches from my lips. "I want you to bite me as you come."

My fangs descended as his jugular pulsed in front of me. A new hunger erupted inside of me. Something dark. Something dripping. Something horny as fuck. I licked my lips, trying to maintain some sort of control. "What's stopping you?"

He laughed. "Isn't it a bit crowded around here?"

My eyes fell on the dark woods over his shoulder. "They don't call it the Wildwoods for nothing."

CHAPTER
FIFTEEN

ez

WATER EXPLODED from my hands in a tidal wave, hitting the Demon Prince and throwing him across the glen.

He landed with a satisfying thud, sputtering for breath, his hands clutching his chest. I pushed myself off the ground, wiping my hands triumphantly. I probably should have gotten the hell out of there, but I couldn't resist watching water drip from his gold mask. The way his soaked, princely gold clothing beneath his silver cloak revealed his strong, defined pecs. The way water droplets pooled at his exposed collarbone.

I squinted, studying him more closely. Something about him was vaguely familiar. I stepped closer, feeling the thread pulling me to him, wanting me to remove his mask to see the face beneath it.

Two figures tumbled into the glen, pawing at each

other's clothing, devouring each other's faces. I immediately recognized the red hair and the side profile of her body as a guy pressed her against a tree.

"Cyn?"

She briefly stilled but began to quiver as her partner slid his hand from her ass to her thigh to her . . .

Anger blossomed inside of me. "Canyon."

This time, she slowly tilted her head over his broad shoulder to see who was speaking. Her green eyes met mine, her face now flushed with embarrassment rather than desire.

"What are you doing here with *him*?"

Canyon broke away from her and narrowed his eyes at me. "We could ask you the same."

No longer terrified of the Demon Prince, or any man for that matter, least of all an ephemeral, I sauntered over to them. They clung to each other as if I would tear them apart.

And FYI, I planned on it. "Don't worry about what I'm doing here. If I ever hear even the hint of aggression wafting off you, I will slam your fucking face into a wall, rip off your testicles, and throw them into a towering inferno."

His Adam's apple bobbed as he swallowed.

Good. He wasn't immune to terror.

As I approached, pain shot up my spine dropping me to my knees. I clawed at my bare back. What in the name of fuck . . . ?

Cyn sprinted over. "What's wrong?"

"I . . . don't . . . know," I grunted through clenched teeth. "Can you see anything?"

She circled around me to my back. "Whoa."

"What is it?"

"You earned Fire and Water."

My eyes shot over to the person who had caused my painful initiation, but all that was left of the Demon Prince was the soaked gold mask. "He's gone."

Cyn looped her arms under my shoulders and helped me stand. "Who is?"

I wobbled, feeling the air whoosh out of me, keenly aware of my assailant's absence. "The Demon Prince."

Who I suspected might be Jace, though I kept that part to myself.

Could Jace be the Demon Prince and a member of the Council? And why did he attack me?

Attack you or trigger two Elements?

But why such extreme measures? Why not tell me and allow me time for my abilities to surface on their own?

He needs you strong now.

Cyn wrapped her arm around me and pulled me close to her. "Are you okay?"

I shook my head, unable to speak. No, I wasn't okay. I was freaked out. Confused. Twisted. I couldn't understand how Jace could be the Demon Prince, but as I worked through the possibilities in my head, I came to only one conclusion. He could be.

"Let's get you back to the room," she said softly. "Just one foot in front of the other," she suggested when I refused to budge or couldn't. Everything was so confusing. A total mind fuck.

"Cyn, what about us?"

Canyon. What was he doing here with my sister? She was supposed to stay away from him. She knew better.

She stopped, still supporting me, but I could feel her nerves wavering, until her body tightened in resolve. "Not tonight."

He reached for her. "But you promised."

I slammed my fist into his forearm. "She said no, so beat it."

His jaw clenched. His eyes flashed. What supernatural being resided in his depths? Of course, it didn't scare me. It didn't worry me. And if he thought he could intimidate me, he didn't know me at all. He deserved a kick to the groin, and I was just the person to deliver it.

Cyn tightened her arm around me, leading me around him and down the path from which they had come. "Dez, don't worry about him. I'll take care of it."

"Humph," I grunted. "Unlikely. The second I disappear you're humping his brains out."

She groaned.

"Cynda, let me help you," Canyon said, ducking under my other arm and taking the brunt of my weight. My muscles tensed at his proximity, but I let him help anyway, feeling pretty wiped out from fighting with a demon prince and earning two elemental tattoos.

Canyon's scent infiltrated my nostrils. "Cyn was right. You *do* smell good."

"Uh, thanks."

I patted his muscular bicep. "Don't worry. You're not my type. I like them dark and twisted, like demon princes and Meditation instructors."

"Dez," Cyn scolded me at my admission.

I might be a tad lust-drunk too. Man, that shit was good. Way stronger than faerie wine. "It's like fucking truth serum coursing through my veins."

"Is that what happened to you? You stumbled off into the Wildwoods drunk?"

"Judgy. No, I got dragged into the woods by the Demon Prince. Didn't you see him?"

"Isn't he a member of the Council?" she whispered in my ear so Canyon couldn't hear.

"Yes, he is, and he defended me."

"Then why would he attack you?" She sucked in a breath. "Oh no."

"What?"

"Payback for your insubordination in his dungeons," she whispered.

"We were imprisoned. Was I supposed to be Miss Merry Sunshine?"

She snorted as the double doors to our wing opened for us. "That's a side of you I'd like to see. You practically threw yourself at him."

"We were thrown into a cell, and may I remind you, it was me who got us out."

"We probably would have been released sooner if it wasn't for your smart mouth. We also weren't completely defenseless," she murmured under her breath.

"Thank you for calling me smart. It was my brains that got us out of there."

She ripped her hand off me. "That had nothing to do with you or your brains. It was your hormones that kept us there. You lobbed sexual innuendoes at the prince like it was your day job."

I stopped, ignoring Cyn's rising anger as I replayed that day. The depth of his fury at his men who imprisoned us, the delight in his mannerisms during our verbal exchange, the way his eyes had followed me when I left the Council meeting. My strength returned to me. I pulled away from Canyon and Cyn, no longer feeling woozy. "I need to find Gage."

Cyn waved her hands back and forth. "Oh no. He's with Red, and they're together. No threesomes allowed."

Canyon's eyes widened, but he kept his mouth shut. Smart guy.

"I don't want to sleep with him. I have to talk to him about something."

She put her hands on her hips. "What?"

She'd never believe me. Plus she and I had made a pact about not going near Jace or Canyon, and while we had both broken that vow, the possibility of Jace being the Demon Prince tilted the world off its fucking axis.

I backed away from her and Canyon. "I can't tell you."

She kept coming at me. Stubborn pain in the ass. "Can't or won't?"

I pressed my lips together, rolling my eyes.

She crossed her arms, unimpressed with my reaction. "I'm waiting."

"Fine. Both."

Her eyes watered and her shoulders softened. "Dez, you can trust me."

"You sure about that?"

"Yes. That is the one thing I am sure about."

I looked meaningfully over her shoulder at Canyon. "What about him. You promised to stay away."

"I did stay away."

"What were you doing with him alone in the woods?"

Her gaze dropped to the floor as she swallowed. "He caught me off guard."

"And what were you going to do with him in the middle of the Wildwoods while you were off guard?"

Her finger trailed along her neck as if following an invisible path. Desire permeated the air around her.

"He's dangerous, Cyn."

Her gaze darkened. "So am I."

Anger rose within me. "You know who his mom is."

"Yet we've been here months and nothing has happened. The only person who accused her of being dangerous is the one person who disappeared from Silverwood Academy over a week ago. Coincidence? I think not," she said, crossing her arms again.

Pieces of the puzzle slid together. "A week ago," I murmured.

"Yeah," she snapped, "one week ago, and you're not worried about your boyfriend, but mine is off limits."

I rolled my eyes. "You sound like a petulant child. Get over it. Fuck some other hot guy."

Canyon's eyes shot to mine. His eyes flashed brightly, but it could have been a reflection of the night-sky ceiling.

"I'll let you take care of him. I'll see you later."

She wrapped her fingers around a cylinder hanging from a long necklace she had hidden under her dress. "You're not going anywhere."

"Watch me," I said, waving at her.

She grinned as she broke something in her hand. The hallway clouded. My vision grew blurry, and I started coughing uncontrollably. She approached me as if in slow motion. I scrubbed at my eyes, but it didn't do any good. It just got blurrier and fuzzier and . . .

Oh fuck.

SIXTEEN

 yn

THE SLEEPING SPELL worked surprisingly well. It was a risk, of course, using it out in the hallway when clearly my sister wasn't about to give me permission to use magick on her, but I had to take matters into my own hands and trust that the faculty, along with the rest of the school, were outside still partaking in the Silver Crescent Moon Festival like Dez and I were supposed to be doing.

I caught her before her head cracked against the floor. Of course, she'd heal on her own, but blood smears would lead any curious passerby to our room, and we didn't need that added attention. We had some rules we needed to sort out, and I was just the sister to initiate that conversation. Just because Dez was my big sister didn't mean she could do whatever she wanted.

Her head knocked into the doorframe on our way into my room. Oops, that wasn't intentional at all. Honest.

I chuckled to myself. Guess I had a passive-aggressive streak in me after all. I mean, after living with my fake parents for almost two decades of my life and dating Derrick for two years, I'd learned a thing or two about it. But what Dez didn't know wouldn't hurt her. However, her headstrong attitude could. She claimed the Demon Prince had dragged her from the party, but I hadn't seen anything, and I feel like that would have been a topic of conversation among the festival goers. Rumors about my sister's outrageous behavior often got back to me, like how she'd barged in on one of Jace's classes. No one knew what she was doing there, but he had quickly ended class before the situation escalated. Situations escalated a lot with Dez around, thus the reason I wanted to knock her out and tuck her in for the night. Aggressive? Yes. Necessary? Absolutely.

"Cynda, what did you do?" Canyon asked, rushing over to help me.

It was cute that he thought I needed help. That I was a weak human rather than an extraordinarily powerful supernatural being. I could use that angle to make myself seem like the damsel in distress.

"Just help me get her to her bed. Then we can talk."

"Yeah, sure."

We carried her over to her bed. I grinned at her unconscious form. Bet she hadn't expected she'd be tucked in at this hour all by herself tonight. I giggled as I covered her with the throw she kept at the foot of her bed.

"What's so funny?" Canyon whispered.

I trusted my potion to work, but one never knew how fast someone of our abilities might burn through it. I flicked my finger at him as I tilted my head toward the bathroom. He followed me inside and closed the door behind him.

"What is it?" he mouthed.

"That," I said, pointing at the door, "is not how my sister expected to spend this evening."

He tilted his head sideways. "And you find it funny that you shot her with a stunning potion?"

"I find it hilarious. She always underestimates me."

His lips rose in a sideways grin as he slowly approached me. "And what if I hit you with a stunning potion with her incapacitated?" His hands shot out and wrapped around my wrists.

Oh shit. A shiver ran up my spine. I sucked in a breath. Maybe Canyon really was the bad guy.

Fuck that. I was a bad guy too.

Twisting my wrists with a sharp jerk, I broke from his grasp as my knee found his groin like a heat-seeking missile.

"Oooof," he groaned, folding over.

But I wasn't done with him yet, not by a long shot. My fingers wrapped around his wrist, wrenching it behind his back. Without wasting any time, I swept his legs out from under him. His body slammed face first toward the floor. I followed him down, my hand still holding his wrist, my knees landing on his back, further nailing him into the floor. When satisfied he was under my control, I bent over to his ear. "What was that you were saying?"

He didn't reply at first. Most likely because of the ass kicking I'd just delivered. Let him think about his words before trying to speak. I waited one ... two ... three ...

"Cynda, you misunderstood. I didn't mean that I was actually going to use magick on you."

I yanked his arm farther around his back. I wanted to make him hurt like his question had hurt me. "Then why did you grab me after you said it?"

"Ouch, Cynda. It feels like you're yanking my arm out of its socket."

"Deal with it. Talk."

"First, using magick on someone is a violation of Silverwood's rules."

"Which I had no problem breaking." I jammed both knees deeper into his back.

He bit back a yelp, but it leaked out.

"Second, I'd never use magick on you. It's against everything I stand for as a pacifist. I'd never hurt you. I wanted to kiss you."

Not the answer I was expecting.

Don't fall for that line of crap, Dez would say.

I jerked his other arm behind his back. He grunted but didn't fight me.

"Why did you grab my wrists then?"

"Considering our current situation, it probably wasn't the best move. I thought you might like someone who takes charge. An alpha male."

I snorted. "I'm not Dez. Besides, already dated one of those and, not a fan."

"Noted. Being a human male in a school created to train future Silver Cloak Brotherhood and Silver Dagger Sisterhood members makes one feel a tad inferior."

I wrenched his arms harder. "A tad?"

He winced. "Ow."

I softened my grip, feeling guilty that I so adamantly pressed my point.

"Okay, a lot more than a tad. I'm a total wuss in this

place. A nobody. A nothing. I am at your mercy. Was that what you wanted to hear?"

His confession spoke to that part of me that always felt like I'd never match up to the standards Derrick set, my friends established, and my "parents" imposed.

"No, actually." I released my hold, leapt off his back, and stood up. I couldn't deny that I loved my new athletic prowess. As a human? Complete klutz. As a Sempiternal? Supernatural Olympic gold medalist.

He lay there with his arms flat at his sides, unmoving.

"Do you need help? Did I accidently break your arms or dislocate your shoulders or something?" I mean, he had complained that it felt like his arm was getting yanked out of its socket. Maybe I underestimated my strength.

"No, just waiting for the circulation to return."

He pressed his hands into the tile floor and slowly pushed himself into a downward dog position before returning upright. He watched me warily as he brushed his hands off. A pang of guilt shot through me. But so did a heavy dose of adrenaline. I liked being able to dominate.

His silver shirt hung open, revealing an impeccable muscular chest. One I'd only imagined seeing. But now, in the flesh, my eyes had a mind of their own, wandering over his abs to the beginning of a deep V, and let me tell you, I wanted to see where that letter ended.

He cleared his throat.

My attention snapped back to his face, meeting his gorgeous green eyes. He stared at me, without saying anything.

"S-sorry for the misunderstanding," I managed to say.

Rather than respond, he reached down and started to button his shirt, or at least he tried to. His fingers couldn't seem to find any buttons. He sighed as he broke his attention from me and dropped his head to search his shirt for them, but he didn't find any. Not a one.

He released the bottom edges of his shirt with a dramatic fling of his hands, his shirttails flying out and revealing more of his chest before feathering back against it.

He glared up at the ceiling, his nostrils flaring, then looked back at me. "Well, I wanted to make a dignified apology to you, but apparently the universe doesn't want to cooperate with me. Again."

I licked my lips and sauntered toward him. "Or, maybe the universe knows *exactly* how you should apologize."

He gave me a sideways grin. "Are you telling me all I had to do was act like the real me? No testosterone blustering? No twelve-pack abs. No impressive biceps."

I trailed my fingers along his arms. "Oh, I don't know about that. They seem pretty impressive to me. And who needs twelve when six work just fine." In an even more brazen move, I traced along his abs toward the top lines of his V.

He sucked in a breath as my fingers hooked around his belt and pulled him closer.

"You don't need to be strong. I'm strong enough for both of us."

"Yes, you are," he murmured, wrapping his arms around me, "and some men might have a problem with that, but I don't. In fact . . . ," he bent down, his nose trailing along my jaw to my ear, "I find it fucking sexy."

Everything in my body tightened. Every lady bit readied for a different kind of conquering. No one ever had referred to me that way before. Derrick had used my body for sex, but I had never felt sexy.

His lips found their way to my shoulder. He bit the dress strap with his teeth and tugged. The strap broke apart. He lifted his head to peek up at me. "Fucking sexy."

Oh my . . .

Wetness exploded between my thighs. His tongue darted in and out as his lips traveled along my collarbone, stopping at the remaining dress strap. His hands twined around my neck.

"When I'm through with you, you will forget every person you've ever been with. Agreed?"

He plucked the strap free, and the dress dropped down, exposing my breasts.

"Yes," I moaned.

His hands cupped them.

"Soon, you will scream my name."

"Yes."

He dragged my dress over my hips and slowly slipped it over my ass, pulling my underwear with it. He stopped his clothing removal midthigh, letting gravity take over. I gasped, standing naked before him. My body quivered with need, shaking with anticipation of what was to come next. His hand slid between my legs, immediately finding my wetness. Fingers seesawed back and forth across it, sending sensations exploding through me.

"And, you will bite me as you come."

I dug my claws into his shoulders, my body convulsing, my fangs lengthening. "Yes."

He bent down and took my nipple into his mouth, sucking it, as he grasped the other and pulled. Consciousness faded away. Control? Lost it when he bit my strap off.

I stilled. That was weird. Human teeth aren't sharp enough to cut fabric.

But all thoughts were abandoned as two fingers plunged into me, dancing in and out in a throbbing rhythm. A new wave of euphoria loosed through me. My body vibrated with need. Climbing. Reaching. Finding . . .

"Bite me, Cyn," he instructed me, so I did.

SEVENTEEN

D^{ez}

Aw, fuck. My temples pounded like I'd downed a fifth of faerie wine. Though the events of the evening were foggy, I was pretty sure I'd only had two glasses. I slung my arm across my head, covering my eyes, trying to numb the pain before attempting to reconstruct the events of the evening. Just a little longer . . .

"Yes," someone cried.

But not just someone—my sister. And it wasn't a conversational "Yes, I'd love a cup of tea." It was a "Yes, I'm getting fucked right now."

I shot out of bed, my mind reacting faster than my body. I staggered, trying to find balance after my feet hit the floor. Waves of nausea overtook me. I held both hands to my head, trying to make the world stop spinning. "Oh man, what happened to me?" I moaned.

In answer, my brain pulled up an image of my dear, sweet sister crushing a vial in her hand and my world fading to black.

Bitch spelled me.

"Yes," Bitch cried again.

Any residual effects of the spell pushed out of me, and my purpose became singular. Get to Cyn and protect her at all costs.

My ears perked at the moans and groans as I pinpointed my sister's location. My fangs dropped, my claws extended, and every muscle in my body coiled, ready to attack. I vamp-sped over to the bathroom door, whipped it open, and threw Canyon against the wall. My mouth twitched at the smell of his blood. He smelled divine. My gaze fell on the two bite marks dripping blood from his neck. Any desire to sample him myself disappeared. I held him in place while my naked-ass sister's body writhed in orgasm, barely aware that Lover Boy was no longer stroking her.

"Are you done?" I growled.

Her eyes shot to mine, then to the person I held captive. She bared her bloodstained teeth to me, growling, "Get the fuck away from him."

I snorted. "Or what? You'll attack me? Been there. Done that. Not worried."

"Why, you—" she screamed, her arms raised, claws out, sprinting at me.

I whipped Canyon in front of me, using him as a shield. It wasn't that I was worried my sister would hurt me. It was just that I wanted to witness for myself what effect he had on her. I couldn't figure out if supernatural blood flowed through his veins from an ancestor or if his mom had spelled him, and now was as good a time as any to find out.

Cyn skidded to a halt and dropped her hands.

"Whew. Was a little worried you were going to rip my heart out." Canyon laugh-squealed, his reaction not faltering. It was pretty wuss-like if you asked me, but then I liked mine dark and twisted, so I was a poor judge.

Cyn's features softened at his confession. "I'd never hurt you," she whispered, raising her hand to cradle his cheek.

He wielded power over her, and that worried me. It was my job to protect my sister at all costs, and keeping her away from Canyon was proving harder than I imagined.

I wrapped my hand around his neck, my claws poking into his skin. "Back the fuck up."

Her face hardened as she glared at me, her pupils elongating into ovals. "Don't you touch him."

"Too late for that, Sister."

A low growl rumbled in her chest. "I'm warning you."

"Noted and not alarmed. You'll have to get through Canyon to get to me."

She threw back her head and screamed in frustration. Her body vibrated as energy built up inside her. Her form blurred and reformed, blurred and reformed, blinking in and out of existence. What was happening?

"Cynda, it's all right. Just calm down," Canyon said in a soothing, low tone almost like a chant. "Breathe in and out. In and out."

Somehow his words penetrated into her brain, and her nostrils flared in and out, her chest rising and falling as she began inhaling and exhaling until her whole body remained in this realm.

"That's it," he whispered. "Just keep breathing in and out, in and out."

Her lips thinned as she focused on her breathing. Canyon pulled toward her, raising his hands to touch her arms as if to fully ground her, but he couldn't get close to her because my claws in his neck stopped him.

Tears streamed down Cyn's face as her pupils returned to normal. Her body quivered, but this time it wasn't because of an orgasm or from anger. Fear, exhaustion, and confusion wrecked her. She clutched her stomach, her body folding in half, revealing the Water element tattoo on the back of her neck. She looked as if she was going to collapse at any second, completely vanquished like I was after the red laser beam incident.

I swallowed hard. Never before had I witnessed another person so broken, so scared, so removed from herself. I was out of my depth. Her actions were so completely out of my comfort zone. But there was someone who could help her.

I released Canyon, and he rushed to her, catching her before she hit the tile floor. In a quick, efficient movement, he swept her into his arms as if she weighed nothing at all and rushed out of the bathroom. I blinked, realizing I'd just given my sister to the enemy. Though as much as I hated to admit it, he no longer felt like that. Canyon had handled my sister's existential crisis in stride while I stood with my thumb up my bum. I followed him into our room and watched as he placed her on her bed and covered her with blankets. He sat down on the edge of it, whispering, "It's okay. Just relax. I've got you."

"Don't leave me," she mumbled.

He glanced over his shoulder at me, raising his eyebrow.

I pressed my lips together and nodded. I was no more prepared to handle my sister now then I was during her episode in the bathroom.

"Thanks," he mouthed to me, before turning back to her. "I'm not going anywhere. I'll be here for as long as you need me."

"I need you," she whispered so softly that even with my vamp hearing I barely heard her.

He chuckled. "I'm right here. Just go to sleep."

"Next to me."

He glanced over at me again. At least he knew who was in charge.

"Fine but over the covers."

He nodded as he lay down next to her, wrapping his arm around her, cradling her head against his heart.

I crossed my arms as I watched them drift off to sleep. My mind raced a million miles an hour, cycling through the many twists and turns of this evening, trying to make demon princes out of yoga instructors and dreadful canyons into harmless meadows.

CHAPTER

EIGHTEEN

ez

I DON'T KNOW how long I stood there watching them, lost in thought, but it had to be a long time.

A hard knock at the door broke me from my headspace. Cyn rustled in bed. Before it woke her up, I rushed over, ready to unleash my fury on whatever asshat had almost interrupted my sister's much-needed rest. My anger quickly dissipated when I saw who dared knock on our door in the middle of the night, and honestly, I should have expected it.

Red's face brightened when I opened the door. She rushed in and wrapped me in a hug.

My eyes met Gage's, who stood behind Red, his hands shoved into his pockets, looking relieved and perhaps a little sheepish.

Alyze brushed past him and enveloped both Red and

me in a giant hug. I tried breaking away, but the siren and the witch were surprisingly strong, and I really didn't try that hard. Eventually they loosened their grips, and we broke from one another.

"We were so worried about you," Red said.

I raised my finger to my lips, quieting them as I tilted my head toward Cyn's bed.

Their heads snapped over to my sister still resting against Canyon's chest, his shirt draped open, revealing a side profile of his tight, lean abs.

They both frowned at me.

"Long story."

Alyze crossed her arms, taking the same warrior stance as I had watching Cyn and Canyon. "We've got all night."

"Can we talk about it in the morning? I'm beat." I stretched my arms over my head to emphasize the point.

Red snorted and waved for Gage to come in. "Yeah, like you'd sleep with the two of them here. Plus, your body's covered with grass, dirt, and"—she leaned closer, examining my torn dress—"is that your blood or someone else's? And why haven't you healed yet? What happened to you?"

My eyes drifted to Gage. "Why don't you ask your date?"

Her long red hair whipped around as she turned to stare at him. "You knew about this?"

He raised his hands. "N—" he started, but she snapped her fingers. Magick swirled around his nose. The tip of it wiggled as he fought the magick, but he really liked Anastasia, so he didn't repel it like he normally would. "A little."

Alyze stomped up to him, coming up to his neck, but that didn't dissuade her from shoving her finger into his chest. "You've got a lot of explaining to do if you want to live to see tomorrow."

Gargoyles were nearly impossible to kill, but I appreciated my friend's effort.

He peeked out of the room, up and down the dark hallway. "Let's close the door."

"Just keep your voices down," I reminded them.

Red shook her head. "You always forget that there's a magick spell for that." She wiggled her fingers and glitter shot out of them. A light purple bubble enveloped us all.

"Right, follow me." I turned around and walked over to my bed.

"What the—" Alyze shouted, then slapped her hand over her mouth as her eyes shot over to a sleeping Cyn and Canyon.

"It's fine. They can't hear you," Red reminded her.

Alyze nodded rapidly. "Right. Right." Her bright blue eyes met mine. "Dez, when did you get your Fire and Water tattoos?"

Gage grabbed my shoulders and spun me around to take in my exposed back. "These both happened tonight?"

"At the Silver Crescent Moon Festival. Well, in the Wildwoods after the Demon Prince dragged me away from the bonfire."

"What?" Red and Alyze growled together.

I smiled to myself. My friends were kick ass.

"Let me start from the beginning," I said.

Gage sat on my desk chair and reached for Red. She skirted away from him with her arms crossed and gave a scowl that would immobilize most gargoyles.

"Yes, lets."

IT TOOK a while to finish recounting the events of the evening, especially because once I mentioned that the only person who wasn't frozen at the bonfire was Gage, Red took forever interrogating his reasoning behind allowing the Demon Prince to kidnap me. It wasn't until I called her off, telling her I trusted Gage with my life, that she finally relented, though she wasn't happy about it. To Gage's credit, he didn't cave to Red, but he also didn't hint that he knew the Demon Prince other than that he was a Council member and a member of Silver Cloak Brotherhood. All of which would line up with my theory that the Demon Prince was Jace, his trusted friend whose identity he would never reveal.

Alyze rested her hands on her crossed knees. "So, let me get this straight, the Demon Prince took you to the Wildwoods and attacked you, but you fought back with Fire. Got your Fire tattoo. But fire doesn't work on a fire demon, so it was only after you accessed your Water elemental power that you were able to get away."

"Pretty much sums it up."

"And before you could confront him, Cyn and Canyon showed up, and the Demon Prince scampered away and hid like the coward he is," Red snapped.

Gage glanced over at her, not agreeing with her assessment of the Demon Prince, but he kept his mouth shut.

Alyze cracked her fingers as she went through everything. "So, if those factors hadn't come into play, would you be captive in his dungeon again?"

My intuition immediately gave me the answer. "He was the one who released us the last time, so I don't think so. And Lilith cast a spell over Cyn and me, holding us to

Silverwood Academy grounds. I don't know if even a demon prince could break that magick."

Red pointed at me. "Good point. So, let's break this down." She began pacing in front of Gage, who was making puppy eyes at her, awaiting her forgiveness, but she was completely ignoring him. "The Demon Prince frees you from his dungeon but then kidnaps you from a large gathering of people, risking exposure on Silverwood grounds."

"Well," I interrupted, "he can freeze time, or whatever he did, so he really didn't risk exposure. No one saw him take me."

She whirled around with her hands on her hips. "Except Gage."

"Except Gage. But there's something else." I licked my lips, unsure how to proceed. Should I share with them my theory about who the Demon Prince really was, or should I discuss it in private with Gage, or should I keep that information to myself for now?

Alyze leaned over, placing her hands on my thighs. "What is it, Dez?"

I breathed in and out, trying to ground myself to the space. I reached for the pagan prayer beads without thinking and ran them in and out of my hands. The crystals immediately warmed to my touch. My eyes fell on the owl charm. Steadfast and watchful. Present yet otherworldly. "Nothing."

Red snatched the prayer beads from my hand.

"Hey!"

I reached for them, but she was already on the other side of the room with her eyes closed, murmuring something. Her eyes snapped open.

"Who gave these to you?"

I looked away from her. "No one."

She stormed back to me. "Who was it?"

My eyes met Gage's. He ever-so-slightly shook his head no.

I didn't want to lie to my friends, but something needled at my brain that I should keep Jace's identity a secret, at least for now. I breathed in and out, steadying myself. "Just a trinket I picked up after a hunt to celebrate my first kill." Not a complete lie, I did steal a gold coin from the pirate's treasure box to commemorate the event.

"I don't believe you. The craftmanship put into this beadwork is from someone skilled in the arts. Someone with an appreciation and admiration for Brigit. Someone who wouldn't leave it lying around for you to steal. And by the way, I never recommend stealing crystals or any other type of bead- or metalwork, because aside from it just being wrong, crystals especially can be tracked."

"They can?" I squeaked out. Then I cleared my throat because I sounded panicked and I wanted to appear calm and collected, and I asked again, "They can?"

She returned it to my clasped hands. "They can, and this one is connected to you."

Jace had given me those prayer beads on my first day of class. Why had he been tracking me since all the way back then?

Weeks later we had marked each other, so even if I didn't have the beads, he could still track me. Probably even easier than with the prayer beads.

I made an oath to protect you, he had said.

An oath to whom?

NINETEEN

yn

MY HEAD POUNDED with the dull ache of drinking too much the night before. Not that I had a lot of experience in that area, but there was that one time . . . and my body never forgot it. (Neither did the interior of the Prius.) But the only thing I had consumed last night was a sip of faerie wine and few shots of lust and desire energy when Dez dragged me around the bonfire. Then I'd broken away and disappeared into the crowd and wound up in Canyon's arms. Oh, and I drank his blood. Again.

Slowly, the events from the evening returned to me. Canyon and me hooking up. Us disappearing from the festival in search of privacy, only to find Dez in the middle of the Wildwoods by herself. The two of us carrying her back to our room. Her lust-drunk babbling about demon princes and Canyon smelling good. Her trying to leave and find Gage. Me hitting her with a stunning spell. Canyon and me putting her to bed. Us disappearing into the bathroom. Him doing things to my body . . .

I stretched like a cat, remembering the way my first orgasm rippled through me.

"Hey, you," Canyon purred next to me.

I stiffened, not recalling how we'd ended up in bed together. My hands landed on my stomach. My bare stomach. They slowly slid up and down my body, searching for clothing, any clothing, only to discover there wasn't any.

His hand stroked my bare shoulder. A moan escaped from my mouth as I remembered how it felt when he stroked me in other places. I peeked up at him. He looked as delicious in the morning light as he had last night in the woods when our chests pressed against one another's as the rough bark of a tree crushed against my back. I licked my lips. Oh yes, I was ready, able, and horny.

"As much as I'd like to return to that memory," he whispered, glancing over at my sister, who sat watching us from her bed with her arms crossed, "I think she'd kill me."

"At least you're not a complete idiot."

I sat up, and my blankets fell away, revealing my bare breasts. Canyon's gaze dropped to them, his luscious lips lifting. My heart raced.

"That's enough," Dez growled, suddenly appearing next to us and ripping him from the bed.

Damn vamp speed.

Annoyance rose in me, soon replaced by fear as I remembered the last time she tore Canyon from me.

"What happened to me last night?"

Dez stood near the door, her grip on Canyon tight, but he didn't appear as frightened as he should be with my sister's hands wrapped around his arms.

"Either put clothes on or cover yourself, because Lover Boy won't be able to contribute to the conversation with his eyes on your tits."

My eyes met Canyon's whose attention had drifted to my chest. Heat rose up my neck as I tugged the blanket up and pinned it in place with my arms.

He pressed his lips together in disappointment but stood at my sister's mercy, completely relaxed as if it didn't concern him that she could stick him with her claws or use him as a chew toy.

"What's up with the two of you?"

Dez's eyes narrowed. "What do you mean?"

Canyon's face brightened with realization. "She means why am I not worried about you killing me."

Dez rolled her eyes. "I don't unalive people on a whim. Plus, it would violate several of Silverwood Academy's rules. The ephemeral isn't worth it." She shoved Canyon away.

He stumbled forward a few steps before finding his balance inches from my bed. His eyes met mine.

"May I sit next to you?"

"No way. There's her chair. Use it if you don't want to lose her favorite body part."

He winked at me and sat down, pulling the chair closer to the bed. He still didn't act in any way fearful of my sister's wrath.

"What happened last night? You two seem almost chummy."

Dez hopped up on her bed. "Oh, I wouldn't go that far, but I possess less of a desire to cause fatal injury to him at the present."

My gaze slid to Canyon, who didn't react to Dez's comments.

"Any reason for the change of heart?"

"Well, after you hit me with that stunning spell . . . ," she cracked her knuckles, "—we'll discuss *that* matter later—"

I raised my chin to demonstrate I wasn't afraid of her.

". . . I awoke to screams of 'Yes' coming from the bathroom, and I do mean *coming*."

My gaze slid over to Canyon, his sculpted chest on display for my ogling. Heat bloomed in my core. His lips rose into a sly grin as if he knew exactly what I was thinking about. Could he smell my desire? Because I could smell his.

Dez yanked Canyon's chair away and pushed him to the other side of the room. "You're not the only one who can smell, Cyn. The two of you are not about to get freaky in here in front of me. You're not getting freaky period, so quit it. Now, shall I continue?"

I tore my eyes from Canyon. "Yes."

"I yanked Canyon off your naked ass, held my claws to his neck, and you freaked out—or should I say blinked out?"

My stomach flip-flopped. Nausea swept through me. A sense of dread crawled up my spine. "What do you mean blinked out?"

"Your physical form faded in and out of existence," Canyon said.

I remembered intense rage coursing through me, and I lost all sense of myself. I stared over at him. "And where did it go?"

He shook his head. He didn't know either.

"You calmed me down," I whispered.

His eyes slid over to Dez as if asking permission to continue. She nodded, her lips pressed tightly together.

"I did."

"You helped me calm down by breathing."

He grinned. "I guess you and I have both learned a lot from Meditation with Jace. Gage is good too."

Dez adjusted her legs on the bed, but I ignored her. Not everything was about her and her misdirected sex life.

"Thank you for helping me."

"My pleasure," he purred in a deep, sexy voice, doing things to my insides that ought to be illegal.

"I'm still here."

"And no freaky behavior," Canyon grinned.

"You." She pointed at him. "I'm starting to like you, and that is bothersome."

He frowned at her. "Why is that a problem?"

"For a number of reasons that are none of your damn business." She leapt off the bed and vamp-sped over to him. He arched backward, surprised at her sudden appearance. His mom was a vamp, but she was a turned one. During my short time at Silverwood Academy, I'd noticed there was a glaring difference between the speed of a turned vamp versus a changed one, and Dez and I were Sempiternals— the fastest of them all.

She raised her hand to his shoulder but didn't touch him. "May I?"

She always surprised me whenever she asked permission.

He nodded. "You may."

She laid her hand on his shoulder, her fingers curling around it. "I really appreciate you saving my sister. Thank you."

His eyes slid over to me, before quickly returning to her. "You're welcome. I would do anything for Cynda."

"Good." She smiled and crouched down in front of him.

"Now, you left the Silver Crescent Moon Festival early. You didn't kiss Cynda."

Fear spiked in me. What was she doing?

"You went to sleep in your bed and stayed there all night."

Canyon's eyes pulsed in and out as Dez stared at him.

"Dez," I shouted as I jumped out of bed, forgetting the blanket.

Canyon turned to me, taking in my naked body. His pupils began returning to normal.

Dez gripped his chin and snapped it back toward her. "Forget everything from last night. Go to your room and get in your bed."

My nose itched as I watched Canyon rise from his chair in a zombie-like state. He didn't even turn in my direction as he walked over and opened the door. Then his eyes met mine. His lips rose in a small smile. I returned it, my heart breaking because I couldn't tell if he was under Dez's compellation or faking it, and I was unsure how I felt about it. I was torn between wanting him to remember what we did together and wanting to keep him safe, because my sister and I were destined to follow a dangerous life, and I didn't want him involved in any of it. He was breakable. An ephemeral. It was better this way.

At least that's what I told myself, but when he closed the door behind him, I wanted to collapse on my bed and cry until I didn't have any tears left to shed. Instead, I remembered who I was and what I was. I raised my chin, my eyes narrowing, my thirst for revenge growing inside me.

"Remember the way we both stared at the door, waiting for Lilith to return and say, 'Kidding, I can't really force you to stay on campus. That's a violation of the rules. Rules I helped create,' but she never did?"

Dez breathed in and out, her nostrils whistling at the force of the oxygen and carbon dioxide she was taking in and blowing out, her own thirst for revenge growing inside her. When she didn't break the silence, I swallowed, realizing my time had come, and I knew exactly what I wanted to do.

"I say we try it."

She turned to face me. "Try what?"

"Make a break for it. Go find Lamashtu and kick her psycho baby-killing ass."

Her purple eyes studied me a long time without saying a word. I began to regret my suggestion. Maybe it was impulsive. Impossible. Irrational. Maybe we should listen to Lilith and keep our heads down and train. Maybe we should—

Her lips split into a giant grin. "I have never been more proud of you in my entire life. Let's do it."

I lifted my chest, her compliment filling me with confidence. No one had ever supported any of my ideas in such a profound way.

"I think we need help though."

Every muscle in her body stiffened. Her eyes flashed red as she looked at me, but she didn't fire her laser beams. Finally, her shoulders loosened, and she cracked her knuckles. "As much as I hate to admit it, I think you're right. Since you're making the decisions, who do you suggest?"

As if in answer, someone knocked on our door. Dez frowned at me as she opened it. Before us stood Red and Alyze wearing tight black long-sleeve shirts, black leather pants, and black combat boots. They stalked into the room, the door closing behind them. Without saying a word, they spun around, demonstrating their backpacks covered with daggers and the knife sheaths dangling from their waists. Red rested her hands on her hips, drawing our attention to her belt loaded with spells and potions.

Alyze swung her blond ponytail over her shoulder as she jutted out her hip. "We're ready whenever you are."

"Uh . . ." was all I could say.

"Seer, remember?" Red laughed.

Dez smiled at her. "And you knew Cyn would suggest the two of you?"

Red gestured to her outfit. "Obviously. Get your asses ready and let's go."

I narrowed my eyes at her. "Do you know where we're going or who we're after?"

She twirled her fingers, and an image of Lamashtu hovered above them.

Dez stepped in front of Anastasia. "Red, just how much can you see?"

She shrugged her shoulders. "Enough. Especially if it involves me in some way, shape, or form, and since the four of us are besties, that includes an awful lot. But to answer the question you're really asking, I have no idea what the outcome of this mission will be. Only that you two needed help and wanted Alyze and me to team up with you."

Dez clapped her hands together. "Right. Get ready, Cyn."

I grinned at her. "I thought you'd never ask."

CHAPTER

TWENTY

DRESSED and prepped for our mission, we stood on the edge of Wildwood Preserves, my entire body crackling with excitement. My little sister had come up with this plan, and I freaking loved it.

Red jumped up and down, barely able to contain her enthusiasm at going on a mission. Of the three of us who had grown up in the supernatural world, Anastasia was the most sheltered. She'd studied her craft. She'd grown her power by complete immersion in nature. She'd manifested her future intentions, but the opportunity for action had never presented itself.

Until now.

"So, how do we get there?" she asked.

I rested my hands on my hips, studying the trees. "Well, last time Cyn and I hitched a ride with Lippincott and

Bladecroft via a portal that dropped us close enough to the crossroads without causing a ripple effect."

"They had also turned Dez into a screaming baby who bit Lamashtu's teat, so unless either one of you is capable of that sort of magick or can portal jump without permission, we need to travel the old-fashioned way," Cyn added.

I crossed my arms. "I'm not traveling by horseback. Besides, that would take forever."

My sister rolled her eyes, her attitude growing with each passing day. I wasn't quite sure if it pleased me or annoyed me. Attitude flowed through my veins, but patience did not.

"Not that old fashioned, and we haven't learned how to ride dragons or griffins yet, though I suspect it's about the same as riding a horse."

I raised my hand, palm out. "Stop right there. I'm not riding anything that shits or eats more than me."

Alyze snickered.

"I was going to say that the animals in the barn and on the grounds are tagged, so if they breach the perimeter, Lippincott, along with security, will know."

"Really? How do you know that?"

Cyn blew air out of her mouth. "I listened the first day of class."

Alyze raised her hand. "Me too."

"Me three," Red added.

I narrowed my eyes at them. "No one likes a told-you-so or a know-it-all."

Alyze's bright blue eyes twinkled in the darkness. "But, it does help to pay attention in class."

I threw up my hand and walked down the path. "Okay, okay, point made."

"Uh, Dez," Cyn called out, "where are you going?"

I stopped and glared at her over my shoulder. "Isn't it obvious? To cross the border to steal a car."

"Or we could borrow one of the Academy's."

I spun around and walked back to them. "Or we could do that. But won't they be traceable like the animals?"

Red looped her hand through mine and followed the border of the Wildwoods. "Or I could disarm it with a spell."

"Or I could remove it permanently," Alyze threw in.

I frowned at her. "What do you know about cars? You lived underwater your entire life until you came here."

"We lived in an underwater city with motorized vehicles, and there are boats in the ocean." She swung out her hip at an exaggerated angle, placed a single finger on it, and winked at me. "I've got the touch."

"That's what I've heard."

Red chuckled with me.

Cyn groaned. "Does it always have to be about sex with you three?"

"Who said we were talking about sex? But, if we were, I'd say you need some," Red teased.

In the cold night air, I could feel Cyn's face heat up, but she kept her mouth shut. I respected her need for privacy about her encounter with Canyon the night before, but I could still tease her.

Red winked at me, patting my arm. "We've got to get her laid. She's too wound up."

"I've been trying, but she won't bite," I said.

"Oh, she bites, but she forgets to ask permission," Red snorts.

Cyn brushed past us. "The garage is this way."

I wanted to ask Red about Canyon and whether or not he could be trusted, but I didn't want to drive Cyn away or cause her to doubt herself when she was calling the shots for this mission. She needed to learn and accept that she was a powerful, fierce woman, a Sempiternal, no less, and all people should fear her.

Alyze hurried to catch up with Cyn, leaving Red and me trailing behind. Of course, I could have vamp-sped, but I didn't want to leave Red in the dust.

A thought came to me. "Hey, can you bewitch a broom, or can you climb on a broom and fly?"

"It's a more advanced skill for a witch."

"So, you can do it."

She clicked her tongue against her mouth. "We aren't supposed to share all our abilities with anyone."

"No," I added carefully, "but since we're besties . . ."

She cackled into the night. "I still can't believe I've got three best friends."

"Three is a powerful number."

"And four makes for a powerful coven."

"Can nonwitches be in a coven?" I had only worked with the occasional witch. I didn't have a lot of background in their true nature and the lives they lived outside of spell making and casting.

She patted my arm. "We make our own rules."

We approached the giant garage at the far end of the property. They liked to keep the modern conventions far away from the magick of the rest of the grounds and buildings. Alyze and Cyn stood in front of a side door. Alyze's mouth moved as she murmured a spell. Sirens possessed magick, much like witches, but their voice was needed to invoke the power, whereas powerful witches like Red could conjure it within themselves without speaking the words aloud. Blue flames burst from Alyze's hand, and she turned the knob. She and Cyn slipped inside.

"I guess we do," I said, pointing at my sister's silhouette waving for us to hurry inside the open car bay.

We soon joined her in front of a black jacked-up jeep, where two long legs were sticking out from the bottom of it. In less than a minute, Alyze slid out, smiled at us, and revealed a small metal beetle in her hand.

"All set."

Alyze and I climbed into the back, Red climbed into the front passenger's seat, and as lead on this mission, Cyn took the driver's seat.

"Buckle up, buttercup," she ordered as the jeep rumbled to life. "It's about to get bumpy."

I didn't bother buckling my seat belt. I was an immortal Sempiternal, but Red and Alyze both did. And that's when it struck me. Neither one of them was immortal. Someday they'd die and leave Cyn and me.

"I'm not dying anytime soon," Red yelled, grabbing the oh-shit bar beside her.

"Me neither," Alyze shouted.

"Let's ride," Cyn thundered, revved up on adrenaline.

My sister was right. It was going to be a bumpy ride, and I was going to enjoy the hells out of it.

She drove the jeep like a backroad rally driver. Again making me proud. My sister proved with each passing day her abilities would make her a formidable adversary to even the most dangerous of supernaturals and a worthy partner for me. Yes, one day we'd find Dad's killer and skin the bastard alive.

Alyze and I bounced around in the back seat, both of us savoring the thrill of the hunt, because Lamashtu wouldn't know what hit her.

"Woohooooooo," the siren hollered.

My ears tingled with her magick. It filled me with even

more adrenaline. I'd be a total junky by the end of this adventure. "Oh yeah!" I screamed, punching the roof.

Red laughed hysterically in the passenger seat, having the best freaking time of her life. I shook my head, smiling, still not fully believing I had not one, not two, but three best friends, and one of them was my sister.

"Oh shit!" Cyn yelled, the brakes squealing and the jeep skidding to a halt, sending me flying into the back of the seat in front of me.

"What the fuck?" I screeched. I clutched my smashed head and slid back into my seat, my neck and back aching from whiplash.

"Oh crap," Alyze groaned.

"I didn't see this part . . . ," Red whispered.

"We're dead. We're dead," Cyn chanted over and over, ever the optimist.

"What's going on?" I leaned between the front seats to see what had caused fear to shoot through the jeep. "Shit," I hissed, realizing there were far more pressing issues than a bruised skull to contend with.

In the headlights, five goddesses stood with their hands on their hips and their eyes narrowed. Mama Morrigan was positioned ahead of the other four, but that didn't mean Rhiannon, Maeve, Brigit, and Lilith were any less angry.

None of us said a word. None of us moved. None of us even breathed. We sat there staring at the five goddesses in all their terrifying glory.

"Did you think you could break through my barrier spell?" Lilith yelled.

Flames rippled from Brigit's red hair. "Or that you could defy my sister?"

"Or that disarming the tracker would go unnoticed?" Rhiannon shouted.

"Or that four of our students could leave the grounds without our knowledge?" Maeve shouted.

Mama Morrigan's eyes narrowed, focusing on my sister and me. *Or that your mother wouldn't know?*

"Return to your rooms and do not attempt to leave Silverwood Academy grounds without our permission," she said, the breath of her words icing the windows of the jeep.

"Do we turn the jeep around and drive back, or should we get out and walk?" Alyze murmured out of the side of her mouth.

"You will walk back," Rhiannon said, answering Alyze's question.

"And you will not discuss with anyone what transpired here tonight," Brigit added.

"Or you will find out why I am the Queen of the Hunt," Maeve threatened.

The four other goddesses broke into maniacal laughter at their sister, sounding especially eerie in the otherwise stillness of night.

"And I thought I was dark," I mumbled.

All four jeep doors flung open on their own.

"You don't know what dark is," Lilith added. "And none of you are prepared to capture Lamashtu. Her power has grown."

Fear shot through me. If we weren't capable of fighting her, why had Lippincott and Bladecroft asked Cyn and me to join their expedition? Cold dread swept through me. And what about Jace? Gage told me that Jace had left to hunt Lamashtu.

I jumped out and turned to face the goddesses.

Cyn tugged on my arm. "Dez, don't," she whispered under her breath.

I jerked free and vamp-sped in front of the jeep. I placed

my hands on my hips and thrust my chest out, mirroring the five goddesses. I would not cower to them. They had embraced me, cherished me, watched me grow. I had honored them my entire life and would continue to do so, but I needed to know one thing.

"Is Jace the Demon Prince?"

Five startled faces stared back at me.

"It is not our story to tell," Brigit finally said.

Red reached for me, but I held firm, refusing to budge. Red respected the goddesses, as did I, but they didn't scare me. They wouldn't smite me down. They wouldn't crush me to my knees and make me bow. They wouldn't make an example out of me for my disobedience.

"And why not? We marked each other. Don't I deserve to know?" I directed my question to the one person who ought to care about me more than the rest of them. Her sisters' eyes skirted to the back of her head before returning to mine.

Mama Morrigan pressed her lips, watching me for a long time. Unfortunately for her, my willful stubborn streak ran strong. Finally, she answered.

"What you deserve and what you need to know are two different things."

"Cowardly response, don't you think? What would my mother say if I fed her that line of bullshit?" I replied, careful to keep my parental heritage secret from Alyze and Red.

The Goddess of Water stiffened. I raised an eyebrow, daring her to reveal our blood tie. At her sides, her fingers twitched, wanting to snap us into a deep sleep but knowing that method was equivalent to the coward's way, and she had already taken that route before. "Lamashtu was exiled to the Demon Realm long ago. However, mortals called her back to the Earthly Realm."

Cyn appeared next to me. "Who would do that?"

Mama Morrigan tilted her head at me. "Would you like to answer your sister?"

The hair on the back of my neck stood on end. A sense of dread overtook me. My mouth went dry. I licked my lips before answering. "The Children of the Sun."

Red released my arm to stand next to me. "But why would they align with Lamashtu?"

Brigit called forth a flame, letting it hover over her raised palm. "My child, you already know the answer."

"Power?"

Brigit clenched her hand into a fist, extinguishing the flame. "Yes."

Alyze slid between Red and me. "But, how did it happen?"

Lilith crossed her arms, frowning at her. "Child, say what you really mean."

The siren looked at me out of the corner of her eye. I nodded.

"Why did the five of you allow it to happen?"

Rhiannon's body shook with rage. "The sacrifices were made in secret. Powerful witches hid their deaths."

Brigit whipped her head toward Rhiannon. "You don't know they were witches. They could have been mages or wizards, even demons. For all we know, unseelie."

Maeve threw out her arms. Power rippled off them, freezing Brigit and Rhiannon. "Sisters, fighting won't stop what's already been set in motion."

Lilith rolled her eyes. "And we've already gone over this."

"Guess you two aren't the only sisters who argue," Alyze said out of the corner of her mouth.

Lilith shook her head at her sisters. "Nor will it be the last disagreement. Powerful women with minds of their own are formidable allies, but we don't always agree."

"No, we don't." Maeve snapped her fingers, glaring at Brigit and Rhiannon, who unfroze.

"The point is," Mama Morrigan said, "the three sets of thirteen sacrifices set into motion a terrible chain of events that we cannot undo, nor can we control."

"For now," Maeve, the master of the hunt, huffed. "Battle strategy is the basis of much of our discussions. Unfortunately the Sisterhood was not privy to those early conversations. A decision we regret. Lippincott and Bladecroft acted on good intel and brought Cyn and Dez with them. They assumed taking down Lamashtu would serve as a good training exercise."

"Training exercise?" Brigit quipped. "Sounds aggressive."

"As it turned out to be. It wasn't until the Demon King became involved that we learned about Lamashtu's fortified power and the sacrifices."

My stomach tightened at the mention of the Demon King but so did my anger. "Don't you mean Demon Prince? He told his men he had not taken on the title."

"Whether or not he accepts the title does not change the reality of the situation. He is the Demon King, and he must start acting in accordance with that position. His days of meditating are over."

Mama Morrigan spun around and faced her sister, her arms in tight fists at her sides. Maeve's eyes widened, realizing what she'd accidently revealed.

Jace was the Demon King.

TWENTY-ONE

 yn

LIKE FOUR CHILDREN who got jumped at Halloween and had all their candy stolen, we shuffled back toward the Academy with our heads down and our tails between our legs. Granted, Dez and I were the only ones with actual tails (or would one day have them once we shifted into our wolf forms, but Mama Morrigan had taken that from us too). After the scolding we received from the goddesses, my ego should have been bruised and my confidence shattered, but honestly, all things considered, I felt pretty amazing. Sure, the mission had ended in failure, but the idea was solid, and the four of us had wound up with a lot more information about the current state of affairs outside of Silverwood Academy.

Supernatural affairs that were complicated and messy.

"Well, that went well," Alyze finally said, breaking the

silence. "Sorry, ladies. I had no idea that removing a tracker would notify the goddesses."

"It makes sense though," I offered. "All the animals wear trackers. I assumed it was to keep an eye on them, but maybe it's to ensure students don't make a break for the border."

"Except that Silverwood students aren't forced to remain on campus. We can come and go anytime we want," Red said.

Dez cleared her throat and gestured at herself then me.

Red glanced at us. "Well, with the exception of you two."

I scratched my head. "So wait a second, students can come and go anytime they want?"

She bobbed the fireball in her hand. "We've been to town a bunch of times since the beginning of the year."

"It was great," Dez added.

I narrowed my eyes at her, feeling the stab of betrayal. "You went too? Why didn't you ever take me? I didn't know we could leave. Well, used to be able to."

My sister shook her head at me. "You never wondered where I disappeared to at night?"

"Figured you were having sex with someone."

Alyze slapped Dez's back. "She knows you well." Dez snorted as Alyze continued. "She was having sex. Just not always on campus."

"But all that came to an end," Red said with an air of mystery. "And now we know why. Well, both reasons why."

I frowned at her. "What do you mean?"

"Well, after your mission with Bladecroft and Lippincott, the two of you got grounded."

"Not that I knew we were even allowed to leave in the first place," I mumbled.

Red pointed her fireball at me. "Don't you even start. You worked in the potions lab every night."

Dez punched me. "You did? You were supposed to stay away from there."

"I cast a spell of protection. And like you're one to judge. You were off gallivanting with Jace, a professor at Silverwood."

"And evidently a Demon King." Her barely spoken words drifted into my ears with the air of truth to them.

"He is, isn't he? That's why there was so much chemistry between the two of you in the Demon Realm."

She inhaled sharply. "He hid it from me. He didn't want me to know the truth about him."

"Or he didn't want anyone to know. Demon relations have improved, but there's still a lot of closed-minded supernaturals floating around," Red offered.

"Like pixies and other faeries. Most of them hate demons," Alyze added. "They'd do anything to get rid of them."

Dez stopped, her eyes widening as she stared into the distance.

I reached out and touched her arm. "What?"

"That's how he found us. That's how he knew we were imprisoned in his castle. He sensed something was wrong with me because of the marking thing. He'll always find me," she snarled. Her venom-laced words hurled angry energy into the surrounding woods.

A twig snapped. Alyze crouched into a fighting stance as she spun around, her blue eyes flashing, scanning the dark woods around us. "Could that be him?"

"It better not be," Dez yelled. "Keep your distance, Demon Boy, or I will show you what pain is."

Red wrapped her arm around my shoulders and

whispered in my ear. "Did your sister just threaten the Demon King?"

"Does that surprise you?"

Her lips rose into a smile. "Actually, no."

Alyze straightened, once satisfied that no one was following us or at least intended us immediate harm. "All clear. Some strange shit going on in these woods the past few nights."

"Tell me about it," Dez growled. Then she yelled, "I will kick anyone's ass who's sneaking around out there."

We continued walking, Red's fireball lighting the path for us, our eyes scanning the trees in case Jace or someone else was watching us. Dez hurled occasional threats into the woods, as if that would keep any predator away. As if she possessed the strength to fight off a demon king.

"I wonder what Mama Morrigan would say if she knew that he forced two elements on you."

Dez smacked me in the forehead. "Quiet, you idiot."

Red flicked her fireball away, quickly chanting a circle of protection. She yanked Alyze inside with us, then latched on to Dez and my arms. "*What* did you just say?"

Oops. Our mother had sworn us to secrecy about her identity. No one could know that we were Morrigan's daughters and therefore demigoddesses (which I was still coming to grips with) other than her siblings and her parents.

Fury rolled off my sister. Her hands fisted at her sides, and her nostrils flared in and out as she stared at me like she couldn't decide whether to pummel me or kill me. Neither outcome was particularly favorable.

Alyze studied me, then Dez, then turned to Red. "I can see it."

Red's face matched her hair. I'd never witnessed her so

angry. She normally kept herself even tempered. This reaction was not what I expected. Dez, yes. Anastasia, no. But right now, in this tight circle, they were twin volcanoes about to erupt.

"Let me rephrase," I said.

"Silence," she snapped, throwing her hand up to stop me from saying more.

Message received on that one. Anastasia lived and breathed magick, and though I didn't think she'd permanently maim us, torture appeared a very real possibility.

Her lips moved as she incanted a spell. I winced, expecting the worst, as did Dez, who had remained quiet, resorting to profound looks of disgust to make it known to our circle I was on her shit list.

Tell me something I didn't know.

A mini lightning bolt shot out of the tip of Red's finger with a loud zap and connected with my mystical third eye, the space at the center of my forehead above my real eyes.

"Holy mother witcher!" I shouted, trying to cover my forehead to break the connection, but the lightning bolt fried my fingers.

"You witch," Dez screamed, also trying to block the lightning bolt on her own forehead, but to no avail.

Alyze's jaw dropped as she watched the laser show.

Red snapped her fingers, and the lightning bolts retreated back into her fingertips. She sniffed them, closing her eyes as she inhaled deeply. She shoved them under Alyze's nose, who had no choice but to smell them too.

Her blue eyes brightened as magick pulsed through them. "It's true."

Dez knocked Red's finger away from Alyze's face. "You mind telling me what the fuck that was?"

Red blinked. "Just confirming your family tree."

I rubbed at my third eye. "You can tell that by a little spell?"

Her lips lifted into that signature devilish smile of hers. "We both know that wasn't a little spell."

I raised my chin. "What was it then?"

"First, let's go over some ground rules. What happens in this circle, stays in this circle. Agreed?" Her green eyes met each of ours.

"Duh," Alyze grunted.

"No shit," Dez growled.

"Obviously, since the two of you weren't supposed to know."

Red's eyes watered, her stance softening. "You don't trust us?"

Dez reached out and grabbed her hands, cradling them to her cheek in a surprisingly gentle gesture. "We do trust you. We trust you with our lives, and you've told me many times that caring for someone doesn't make them weak, it makes them strong."

Red smiled. "And you finally believe me?"

Dez winked at her. "Debatable. But that's not why we didn't tell you who our mom is."

"Why didn't you?" she whispered softly.

"First, we only found out a few weeks ago, and it's not like we've had a lot of mother-daughter bonding time as a result."

Alyze slapped her own thigh. "That's why there are always crows watching our outside classes. I figured they were keeping an eye on the students, or they were wild with a nest nearby."

"Nope, that's Mommy Dearest spying on us," I added.

Dez's purple eyes met mine, nodding tightly. "I throw sticks at them and yell when I'm in a mood."

"Which is all the time," I murmured.

She blinked, turning back to Red and Alyze. "Second, having a mother who is a goddess makes us . . ."

Red and Alyze gasped. "Demigoddesses," they said.

I pulled my hand to my chest. "Big Percy Jackson fan, so I thought it was common, but . . ."

Red shook her head aggressively. "It's not common. Not at all."

Alyze furrowed her brow. "Morrigan, in addition to all her other titles, is Queen of the Shifters. So that's how you can be pure Sempiternals and wolf shapeshifters. But you've never changed at the full moon, have you? Or . . . ," she grabbed my bicep, squeezing really hard. Frick, she was really strong. "Or you kept that shit from us too."

"No. That shit got locked up by Mommy Dearest the night of the full moon, just as we were turning." Dez glanced at me. "Well, fighting each other and forcing the shift."

Red twirled around, reminding me of a ballerina or perhaps a pixie, but a nice pixie like Tinkerbell instead of a dark, nasty one like Azalea. "I just figured the full moon brought your wolf to the surface, but it went back to sleep after the moon phase."

Dez smacked the side of her head. "Beasts can do that, can't they? I forgot about that."

I frowned at her. She seemed far too excited about something she already knew. "Mom put ours back to sleep. You know that. You were there."

She shook her head and began edging away. "Not the same though. I gotta check something out."

The minute she slipped through Red's protection

barrier, the air blurred around her. On instinct, the three of us started following her, the circle moving with us. We were so in sync with one another, it truly was beautiful. She picked up her pace, and we had no choice but to keep up with her or get left in the dust. What was she so excited about?

"Now? It's like the middle of the night."

"Yes, now. Laters, baby." She waved and vamp-sped away, leaving us dumbfounded.

Alyze tapped her mouth with her finger as Dez disappeared down the path. "Your sister knows how to make an exit."

"And an entrance," Red added.

That she did, but her departure made no sense. "What is she looking for, and why didn't she ask for help?"

Red wiggled her fingers and the circle lifted. The three of us took off down the path. Of course, I could catch up to my sister, but I didn't want to leave Alyze and Red behind, especially after the events of the evening.

"Only she knows," said Red, "and when she's ready, she'll tell us."

"Seer thing?"

"No. Friend thing."

"And thank the goddess for that."

TWENTY-TWO

ez

I STOPPED at the entrance to my wing. The feeling I was being watched washed over me again. I glanced over my shoulder and stared across the fields toward the Wildwoods I'd just come from. Alyze, Red, and Cyn walked toward me, but none of them seemed in too much of a hurry to catch up. I scanned the edges of the Wildwoods. A shiver ran down my spine at the prospect of meeting a pair of red-rimmed gold eyes, but there was nothing that I could see or sense.

I quietly opened the door and slipped inside. I wasn't doing anything illegal. Yet. But my intended destination would cause some potential backlash, especially if any of the goddesses caught me, but it was worth the risk.

I crept down the dark hallway, the stars shining down and illuminating a path for me. The other Air students were tucked away in their beds, getting a good night's sleep like the obedient little initiates they were. And those that weren't were probably doing something Lilith would approve of.

As I approached the center of the star, I immediately turned left and climbed the stairs. The library was open twenty-four hours a day for students and faculty alike. One never knew when the muse would hit, and a book could offer guidance or provide divination assistance. Of course, I spent a lot of time in the library after hours, reading up on whatever topic struck my fancy, but I liked to keep my nerdy tendencies secret. As a badass Sempiternal, my reputation rested on acting like I knew everything.

Ancient magick pulsed through my fingers as I pushed through the library's intricately carved oak doors. The Celtic symbols and pastoral scenes spoke to my soul in a way that little else did. I peeked around to confirm I was alone. The desk lamps were dark, and the tables were unoccupied. I loosed a breath, my energy surging through me. It always took more energy to compel late-night readers. Their will was filled with insight and knowledge, making them much more difficult, though not impossible, to bend. I needed my full energy charged and at the ready for what I had in mind.

I tiptoed across the rows of books, keeping to the shadows. I wound through the stacks of new fiction, fantasy, romance, romantasy, and paranormal romance. I sneaked past my favorite chair overlooking the courtyard below and continued through to the nonfiction sections, the bookshelves getting older the deeper I went. Like all aspects of Silverwood Academy, the library was much bigger than it appeared. Much like Hermione's handbag. The star-shaped library seemed like a structural impossibility, but then, most every aspect of Silverwood Academy grounds appeared impossible until immersed in it.

At the point of the Air triangle of the star, farthest from the library's entrance, resided the restricted section, the only portion of the library off limits to students. Only professors, gods, and goddesses were given direct access, along with all members of Silver Dagger Sisterhood and Silver Cloak Brotherhood and individuals who were granted special permission. I had prowled past the entrance numerous times, but I'd never attempted to enter. A magickal handprint pad allowed entrance to qualified individuals. Since technology didn't work well on Silverwood Academy grounds, the entrance responded to a magickal signature, if you will. It recognized those who possessed it and denied those who didn't. I wasn't exactly sure what would happen to the individual who tried to get in but didn't qualify, but a security detail of screaming bean sídhes would alert everyone on campus of the perpetrator. Rumors of red dye smoke bombs were also thrown around, thus the reason no student in recent history had tried to get in. Until now.

But there were only two copies in existence of the book I needed. One was locked away in my father's bunker, a place I hadn't been to since he died and still wasn't keen on visiting. Plus, without a portal, it would be a three-day drive or a four-hour flight. And since I couldn't leave the campus without alerting five goddesses anyway, that left me with the only other option.

I stood in front of the magickal hand pad, licking my lips. The blood of a goddess ran through my veins. That made me a demigoddess. An anomaly in the supernatural world. Adrenaline buzzed through my body, giving me confidence. I could do this. I could do this.

I pressed my hand against the hand pad. It whirled to life, flashing blue as it read my magickal signature. Power zapped along the palm of my hand. My natural instinct was to jerk it back, but my intuition told me to keep it there. My Water tattoo tingled with energy as blue switched to white. A phantom energy tickled where my Spirit tattoo would one day be as white turned to green. The ghost of my Earth tattoo vibrated as green became red. Heat shot through my Fire tattoo, the constant reminder that the Demon King had forced two elements to surface. With my hand firmly held against the hand pad, I waited for the final elemental tattoo to vibrate. My other hand possessed the Air brand, but I had yet to receive my Air tattoo. The location on my spine where it would one day sit came to life, less intense than Fire and Water, but more alive than Spirit and Earth. I waited as the hand pad cycled through the other colors again, spending more time on red than any of the others.

Oh crap, this might actually be the worst idea I've ever had. The Council had warned me that if I got thrown into Silverwood Prison a third time . . . well, I wouldn't make it a third time. I winced, waiting for the screams, not worried as much about the red dye that would stain my hair, face, and skin as much as I was about the smoke bomb and how it would sear my throat and lungs as if I'd inhaled thousands of tiny knives. I considered turning and running, but that didn't fit into my genetic makeup. Badass did.

Finally, the hand pad lit to yellow, and the door swung open. Without hesitation, I rushed in before the hand pad changed its mind and sent the bean sídhes on me.

Once both feet were firmly rooted inside the space, the door slammed shut behind me. I didn't think too hard about how to get out—I'd deal with that after I found what I wanted.

Dozens of magicked candles blazed to life upon my entrance. Fire and books created a dangerous combination, but not when magick was involved. The space reminded me of an old study. Huge hand-knotted Persian rugs covered the floor. Thousands of ancient tomes filled the mahogany bookshelves that lined the four walls. Each volume thrummed with magick. Powerful energy resided in this room, much more than in my father's bunker library.

Silverwood Academy didn't ban books. We weren't heathens like many mainstream American asshats. Books didn't cause girls to fornicate or boys to masturbate. Books didn't fill a person's mind with poison. Books provided entertainment, escapism, and information. Only fucking assholes believed otherwise.

The restricted section merely prevented the untrained from handling power they weren't prepared for. It protected their life and anyone who came into contact with them.

Corrupted energy seeped through the air from a far-off corner. That's where Maleficium—dark magick—spell books and grimoires lived. I took off in that direction, not because I planned to memorize terrible spells that burned the skin of my enemies, but because the thread of intuition tugged me toward that section. I sensed that the book I wanted was tucked in that corner, even though it had nothing to do with Maleficium.

And there it was. The black spine was well known to me, as was the red foil title. I grunted knowingly as I grounded myself, casting a protection spell around me before pulling the volume from the shelf. For particularly powerful books, especially of the evil type, precautions must be made before handling. Since I'd spent much of my early life reading powerful books, grounding and protecting came naturally. A second nature to me.

Someone had tried to hide it, figuring most people wouldn't be able to sense it, but I could. The book's signature reminded me of my father's bunker. It also reminded me of Jace.

The black book vibrated in my hands as if recognizing me. Or perhaps it was happy someone had pulled it from the Maleficium section, ridding it of the corrupted energy. Yes, powerful books possessed a brain of sorts, or at least a memory of the past.

I held the book against my chest and headed over to the long mahogany table. Piles of books lay scattered across it. My lips pressed together in a tight line as I frowned at the haphazard manner in which the books were heaped and stacked on top of one another. The spines of those old books had better be magicked so no harm would come to them, because if not, the librarians would skin this person alive. I knew I would if I caught whoever was researching . . . I leaned over, my eyes roaming the open pages. An upside-down pentagram with the face of a goat was sketched on one page. Someone was studying Lucifer and how to summon him. Good luck with that. His daughter kept him too busy with her shenanigans nowadays for him to answer a summons, although he considered me a bad influence, but whatever.

And I never really thought about it, but obviously the whole summoning of Lucifer with Maleficium that caused my mom to go into early labor with Cyn must have been an elaborate hoax by my dad, mom, and Lucifer.

Figures.

I glanced at a few more of the books. Malevolent spirits crept across pages. Skulls and rats and bubbling cauldrons.

Who in the name of the goddess had pulled out these books?

I glanced down the rows of shelves to double check that I was alone. I even closed my eyes to shut off that sense as I inhaled deeply to ensure no one was cloaked in here. When my senses came up clear, I opened my eyes again and gently pushed a few book piles aside, careful not to disrupt them. I wanted to enter and leave with the least amount of disturbance possible.

I rested the book on the table as I pulled a leather chair over. Once comfortably seated, I drew the book closer and flipped through the pages, trusting bibliomancy to give me the section I desired. The large, yellowed pages fell open, revealing exactly what I wanted to reread. It had been five or six years since I had last read the section, but the words were burned into my mind and, in a way, burned into my heart.

Demon Realm and the Lost Demon King.

TWENTY-THREE

ez

I READ until my brain hurt. Then I read some more, until my head hit the table in total information overload. Exhaustion swept over me, inviting me to take a little nap before continuing with my reading, but my conscience reminded me that if I fell asleep in the restricted section, I could be caught, and the parties would end. Well, the late-night reading sessions, anyway.

Rereading the passages about the Mad Demon King as an adult, and the fact that I was most likely tied to the new Demon King, gave me fresh perspectives. At fifteen, my reading habit included curling up on the old recliner under a thick, cozy blanket with a steaming mug of peppermint tea, perusing the accounts of the Demon Wars, the devastation of his realm, and the Mad King's acts of slaughter as fictionalized tales, ones meant to entertain, not as a history lesson.

The Demon King had killed all his offspring to protect his throne. Not because of some oracle making a prediction. Not because a seer foresaw his death. But from paranoia.

If I wanted to find a way to break the marking with Jace, I had to keep going. No matter how tired I was. I closed my eyes and took a few deep breaths in hopes of energizing myself. Just a few more seconds . . .

THE ONLY LIGHT *in the room came from an old yellow glass lampshade, one of the only family relics we took from move to move. Once an oil lamp for a prior generation of Wickershims, it had been repurposed as an electrified light that cast a soothing presence when I was stuck home by myself. Dad had promised he'd be home in a few days, but it had already been a week. Alexander Logan babysat me as a child, but now, at fifteen, I was stubborn and arrogant and determined to prove to my father and the world that I could stay home alone. I was familiar with a blade and not afraid to kill a baddy if one dared cross the bunker's threshold. I patted the sword propped up beside the worn chair. Of course, most baddies would blow up if they approached the perimeter of the bunker. Dad had powerful witches and warlocks ensure that no foe could enter. An elder faerie had also cast an impenetrable curse around the ground that would cause anyone with ill intent to turn around and leave, forgetting their name and what they were doing there for at least a week.*

I tucked in under the blanket, the book splayed across my lap, fascinated by tales of the Mad Demon King. He slaughtered his young to ensure he always remained in absolute power. A narcissistic psychopath if I ever saw one. My eyes slipped shut, and dreams of a blackened, dead landscape appeared before me. A man—no, a monster—stalked toward me. An enormous crown lay upon his head, and his gold eyes were rimmed with red. A maniacal grin on his lips revealed blood dripping from his teeth. Every instinct inside me told me to run, but I was paralyzed, completely frozen. He reached out for me, grasped my arms, and shook me.

"Dez," he said. "Dez, wake up."

I startled awake, my heart racing, to find my dad watching me, concern in his pale green eyes with flecks of purple.

"Are you okay?"

When I finally caught my breath, I shook my head in confirmation. "Nightmare," I whispered, sounding more scared than I intended.

He glanced down at the book in my lap. Frowning, he picked it up and set it aside then sat down in the chair across from me. The old glass lampshade cast a soft glow over his face.

"Why did you pick that book?"

Every book in the bunker library was available to me. If there were spell books, grimoires, or volumes he didn't want me to read, I didn't know about them—which was smart on his part, because when he was away on a mission, I totally would have torn the bunker apart in search of them.

I adjusted my blanket, covering my arms. The fire had gone cold, and even though the bunker was deep underground and kept an even temperature, it was still chilly. I told him the truth.

"It called to me."

As a member of the Brotherhood, he didn't find my answer weird at all. He encouraged me to always listen to my gut, and at that time in my life, I did. It wasn't until after his murder that my desire for revenge replaced my intuition and my common sense, and occasionally got my ass kicked.

"And why do you think that is?"

"I don't know. It just seemed like a story I should read."

He dropped his chin as he looked at me. "But it's not a story, is it?"

I shook my head no, giving him the answer he wanted to hear, but the exploits of the Mad Demon King still felt like tales to me.

"What happened to him? Is he still around?"

He rested his back against the chair and pushed out the reclining section before sharing his own exploits in search of the Mad Demon King. He had disappeared a few years before I was born and hadn't been seen or heard from since.

"Of course, there are plenty of rumors on his whereabouts, but there doesn't appear to be an ounce of truth in any of them."

"And what do you think happened to him?"

He breathed in and out deeply, contemplating my question. "I tend to believe that he disappeared into the Aether Realm in search of absolute power. A power no living being could destroy."

My heart raced at the prospect of an all-powerful being.

"But . . ."

He rose from his chair. "But nothing. It is time for good little Sempiternals to go to sleep."

I rolled my eyes as I stood up next to him. "Dad, I'm not a little kid anymore."

He curled his hand around my head and kissed my forehead. "I know that, sweetie, but you will always be my baby girl."

I smiled, feeling warm and safe and loved.

Suddenly, the feeling I was being watched washed over me. Not in danger, but not entirely safe either.

I GASPED AWAKE, shooting upright in my chair. The soft glow of the yellow lampshade was gone, replaced by candlelight highlighting the outline of the very person I was researching. He wasn't wearing a gold mask nor was he dressed like a demon king. His pupils danced across gold landscapes in the candlelight as he stood across from me with his arms crossed, his shoulders tense.

"Jace." My voice came out in a breathy whisper. A single tear trailed down my cheek.

He sighed, his stance softening, until suddenly he jerked his chin up. "What are you doing here?"

Annoyance surged through me. I narrowed my eyes, swiping the errant tear away. "I could ask you the same."

He stepped back, as if shocked by my question, before regaining himself. "What's that supposed to mean? I'm faculty. I'm permitted in here. You, however, are not."

"Says who?"

His nostrils flared in and out, as if trying to retain his composure. "Silverwood Academy for one. Ten gods and goddesses for another."

I grinned at him. "You're cute when you're annoyed."

He straightened. "Excuse me?"

"You heard me. I think you're cute when you're pretending to be angry at me for breaking the rules, but you're forgetting one thing. Well, several things, actually, but let's start with one."

"And what's that?"

"I know who you are."

He sucked in a breath, his pulse quickening, his eyes darting around the room until he realized he'd reacted exactly as I'd hoped he would. He cleared his throat, trying to play it off. "I should hope so, since I'm your professor."

I snorted. "Cut the crap, Jace. Or should I say . . . ," I glanced down at the book, as if searching for the name I already knew, that I remembered from my dream, that I remembered from reading the passage all those years ago, "Asmodeus."

He rushed over to the table. "You shouldn't be in here. How did you get in?" He snapped the book shut and tugged it to his chest as if he could hide the contents of it, but they were already ingrained in my brain just as his delicious earthy scent was.

"You're smart. You already know the answer."

He glared up at the ceiling, his arms wrapped around the book. "I am not playing games with you. Tell me how you got in."

I patted the empty seat next to me. "Let's have a chat, shall we?"

He pressed his lips together, shifting his feet.

I smiled at him. "You don't trust me? You told me to trust you."

He held up a finger. "I told you not to trust anyone."

"A warning I should have taken into account before showing up at your bedroom." I rose from my seat. "A warning I should have listened to before chasing you into the Wildwoods." I stalked toward him. He remained rooted to his place, the book clutched in his hands. "A warning I should have heeded when someone froze time, ripped me from the Silver Crescent Moon Festival, and forced two elements upon me."

"Dez, I—"

I stopped within three inches of him. His eyes darted from my lips to the book to my eyes and back to my lips.

"Apologize? You're sorry? Don't know what I'm talking about?" I leaned in, my lips a breath's width away from his. He sharply inhaled, but he held his ground. "Shouldn't have kissed me? Fucked me? Marked me?"

His entire being quivered, as if fighting every impulse to

take me then and there or run in the opposite direction. His chest rose and fell as I backed away from him, returning to my seat.

"You could have told me."

He blinked several times, composing himself, trying to return his attention back to the conversation and not where he wanted his lips to land.

I patted the seat again. "Sit."

He sighed. "Fine." He placed the book back on the table and sat in the chair next to me.

I flipped it open to the part I wanted to discuss with him and pushed it toward him. "Now, let's start here."

He leaned over and glanced at the picture of a lonely castle forged into a rocky mountainside. He settled back in his seat, folding his hands across his stomach. "What do you want to know?"

"Everything."

Searing pain tore into my spine. I clawed at it, trying to either rip it off or calm it, because I knew what was happening this third time around, and let me tell you, it wasn't no charm.

Jace's hands wrapped around my waist, pulling me onto his lap. "Breathe, Dez, breathe." His touch calmed the fire raging inside me that was somehow erupting to the surface. "Don't fight it."

"But it hurts," I cried through clenched teeth, pure agony destroying any sense of composure.

He cradled me in his lap. "Because you're fighting it. Just let it happen. Allow the element to appear without resisting it."

"I'm not— OWWWWW!" I screamed, arching my back.

His hands ran up and down my spine. "Just relax. Allow

the element to come. Listen to my words, focus on my voice, just breathe . . ."

His words soothed me as much as his touch. I breathed in and out, allowing the element to take control.

"That's it," he whispered, his nose skimming across my jawline.

When the pain finally subsided, I collapsed against his chest. It had been a much longer day than I realized, and I couldn't remember the last time I'd fed. I felt weak, hungry, tired. Completely spent. We sat in silence for a long time, neither of us saying anything. My head rested against his chest, and my eyes grew heavier by the second, until —nothing.

TWENTY-FOUR

 yn

ONCE WE GOT INSIDE, Alyze and Red dropped me off at my room then left for their rooms in the other wings. But I wasn't ready to go to bed. Not with the adrenaline coursing through my body. I'd never been so scared and excited at the same time in my life, and it was kinda a rush.

I waited until they were gone before carefully creeping back into the hall. The ceiling was still black with only a faint hint of stars reflecting the late hour—or early morning, depending on how one looked at it. I worried that Red might see me leaving my room, but her visions were tricky, and she didn't see everything. Our encounter with the five goddesses had demonstrated that all too well.

I inhaled deeply, searching for Dez's scent. I'd never tracked a person before. It added to my rush, adrenaline grabbing ahold of any tiredness and saying, *Let's hunt.* For the first time, I felt like a hunter. Of course, I wasn't hunting an actual baddie in a manner of speaking, but Dez's villainous side would serve as an adequate placeholder. I caught her scent immediately and crept down the hallway, following it. She had seemed intent on getting back to check on whatever it was she wanted to check and had left so suddenly, none of us could react quicky enough. The last time she tried to ditch me, to talk to Gage about perhaps the same mysterious "something," I had spelled her. Now I was super curious about where she was. I followed her trail to the center of the star and briefly lost it, until I picked it up again and followed her scent up a flight of stairs to the entrance of the library.

Well, surprise, surprise. Dez always acted like she knew everything, but I guess even the great Deziree Wickershim needed answers sometimes. My hands hovered over the thick carved-wood doors, picking up my sister's energy signature.

She had left us out in the Wildwoods to go study? To find a book? That didn't sound like her at all. I pushed through the double doors. The soft light of dimmed torches lit the space, further proof of the late hour and the lack of people in the library. I glanced around, searching for my sister, but I didn't see any sign of her. I inhaled deeply, finding her scent once more. She had stuck to the edges of the library, staying close to the rows, like she didn't want to be seen.

Very unlike her.

I followed her trail deep into the Air wing until I reached the restricted section.

She didn't.

Yet, there was a little voice inside my head whispering, *She did.*

I stopped at the handprint pad and stared at it.

She couldn't have. There was no way she could get inside. Dez was powerful, sneaky, and rebellious—and incredibly talented—but there was no way she could override the security measures in place to get into the restricted section.

Of course, I knew she would have wanted to. A locked door was a challenge she couldn't resist. But the security devices in place specifically prohibited any student from getting in unless accompanied by a professor, and the one professor who might succumb to her wiles was away on assignment.

I stood for a long time at the entrance, listening for any noise or sign of life from anywhere in the library, but my spidey senses picked up nothing. Only once did I swear I heard a footstep, but I knew it was my imagination getting carried away.

I shook my head. I must have lost her trail, or she'd backtracked. I gave the hand pad one parting glance before heading off to search for her somewhere else.

I wandered deep into the recesses of the other elemental wings but didn't catch her scent anywhere. My sister-instinct had disappeared completely.

With a heavy sigh, I left the library, the long day finally catching up to me. My bed called to me, and don't even get me started about my pillow. That baby promised to cradle my head and send me straight off to my dream space.

Cedarwood and mint filled my nose.

The apex of my thighs clenched, remembering the orgasm Canyon had given me. The desire to see him overrode all sense of tiredness. I inhaled deeply and turned right, following his trail down the Spirit hallway. I didn't have any classes down this wing since Jace had changed my schedule, but it wasn't like you could get lost in this school. Every wing led to a point—either a door to outside or a stairwell, or you could turn around and head back the way you came.

My ears tingled as soft whispers reached them. My heart pounded at the prospect of getting caught by one of the professors, or worse, a goddess and getting scolded again for not returning to my room and being the obedient daughter they wanted me to be. I pressed against the wall, attempting to make myself invisible as I stared down the dark hallway. I tried to make out who was talking, but they were too far away, and the ceiling stars weren't bright enough to illuminate them.

I closed my eyes and listened.

"I don't want to do it anymore."

"You promised."

"That was before . . ."

It sounded like Canyon and someone else. A voice I didn't recognize. Not that I could hear much. I tilted my head, leaning my body sideways, trying to get closer without drawing attention.

". . . blood vow."

The hair on the back of my neck stood up. What the . . . ? Blood vow?

I shimmied down the hallway, clinging to the wall, desperate to find out who was talking. As I opened my eyes and ventured farther, I lost track of the conversation, but I didn't have a choice. My intuition told me their identities were everything.

Paper crinkled as my back hit a flyer, sounding like a gunshot in the silence.

"Who's there?" a woman called out.

"Shit," the male voice cursed in a low hiss.

Footsteps hurried in the opposite direction, confirming what I already suspected. Whoever was speaking was planning something unsavory, and they didn't want anyone overhearing their conversation.

My nerves lodged in my throat. Not that I was naive enough to believe everyone at Silverwood Academy possessed good intentions—Azalea and her gang were proof of that—but the goddesses and gods had selected each and every one of us. That had to mean something.

Right?

But there was no time for an existential crisis. I had two choices. Blow my cover and find out who was talking or run away and hide like a coward. I'd spent my first eighteen years cowering to assholes. No more of that shit. Fierce power coursed through my veins.

And if one of them was Canyon . . .

No, I refused to let my mind go there. He couldn't be involved in anything shady. Not after what we'd been through. Not after what he meant to me.

I tore off down the hall. A door slammed shut as someone disappeared into one of the rooms, but instinct told me to focus on the shadow in front of me. The identity of the shadow in front of me was everything.

The double doors at the end of the corridor flung open, casting a faint light over the deserter. Male. Wavy hair. Low to mid-twenties. Wearing a flannel and jeans. My mind itemized every characteristic without me even thinking about it. The resemblance to Canyon was uncanny, but there were also dozens of other male students who could fit the description. I shifted into vamp speed. That bastard wasn't getting away.

The tip of his head disappeared down the stairs as I dashed through the doors. Whatever supernatural he was, he was fast. However, I was faster and could jump. I leapt down two flights of stairs, snagging his shirttail just he pushed through the doors to the courtyard. The flannel tore as he broke away from me, but not before I caught his scent —cedarwood and mint.

My heart skipped a beat. "Canyon?" I clutched the fabric scrap in my hand.

He stopped and slowly turned around, his chest rising and falling as he tried to catch his breath. "Hey"—gasp—"Cynda," he finally managed.

My lady bits squirmed at his low, raspy voice, but my instincts screamed at me to remain on guard. To not get distracted by his pretty eyes and his heaving muscular chest.

"What are you doing? Why did you run?"

His eyes skirted away from mine as he swallowed, then he turned his attention back to me. "You caught me."

I straightened. "Excuse me?"

He inched toward me, his mood impossible to decipher. "I was planning a surprise for you."

Warning alarms went off in my brain, but something about his presence brought me to my knees.

Keep it together, Cynda. Keep it together.

My muscles tensed, preparing for battle. I raised my chin. "What surprise?"

His lips rose in a mischievous grin as he continued his advance, his entire being boxing me in. "What kind of surprise would it be if I told you?"

I backed away, every instinct warring with my hormones. I held up a hand. "Stay back," I whispered in a shaky voice.

His green eyes pulsed as his pupils enlarged. Was he trying to compel me? Spell me? My muscles loosened. My brain screamed at me to run. However, the rest of me stood frozen in place.

"Oh, I don't think you want me to keep my distance. In fact, you want me to take you right now."

Wetness exploded between my thighs. What the fuck was happening to me? "N-n-n-no," I stuttered.

"You can lie to yourself, but you can't lie to me."

His attention darted over my shoulder and his eyes widened. "No," he yelled, yanking me to his chest.

And everything went black.

TWENTY-FIVE

I STARTLED AWAKE, sensing a nearby steady heartbeat. A heavy arm curled around my waist, keeping me tucked into the hard lines of a muscular chest. I slowly twisted my head to look over my shoulder, fairly certain of whose bed I was in but still needing confirmation.

A single gold eye peeked open. "Hey, you," he whispered, tugging me closer, as if this sleeping arrangement was a common occurrence. As if we often snuggled. As if we were a couple.

Rather than leap out of bed and dart away, which was what I'd always envisioned I would do if I found myself in this situation, I allowed him to spoon me while my mind replayed the evening's events.

It had all begun fairly ordinarily—well, what I wanted our everyday life to be—preparing for a hunt, going after a monster, Alyze and Red joining in to form the greatest future Silver Dagger Sisterhood team this world would ever encounter. Defying Lilith was not something I'd intended nor was it something I wanted to make a habit, but when Cyn suggested it, I latched on to her rebellious idea, proud to call her sister. Of course, that course of action had ended in a failed result when Mama Morrigan and the other four goddesses caught us.

With our tails between our legs, we made our way back to Silverwood Academy, along the way sharing with Alyze and Red our parentage—and that's when epiphany had struck—a way to break the marking link between Jace and me.

He stirred beside me, as if sensing I was thinking about him.

I had left my team in the Wildwoods without informing them of my intentions. They'd already gotten into enough trouble. Plus, they couldn't help with what I planned to do. I smiled to myself at the rather impressive feat of sneaking into the restricted section of the library given the seemingly impenetrable hurdle of the magickal hand pad. But, when the blood of a goddess flows through one's veins, you might as well use it.

I had found the demon book in the Maleficium section rather than with the other demon and other realm books. Someone had put it there to ensure that no one found it.

Someone?

Jace. Jace had hidden it, so no one would read it.

No one?

Me? He didn't want me to read it. I tasted that idea, rolled it around in my mouth, chewed on it, but it didn't feel right. He wasn't worried about me finding it and reading it. He had been surprised that I had gotten into the restricted section in the first place. So, who had he hidden it from?

My mind raced through the possibilities until settling on the very person he had warned me to stay away from.

Goldwell. He didn't want Goldwell to read it. But why not? It only contained the accounts of his dad's cruel reign, the murders of his siblings, and the devastation wreaked on the Demon Realm. It didn't make any sense, and honestly, the reason behind why he hid it mattered little. What mattered was that Jace had been about to tell me about his past until horrible pain had seized me. I reached behind my back, fairly certain of which elemental tattoo I had acquired but not entirely sure.

"Air," he sighed, his chest rumbling against me.

"Really? Why did it hurt so bad? Air selected me along with Lilith. I figured it would be the easiest one."

He chuckled. "It usually is, but not when you fight it."

"I didn't—"

"You always fight. You're a warrior whose shield is always at the ready."

Well, at least that was true. A sense of pride filled me that this man lying beside me called me powerful and strong.

"But how—" and then it hit me. "Oh, because I wanted to know everything about you. Plus, I bypassed the security to get into the restricted section, using my head again. I gotta say, it was a different type of pain compared to my initiation. I had yanked two daggers out of the windstorm and fought my way through it."

He laughed this time. "Of course you did." His hand traveled from my waist to my back, massaging small circles around the three tattoos along my spine. "They're beautiful. You're beautiful."

Cradled in Jace's arms, snuggling under the blankets, in all my adult life, I'd never felt so safe. It reminded me of being cocooned in the bunker with my dad. Times when it was too dangerous to live in random houses and apartments, hunting—insert evil villain of the day here—because—insert second evil villain here—searched for us. I always figured they were after us because of someone Dad had unalived or something he had dug up, but now I wondered if evil could sense the daughter of a goddess, a demigoddess, and that's what had put our life at risk. And that's what had killed my dad.

"What are you thinking about?" he murmured.

"How do you know I was thinking about things other than being in the same bed as you?"

"You bite your lip, and your entire body stills as you singularly focus on that one thing."

And, cue the awkward silence. I prided myself on not having any tells, but then again, I'd never stayed in the same bed with any of my conquests.

"How long have you watched me?"

His hands slid around my waist again, as if ensuring that I couldn't slip away. At least not until he released me. "Are you making stalking accusations again?"

"The thought had crossed my mind."

"If that makes it easier for you to accept, then yes, I've been aware of your existence for a long time."

I remembered Red telling me that the prayer beads tracked my whereabouts. And then, I had made it even easier for him to track me by getting caught up in sex and marking each other. I needed to be more careful in the future. Learn how to ground myself before fucking someone, so I didn't have baddies chasing me through some invisible marking thread.

"Can I ask you something?"

He leaned closer to me, his breath hot on the back of my neck. "Sure."

"Would you have picked me if I was a no one?"

He stilled, his muscles tightening around me. I spun around, wanting to see what his other tells were, since we shared at least one.

"Well?"

His gold eyes snapped to mine, suddenly aware I was watching him.

"You always surprise me."

"That's not an answer."

His lips rose in a mischievous grin, his dimple popping to attention. "Actually it is."

"How do you mean?"

"I guess I should probably start from the beginning."

"That would be a refreshing change since you've always evaded sharing anything about yourself."

"You *are* direct, just like your mom."

I froze. No one except the sisters knew who my mom was, right? Well, them and my dad.

"What do you mean like my mom?"

"Morrigan," he mouthed.

My face screwed up. How did he know that?

"Let me tell you my story, and then you'll understand."

"Tell me everything," I whispered to him across the pillow we shared. Now this was my idea of pillow talk.

"So," he paused, "you've already figured out that I'm the Demon Prince."

"I pieced it together. You're not great at undercover work. I hope you didn't spend a lot of time spying for the Brotherhood."

His eyes rimmed red, his demon rising in anger at the

VAMP AWAKENED

slight. "Actually, no one knows my true identity outside of Gage, the gods and goddesses, and . . ."

"Me." I winked at him, clucking my tongue against the roof of my mouth. "But if your father is the Demon King, how did you survive?"

His chest rose and fell as he focused on his breathing to slow his racing heart. "I never knew my father. He disappeared before I was born. When my mother discovered she was pregnant, she fled the castle."

"But all those demons called you Master or King. One told me you'd been away for a long time, and that I shouldn't upset you and make you go away again."

His face broke into a smile. "Jeevs."

"But how did he know you?"

He bit his lower lip, his eyes watching me, contemplating his next words. His meditation tricks gave him a ridiculous amount of patience. My patience didn't come close.

"Out with it."

"When I felt you blink out of existence . . ."

"Excuse me?"

He cleared his throat. "The night of the Lamashtu mission, you blinked out of the Earthly Realm, but our tie didn't disappear, so I knew you weren't dead. I tracked you to the gate, and I went through it."

My eyes widened as I remembered what Bladecroft and Lippincott had told Cyn and me about the gate. "And only a demon can enter."

He pressed his lips together. "Uh-huh."

"You risked exposure for me?"

"I will always choose you."

I pulled away. "Whoa, that's . . . ," I paused, trying to find the right word but unable to, "a lot."

219

He reached for me, drawing me back to him. "And I mean every word."

My desire to hear his story overrode the overwhelmingness of his confession. "We'll circle back to that. How did Jeevs recognize you?"

"I have my mother's hair and my father's eyes."

"Don't get me wrong. I enjoy wrapping my fingers through your sexy locks as much as the next woman"—he laugh-snorted at that—"and your eyes, totally dreamy. Angelic, in fact. The red gets a tad creepy, but I'm okay with creepy."

He nuzzled his nose against my forehead. "Of that I have no doubt."

"But neither one of those characteristics, or even your ability to enter the Demon Realm, explains how he recognized you."

"I stormed the castle and announced myself as the long-lost prince."

My forehead scrunched, skeptical of his response. "And they believed you?"

He snorted, shaking his head. "It takes a lot to convince you, doesn't it?"

"I spent my life as a hunter. Of course I'm skeptical. Proof speaks volumes."

"You want proof?" He dipped his head toward me, his lips mere inches from mine, and as much as I enjoyed kissing him, I wouldn't be deterred.

"I want proof."

"Fine." He shifted his body, wrapping his leg around me. I frowned, unsure where this situation was going, his earthy scent overwhelming my senses. He hovered over me, his legs straddling my hips, his hands resting on either side of my head. His bare muscular tattooed chest bulged in all his gloriousness, and his long raven locks rimmed his face. He raised an eyebrow. "You sure you're ready for this?"

I wasn't sure of anything at the moment. I was torn between wanting to ravage him and wanting to know all of him. My heart raced, and I forgot how to breathe. I nodded, afraid my voice would betray me.

"Okay," he said, as if he didn't really believe me but would oblige me anyway.

He sat up, his hands resting on his hips, accentuating his narrow waist and broad chest. I licked my lips, thinking of all the parts of him I'd like to taste. He flung his arms out. Gold light blasted from his chest, temporarily blinding me. When I opened my eyes, kneeling before me was the most glorious creature I'd ever seen.

CHAPTER
TWENTY-SIX

D^{ez}

BLACK WINGS STRETCHED from his back. Sharp talons pricked out from the tips of each wing. Thick gold horns jutted out of his head. His gold eyes rimmed red, exposing the beast within. The beast he now revealed to me. His tattoos whirled along his chest as if alive in this true form. I looked from wing to wing, from horn to horn, from chest to face without uttering a word.

"Say something," he whispered.

"Wow," was all I could manage. Emotions welled up in my chest, making it impossible for me to speak.

His wings lowered, folding into his back, and his shoulders rounded. "Wow, as in you are the most hideous beast I've ever seen?"

"Hideous?" I laughed, unable to believe that he could

222

think such a thing about himself. "Or, wow, I've never seen anything so magnificent, so defyingly beautiful."

His eyes widened, and that gorgeous, confident smile reemerged. "Defyingly beautiful? Really?"

I pushed myself up on the pillow to get a better look at him. "Really." I raised my hand. "May I touch them?"

He pressed his lips together, nodding slowly. His wings unfurled from his back.

I leaned forward, my fingers caressing the leather membrane-like wing. He shuddered and gasped as his nostrils flared in and out. I yanked my hand away.

"Did I hurt you?"

He shook his head, grunting, "No."

But I didn't believe him. It seemed my touch had pained him or burned him or something. "Are you sure?"

His chin dropped to his chest, and he laughed to himself before he answered. "Positive. No one has ever touched them."

"Really? Why?"

He swallowed hard, his Adam's apple bobbing up and down. "I've never shown anyone my wings before. Well, other than Jeevs and the other demons in the castle."

"You haven't? No one?"

"No one. Go ahead." He angled his wing for me, encouraging me to touch it again.

I swallowed, not willing to consider the implications of his admission and only too curious to touch his wings again.

He took a sharp intake of breath as my fingers slid across his skin. I stopped moving and eyed him, double-checking that my touch didn't cause him pain.

A purr rumbled from his chest. "Keep going."

I stroked the smooth leather membrane, trailing my fingers along the veins.

"That feels . . ."

I stopped my exploration, awaiting his answer.

". . . incredibly hot."

"I agree" I said. "I'm getting incredibly hot as well."

"Well, isn't this cozy," a voice growled.

We both stilled, our eyes meeting like we'd just been caught with our hands in the candy jar. He slowly turned to look over his shoulder as I bent around his waist to see what Mama Morrigan was doing in Jace's room.

Dressed in blue leather from head to toe, she looked ready for battle. The daggers strapped to her waist along with the two swords sticking out above her shoulders from the sheath on her back only confirmed it. I immediately went on edge.

"What's going on?"

She stomped toward us. "You mean aside from the fact that the Demon King is straddled over my daughter with his wings out?"

Jace cleared his throat, folding his wings back in as he climbed off me to stand beside the bed. "I can explain."

"There's no time for explanations, apologies, or excuses." She pointed at Jace, then me. "I will deal with the two of you later. Right now there's something more important going on."

And that's when I felt it. Felt the missing part of me. Jace and his wings had distracted me from the feeling that something was off. Someone was missing, and not just someone.

"Where is my sister?"

Mama Morrigan's nostrils flared. "She's gone."

My pulse spiked into hyperdrive. "What do you mean she's gone? Where did she go?"

"I don't know. I went to your room to talk with both of you, and it was empty." Her gaze fell on Jace.

"It's not what you think—" he started, before she threw up her palm and blue light shot from it.

I leapt in front of him, throwing my own blue fireball at her. It bounced off her chest. I growled in frustration and whipped around to check on Jace. His gold eyes rimmed red, and his lips were pressed together, but otherwise he appeared unharmed.

"Are you okay?" I pressed my hands to his chest, but he didn't answer, or couldn't.

"He's fine," Mommy Dearest said. "I just needed to speak without interruptions."

I whipped back around but stayed close to Jace just in case she shot another fireball at him. "Is your ego that fucking huge?"

Her purple eyes brightened, and her hands fisted at her sides. "Your sister is missing."

Right, that.

I quickly shifted gears. "How do you know? Maybe she's off with someone." I gasped. "Oh no, maybe she's off with Canyon."

"Already checked his room. She's not there, and neither is he."

I remembered the spell Lilith had cast over us. "She can't leave the grounds, though. Lilith made sure of that."

Mama Morrigan pressed her lips together as if debating something. "That's actually not true."

Anger flickered back to life. "What do you mean?"

"She can't actually prevent you from leaving campus.

That *would* be a violation of Silverwood Academy rules, which even she can't break."

My eyes narrowed. "So she lied?"

She winked at me, unapologetic. "Bent the truth."

"Apparently a common theme among the goddesses."

Mommy Dearest's shoulders tightened. Jace wrapped one hand around my shoulder, pushing calming vibes into me, as his other hand sent yellow calming energy at my mother. She failed to notice, however, because her attention was focused on me. Rage swirled around her.

She shook her head, clearing the intense emotions her daughter managed to stir in her. She snapped her fingers. "Thank you, Jace, for reminding me what was important, and what"—her purple eyes settled on me—"will be discussed at another time."

"You're welcome, and if I may be so bold as to point out the similarities between you two . . ."

She pointed at him, and her lips rose in a smile. "I suppose after raising you, you'd know that better than just about anyone, aside from my sisters."

Betrayal stabbed me between the shoulder blades. "You raised Jace?"

She shrugged as if it wasn't a big deal. "Along with my sisters. After what he revealed to you, you can understand why."

I stepped away from Jace, seeking to latch on to my anger. His presence and touch dulled its point. "No, actually, I don't. Not when you abandoned Cyn and me."

"I didn't aban—"

"Ladies, focus!" Jace thundered, his alpha testosterone shooting across the room, hitting both powerful women, wrapping us in a blanket of submission magick.

"What the fuck?" we growled together.

"Cynda is missing. Nothing else matters at present. Do you both agree?" His head whipped back and forth between us, settling first on Mama Morrigan who was the most likely of the two of us to break free from his magick.

"Yes," she ground out through clenched teeth.

His gold eyes met mine, and he raised an eyebrow. A very sexy eyebrow.

"Fine," I conceded.

He snapped his fingers, and the blanket of submission disappeared.

Mama Morrigan pointed at him again. "We will discuss your use of magick on me later. For now, we search for my missing daughter."

My mind immediately shifted into work mode. "I'll check her favorite haunts on campus."

"I don't believe she's within the Silverwood boundary—"

I glared at her criticism of my plan of action.

She pressed her lips together, realizing her overstep was on tenuous grounds. "But that's a good start. Covering our bases is smart."

Jace stepped up beside me. My heart sped up at his proximity.

"I'll go with Dez and protect her."

I punched his shoulder. "I don't need protection. We'd cover more ground if we split up."

Mama Morrigan ignored my reaction, her mind lost in thought. "Yes, yes, please do, Jace." She stared at me as if she wanted to say more, then cleared her throat. "I'll search for Cynda's trail. Where was the last place you saw your sister?"

"I left her, Alyze, and Red in Wildwood Preserves. The building was within sight."

"Okay, that's a start."

Blinding energy shot from her. Instinctively, I covered my eyes. When I pulled my hands away, a large furry black wolf stood where Mama Morrigan once did.

Right, Queen of the Shifters.

"We'll probably get along better this way," I said as I reached over to scratch her head.

She raised her hackles and bared her teeth, snapping them at my hand.

"Or not." I pulled my hand away. "But you forget, if you hadn't locked up my wolf, I'd be able to help you."

The wolf dropped into a low crouch, snarling at me.

Jace pulled on my arm, tugging me away from my mother. "Dez, let's get going." He opened the door and stepped back. "After you," he said to the wolf, who bounded through it.

I stepped out into the hallway in time to see the tail end of Mama Wolf as she rounded the corner.

"It's true, you know."

Jace closed the door behind him. "What is?"

"Both things. It would be helpful if I could turn into a wolf whenever I wanted. *And* I can protect myself."

He sighed as he shoved a sword into a scabbard at his waist. "I swore an oath."

"Humph." I crossed my arms. "We can discuss oath swearing later along with a number of other things."

Heat percolated between us as he sidled up next to me. "So, there *will* be a later?"

Wetness bloomed between my legs. I glanced up at him, swallowing, remembering how mesmerizing his wings were, how mesmerizing all of him was, but my sister was missing, and until we found her, nothing else mattered.

I gestured to his weapon. "Do I get one of those? Or at

least a dagger or something?" I looked around. "And where did it come from?"

He winked at me as he reached into thin air, withdrew a silver dagger, and handed it to me.

I'd heard about individuals who'd mastered Spirit, sometimes called Aether, who could store items in it. But that ability was rare. Only a few in all of history could do it. I swallowed, realizing the implications and remembering that the Mad King had disappeared into the Aether Realm, the origin of Aether and ultimate power.

Jace frowned at me, aware I was studying him. "What?"

His question jerked me out of my daze. There was far more to Jace that met the eye, as there was far more to me and Cynda.

An idea came to me. I took off down the hall, intent on finding my sister.

"Hey, wait up," he called after me.

I ignored him. He could either keep up or catch up—it really didn't matter to me either way.

I clutched the silver dagger handle in my hand. Intent on two things: finding Cynda and killing whoever had taken her.

"Where are we going?"

"I think I might know where she is," I replied before shifting into vamp speed. I took off down the halls, finally stopping at me and Cyn's room.

"What are we doing here? Morrigan already checked here."

I could feel his hot air on my neck. I frowned over my shoulder, surprised that I hadn't lost him. His demon speed matched my vamp speed, a fact I wasn't proud of. Must be because of his age. I hadn't reached my maximum potential in terms of Sempiternal speed and ability, but I far exceeded the other Sempiternals and vamps.

Instead of answering, I pushed into the room, giving it a cursory glance in case Cyn had shown up while we'd been talking with Mama Morrigan, but it was empty. I closed my eyes, absorbing the energy in the room and trying to get a read on my sister's whereabouts.

The door quietly closed, and Jace's earthy scent filled my nostrils. My body thrummed at his presence. He shifted closer but didn't touch me or speak, respectful of my current state of trying to sense my sister.

"Huh," I said under my breath. I hurried to the bathroom and pushed open the door. I stopped in the middle of the room at the exact spot where Cyn had her episode. I closed my eyes again, focusing on the energy there. "Huh."

Jace hovered nearby. "Did you find something?" His words sent shivers down my spine.

I opened my eyes. "I think I did. Well, I remembered something."

"What?"

I swallowed, realizing the possible implications of my sister's new ability and who knew about it. Panic shot through me like a shot of whiskey, but instead of liquid courage, it riddled me with all-consuming fear. My legs wobbled as reality set in, and I realized how weak I was, how long it'd been since I'd fed, which only contributed to the paralyzing fear. "Oh no."

Jace caught my arms. "Dez, what is it? What did you see?"

"I think I know who took Cynda and why." Tears streamed down my cheeks, a flood bursting from a floodgate.

"Who?"

I didn't answer. I couldn't answer.

He squeezed my biceps tighter. "Dez, who?"

"The Children of the Sun."

He cursed. I cursed. And Cyn was cursed.

CHAPTER
TWENTY-SEVEN

yn

MY HEART RACED as my brain replayed everything that had happened. Me catching Canyon's scent down the Spirit hallway where I overheard parts of a conversation that suggested not everyone at Silverwood Academy possessed good intentions. The people who were talking fleeing when they realized they weren't alone. One disappearing into a room. The other racing down the stairs and dashing outside, but not fast enough to lose me. Me ripping Canyon's shirt when I caught him. Him turning the conversation into something else, something more sexual. My stomach roiling at the look of alarm on his face when he realized we weren't alone. Him tugging me into his chest as if to protect me. Then everything went black.

I kept still, careful not to move. Whoever had knocked me out believed I was unconscious, and I wanted to keep it that way until I figured out my situation. I scanned my body first, checking for injuries. The back of my skull hurt, but it wasn't life threatening. I doubted I even had a concussion, especially with my fast Sempiternal healing. I focused on my arms and legs. It didn't feel like I was restrained, at least not with physical bindings like chains, ropes, or zip ties. My back pressed against a semi-solid surface. Not hard floor, but not a bed either. Something in between.

With my body scan complete, my enhanced hearing kicked in. I caught a single heartbeat nearby, pulsing in a steady rhythm, signifying neither prisoner nor worried captor. Whoever it was seemed calm and collected.

I focused harder on my surroundings. There was another heartbeat on the other side of the room. Fast, angry, annoyed, reminding me of a bat trying to get out of a cage.

When Dez and I were imprisoned in the demon dungeon, my sister had called on the elements to discover our location. It gave her a clear impression of our surroundings and potential ways to get out of them. We soon discovered I could bend metal, and we came up with a plan of escape. We wound up not using that ability because the Demon King showed up and released us. Of course, Dez had infuriated him, provoking him to the point in which I feared we'd be locked back in the cell, but he ultimately let us go. Knowing now that Jace was the Demon King put a lot about that situation into perspective. Dez and I could deal with the ramifications of Jace's identity another day. Right now, I needed to figure out where I was.

I called on Earth to guide me with a location. It rustled deep below me and all around me, suggesting I was above ground, but that was all the impression I got.

I called on Fire, searching for the embers of a flame. In the distance, I sensed a series of small fires. Candles perhaps? Or torches? I couldn't decipher which. In either case, it wasn't a definitive enough answer, and I wasn't sure how it could help me.

I called on Water. It surrounded me, in all forms. The blood of whoever was nearby. The gentle flow of channels, pipes maybe, stopping and going.

I called on Air. A soft breeze swept over my face, kissing my cheeks. There, but not enough to tell me anything.

Spirit, could you aid me? Give me an answer as to where I am?

You are home.

I winced, my mind immediately going to the house I grew up in with my adoptive parents. Did they even miss me? Did they think I was dead? Did they even care?

The answer was no. No, they didn't.

I inhaled slowly, following the steady ebb and flow of breath, trying to sense if I was indeed in my childhood home or someplace else. I didn't smell the harsh scent of Meadow Fresh, my adoptive mom's chosen fragrance for detergent and air freshener. Or the strong musk of the aftershave my adoptive dad dabbed on his neck every morning. I did, however, catch the faint hint of cedarwood and mint, but that could still be residual from when Canyon had crushed me to his chest.

"Is she awake yet?" a woman's voice asked, sounding annoyed. The person on the other side of the room.

"Not yet," someone else replied softly.

Tingly warmth ran through me, my body immediately recognizing and reacting to Canyon's voice. He sounded nearby and, dare I say, concerned. That had to be a good sign, right?

"Well, I need to wipe her memories before she rats us out."

Us, as in her and Canyon? So maybe his presence didn't mean we were on the same side. Maybe Dez and Jace were right, and I shouldn't trust him.

"I warned you it was dangerous," he said in a low, deadly voice.

What was?

"You're the one who broke ranks."

"Quiet, you two," a third person hissed, sounding far away. Somehow I'd missed her heartbeat. My ears pricked, recognizing the voice as belonging to the woman from the Spirit hallway. "Outside."

A lock clicked open, followed by the creak and groan of rusty hinges as the woman, the leader if I had to guess, opened a door.

Footsteps paused next to me, bringing with them the scent of cedarwood and mint. My breath hitched at Canyon's sudden presence beside me. I quickly recovered so as not to give myself away. He patted my arm. "Be back soon," he whispered before shuffling away, sounding as if he was dragging one leg across the floor. Was he injured? And if so, had he hurt himself trying to save me from whoever took me? Was that what the other woman meant when she accused him of breaking ranks?

The distinctive sound of a jail cell door slid open, then closed again, answering one of my questions. I was in fact locked in a cell, but my initial impressions didn't indicate any of the typical trappings of a prison or dungeon. Considering I'd already been imprisoned twice, I was something of an expert.

Canyon's footsteps were soon followed by another set,

and then the heavy door banged shut and a lock slid into place.

I peeked an eye open, keeping it half-lidded in case someone had stayed behind.

Empty.

I jumped up, quickly taking in my surroundings. I was locked inside a small cell, maybe eight by eight, which was tucked into a corner of what looked like a Silverwood Academy faculty office: hardwood floors, intricately carved built-in shelving loaded with textbooks, and crown molding encircling the ceiling. A large desk sat opposite me with piles of books and papers scattered across it. But it was what was behind the desk that I was most interested in —a large window. That was my exit.

I rushed over to the cell bars. My palms warmed as I grabbed hold of them and pulled out. The metal bent at my will. But rather than celebrate, I pulled harder. The clock was ticking. I didn't know when my captors would return, and I didn't want to get caught red-handed.

Ha! Red-handed. Because my hands were red?

Never mind, not important.

Once the opening was wide enough, I stepped through, careful of my footing so as not to alert anyone of my escape. I smiled as the bars returned to their original shape.

Yes! Another win. No one would figure out how I'd gotten out of the cell. They'd assume they forgot to lock the cell door. Which ... come to think of it, I don't remember Canyon locking it. Did he leave it unlocked purposely so I could escape?

I shook off the thought. It didn't matter. I couldn't trust him, and I needed to stop hoping he was on my side. Sure he had given me my first orgasm, but that didn't mean I owed him anything. Hells, I could give myself one.

Focus, Cyn. Focus.

I vamp-sped over to the window and pressed on the frame, pushing against it and up. Nothing happened. My hands searched for a latch or something. I glanced at the leather desk chair. Worst case, I could throw it at the window and jump out.

My heart raced. Adrenaline coursed through my veins. Any second my captors would return and discover me out of the cell.

As if manifesting my fear, the lock clicked and the hinges groaned as the door opened.

Shit. Without thinking, I ducked behind the desk. Every muscle in my body tensed. My pulse shot into hyperdrive. I couldn't breathe. Like I forgot how to. Like my lungs forgot how to pump oxygen through my veins. Like I forgot my own name.

"She's gone," the woman who accused Canyon of breaking ranks screamed.

Footsteps hurried in.

"What do you mean she's gone?" Canyon asked.

"Look at the empty cell."

"Crap," he cursed under his breath, though there wasn't any venom to it. It was more like he was acting upset, but he really wasn't.

Quit it, Cynda. Stop trying to make him the good guy.

"I'll search the room. You tell . . . ," he paused as if torn about saying any names, "the appropriate people about the missing prisoner."

My heart broke a little. He suspected I was still in here and didn't want me to know who else was involved.

"Look around, dipshit. She's not here."

"Then I'll search for evidence," he spat.

She snorted. "Like you have any special abilities. If it wasn't for your—"

"Enough," he roared, silencing her, casting an alpha-like presence over the room. I shuddered as it wrapped around me, causing an intense ache between my thighs. I clenched my legs together, trying to keep myself from sighing in pleasure.

Seriously, what was wrong with me? It was one freaking orgasm.

"You're lucky you're sexy as fuck," she sneered.

Mine, a voice snarled inside me as a wave of jealousy blasted through me.

She-Wolfie? What was she doing here? Mama Morrigan had locked her up.

We're ripping out her fucking throat is what we're doing.

Easy, I whispered. *We've got to get out of here.*

After her intestines fall out.

The possessive type. Got it. *Let's escape first, then plan revenge.*

"It's never going to happen, so do what you're told," Canyon told her in a cool, detached voice.

"Fine." She stomped out of the room, the heavy door slamming behind her.

He waited an impossibly long time before calling out in a low, husky voice, "Cynda, are you here?"

Over here, baby, She-Wolfie howled in my head.

You need to stay quiet. We don't know if we can trust him or not.

We don't need to trust him. We need to—

Easy, She-Wolfie, easy. We need to escape. That's what we need to do.

For now, she purred.

Oh goddess. I rolled my eyes. My inner beast was as horny as my sister.

"Cynda, you can trust me."

Said every untrustworthy bad guy ever.

The floor creaked as he approached the cell and tried the cell door. It didn't open.

"Huh," he said under his breath. "I didn't lock it. She must have."

She. The one who hit on our man. Rage rushed through me.

Priorities, I reminded her, and she settled down. I pictured her resting her furry head on her paws like a good little wolf.

I am not little.

Like a good big wolf.

The lock jiggled as a key slid into the mechanism. The cell door slid open, and the floor creaked as he entered.

"Cynda, please talk to me. Show yourself."

I stilled. He thought I went invisible. I had blocked that incident from my mind, compartmentalized it to address at a future date (meaning never).

I could hear him searching around the cell. I pictured him with his hands out, blindly swinging around trying to find me.

And rip our clothes off.

I ignored She-Wolfie. If I could go invisible, I could sneak out of here. I groaned, remembering the other captor had slammed the door shut behind her. There was no way to get out without tipping off my whereabouts.

"Huh, she's not here." He walked out of the cell, sliding the door closed behind him. "Did she lock the cell behind her? Could she walk through the bars when invisible?"

The floor creaked as he approached the desk. "Cynda, come out, come out wherever you are."

Panic returned, but I focused on my breath as I wildly glanced around for someplace to hide. Under the desk maybe. Behind the curtain. Flat on the floor.

Naked in his arms?

Not helping.

Energy flickered through my body. I wasn't sure what was going on, but something definitely was. I didn't remember much of what had happened the night I blinked in and out of existence. My body had writhed with orgasm when Dez ripped Canyon away from me. She had glared at me, holding Canyon by the throat. Uncontrollable anger had coursed through me. The most intense emotion I'd ever felt.

I closed my eyes, trying to find that intense emotion again. Dez wasn't here to piss me off.

No, but that bitch flirted with our man. Jealousy combined with rage is a beautiful thing.

And it was, at least for what I needed at this moment.

My fangs elongated. My claws curled into the wood floor. My body arched and spasmed.

"Gotcha!" Canyon leapt behind the desk.

TWENTY-EIGHT

yn

"Huh, I could've sworn she was here." Canyon scratched his head, looking confused and gorgeous. I slowly edged away from him, backing around the other side of the desk, careful not to make a sound.

He walked over to the window. He pressed his hands against it and pushed up, mirroring my earlier movements, but the window didn't budge.

"Huh, she didn't go out that way. Must be spelled shut," he said to himself. He turned around, his hands in his pockets, and stared out into the room. "So where is she? How did she get out?"

"Cynda," he called out, louder this time, not quite in his alpha voice but close. She-Wolfie whimpered but remained quiet. Why she was attracted to him was beyond me.

Canyon wasn't a shifter. Well, it wasn't completely beyond me. I mean, I was a woman with needs, and he'd met them brilliantly. He was also super smart and kind and caring.

And possibly a murderous asshole member of the Children of the Sun.

Right, and that.

"If you're here, just listen to me. You don't have to be scared. She's gone. No one knows what you're capable of. I didn't tell anyone. Not after what we've been through. That night in your room was the best night of my life."

A wave of dizziness overtook me. Probably hunger. I couldn't remember the last time I'd eaten regular food. I certainly couldn't remember when I last fed. Oh wait, it was with Canyon, during my orgasm. My mouth watered. My fangs tingled.

Dez warned me about not going too long between feedings. Nausea rolled through me. I'd never felt so weak before. Not since I first turned. What was happening to me?

Canyon stepped out into the middle of the room, his back to me. And what a fine back it was.

"I can feel your need," he purred.

She-Wolfie whimpered again.

He slowly turned, scanning the room before his eyes rested on me. His lips rose into a sly grin. "There you are."

And I collapsed on my side, the hunger unbearable.

He sauntered over and knelt down beside me. He scratched at his throat, emphasizing his carotid artery. "Is this what you want?"

She-Wolfie and I whined together.

He curled his arms around me and lifted me to his chest.

"You want me to be the hero, don't you?"

My body shuddered in reply. He dipped his head down to my ear.

"What if I'm the villain?"

CHAPTER
TWENTY-NINE

ez

JACE and I stood stock still, our bodies quivering with rage. Once the words left my mouth that the Children of the Sun were involved with Cynda's disappearance, we both knew it to be true.

He gently squeezed my arms, pulling me back into the present. "We'll find her. I pledge all the resources at my disposal to use in the search for her."

I pulled away in surprise. He'd just promised his entire demon army, but he hadn't even fully accepted his position as king yet. I peered up at him, his gold eyes watching me.

"So, you're taking the crown?"

He sucked in a breath, his nostrils flaring. His chest rose and fell, gathering himself before he answered "Yes" with a finality that reminded me of the proverbial nail in the coffin.

My heart warmed at the gesture. I didn't do romance. I didn't swoon for the handsome hero. I always preferred the morally grey tattooed bad boy. But Jace's admission was the freaking sexiest thing I'd ever experienced. Well, after his wings and horns. But the gravity of the situation and the possible implications were not lost on me.

"You'd do that for me?"

His lips rose in a crooked grin. "You really don't get it, do you?"

I frowned at him. "Get what?"

His head dipped toward my ear, his nose trailing along my jaw, his hot breath fanning across my neck. "I'd do anything for you, Dez."

Wetness bloomed between my thighs. The air shifted from pure, honest confession time to something much more sexual. I pressed my body against him, remembering his wings and horns, and how we'd been interrupted.

"I liked touching your wings."

"You've no idea how erotic it felt."

"We could revisit that feeling right now and see where it plays out," I purred.

He groaned in answer as his wings popped out. I reached out to touch them, no longer asking permission. As my finger hit membrane, a wave of dizziness hit me.

"Whoa." I pulled away, grasping my head, swaying from him. Another wave of dizziness overtook me. I tipped backward, losing my balance, losing all sense of everything.

His arms wrapped around me, catching me before I hit the floor. "Dez, what's wrong?"

My energy dropped away from me like a torrential rainstorm. I envisioned what was happening and tried to stop it, but I couldn't. I'd already been drained and was too weak to try again, completely vanquished. "I . . . don't . . .

feel . . . so . . . good," I moaned, barely able to get the words out.

He swung my legs up, cradling me to his chest. I leaned into the heat of him, shivering.

"You're ice cold," he hissed. "When was the last time you ate?"

I couldn't remember. Cotton balls filled my brain. My tongue felt like sandpaper, thick and swollen. I smacked my lips together to speak, but nothing came out.

"Damn it, Dez. Why did you go so long?"

I shook my head. It hadn't been that long. I'd gone longer before and never felt like this.

"Drink," he ordered, adjusting his hold, lifting me up to his neck.

His jugular pulsed in front of me. My fangs descended. My mouth watered. My body longed for it. But a warning bell rang through my foggy brain.

Girl, don't do it, it warned. *If you drink from him, there could be consequences. Remember your rules. No biting during sex or after. No feeding off energy during sex or after. No biting or feeding off of Jace. No emotional attachments. Period.*

I snorted at the irony of the last rule. I'd become too invested in too many people since arriving at Silverwood Academy. I would have been better off on my own like I'd spent the last three years before entering the Change—a kick-ass Sempiternal bounty hunter. The only reason I attended Silverwood was because of my dad and the prospect of joining Silver Dagger Sisterhood one day. And now look at me . . .

My vision flickered as I slipped in and out of consciousness.

Jace pressed his neck against my mouth. "Drink," he growled.

I closed my lips, fighting the overwhelming urge to bite him and feed.

"Damn it, woman, why must you act so stubborn all the time?"

A sarcastic retort would have been my typical response, but I didn't even possess the energy to talk let alone formulate a witty comeback.

"I don't want to force you," he cried. "Removing someone's will violates everything I believe in."

I shuddered as my internal organs began shutting down.

"But I will make you drink if you refuse." The threat hung in the air, but he wavered. "Dez, I understand your reservations. You don't want to drink from me because I'm a demon. I get it. We're evil. The villains in every story. But if it's a matter of life or death, shouldn't you choose life?"

What a freaking idiot. He thought it was because he was a demon? Please. I couldn't give two shits what he was. The truth was, if the Sempiternal rumors were true, and if I fed from Jace, we could wind up bound together, because I just might care about him as more than a passing fling. And if those rumors were indeed true, the bond could be permanent. No chance of breaking it. I couldn't take that risk. I refused to be bound to anyone.

I stilled. That was it. That was what was happening to me. It wasn't me who'd gone too long without eating, it was Cynda. I'd sired her. I could feel her emotions. That was how I always knew when she was in trouble. And even though I couldn't tell exactly where she was, I had a sense of it. She and I were bound together. So, if I ate . . . would it help her?

My muscles seized as my body continued shutting down.

"Dez, hurry. You don't have much time left," Jace cried.

But there was too much at stake. We'd already marked each other. What if we became permanently bound together? What were the long-term ramifications of such an action?

"Bite," he roared, his alpha voice ripping through the air, just as blackness filled my consciousness.

I snapped back to the present, and before he could finish his order, I bit into his neck.

Not today, Alpha.

He sighed in relief as I drew energy and blood from him. My depleted stores needed both. His demon blood energy raced through my veins, giving me life. Almost immediately I felt better and was tempted to stop, but I wasn't feeding for myself. I was feeding for Cynda. She needed help, and if my theory was correct, filling my energy stores would help her. Maybe even save her.

I'd fed from pretty much every type of supernatural since becoming a full-grown vampire, but I'd never fed off a demon. Not because I had a problem with them, but because there'd never been an opportunity, and of course I had purposely never drawn from Jace. But holy sparkly blood energy! I felt like my veins were filling with glitter and I could fight the freaking world—and win with just my fists.

His chest rumbled as I drew from him. The venom I released from my fangs induced carnal desire, an aphrodisiac to many. From the sounds of it, Jace was enjoying himself, more so than anyone else I'd ever fed off of. I tried not to overthink the implications, attributing his reaction to the intense sexual chemistry between the two of us and not something more.

When I finally felt sated, I licked the marks, sealing

them back up. He shuddered as I pulled away from his neck and collapsed into his arms. I would allow myself a moment to feel safe and nestled in his cocoon before dropping the truth bomb on him about me and Cynda being bound together. But first, I wanted to confirm it.

I closed my eyes and pulled on the thread that tied me to her, similar to the marking tie Jace and I shared but somehow different. Life vibrated through the cord, but it was tenuous at best. She needed to feed on her own soon. The proxy feeding had worked well enough for immediate relief, but it wouldn't continue to sustain her as it had sustained me.

"Better?" he whispered.

"Uh-huh." I sighed, opening my eyes as I lifted my head. "Much better. You can put me down now."

His fingers curled around me, as if unwilling to release me.

"Jace," I said gently, not wanting to scold him but also warning him that I wasn't his possession.

"Right," he nodded, carefully lowering my legs until I stood on my own two feet. He stayed close, his arms ready to catch me if I fell, but his concern was unwarranted.

In fact, I felt amazing. I smiled up at him in absolute wonder.

"You feel okay then? Not repulsed that you drank from a demon?"

I swatted his chest. "Would you stop with that shit. I don't care if you're a demon. I don't care what you are."

"You say that now, but why didn't you want to feed from me?"

I could feel my cheeks blush, which was a surprise reaction. I wasn't embarrassed of the reason. Well, mostly.

He ducked down so we stood face-to-face. "What is it, Dez? Tell me."

His forehead pinched in worry. I raised my finger and pressed it into his third eye, an intimate gesture given his dedication to meditation. I squeezed my lips together, contemplating what I wanted to tell him.

"What is it?" he whispered, sounding almost fearful.

His concern literally pained me. I cleared my throat.

Nope, not going *there* today. I shoved my hands in my pockets.

"I think by killing my sister and forcing the Change, I might have sired her, thereby binding her to me."

He blew out a sigh of relief and straightened, rubbing his hand along the back of his neck. "It's possible."

"And a few minutes ago, when I collapsed, it wasn't because I haven't eaten in a long time."

His gold eyes met mine, his eyebrow raised as if doubting me.

Annoyance grew within me. "I fed at the Silver Crescent Moon Festival. Feasted, actually, until I was rudely interrupted and forced into two elemental acquisitions."

His nostrils flared as he glared at me. "You gained three elements, and you didn't eat?"

I put my hands on my hips. "Don't even start with me. We're not talking about me."

His jaw tightened. "What are we talking about then?"

"Cyn. We're talking about my sister. I felt her. Her emptiness. She hasn't eaten since she bit into Canyon, and she's still new. She needs to feed more often than a seasoned Sempiternal."

He frowned at me. "You're not *that* seasoned."

"I. Know. My. Limits. Don't. Push. Them," I ground out.

"You drive me mad."

"Welcome to the club, Demon Boy."

He snorted. "I am no boy. I'm all man, as you well know."

I spun around, storming away from him. "We keep talking in circles. I don't have time for this."

He chased after me. "Where are you going?"

"To find my sister?"

"How?"

"The same way you and I always find each other. Cyn and I are tied together."

He grabbed my shoulder and skidded to a halt, causing me to stop with him. He spun me around to look at him. "That's why you didn't want to feed from me. It could further cement our relationship."

I rolled my eyes, not wanting to have this conversation right now with my sister missing. It was too late now anyway. I'd only find out the next time I fed on someone else. I'd either keep the blood down or puke it all over the floor.

"Something like that. Now, can we go?"

"We're marked, Dez. What difference does it make if you feed from me? You almost died." His face pinched together as if the mere thought of my death hurt him. Hells, for all I knew, maybe it did.

"Because Cyn almost died, and she needs us to find her. She was on campus and now she's not. I can feel it. And I don't want to be bound to you."

"Bound?" He dropped his hand from me. "What the—" Then his eyes widened as realization dawned on him. I could read his mind as if it were my own. "So, the legends *are* true?"

I looked away from him. "I don't know."

He lifted my chin so we stood face-to-face, sharing the same air. "Yes, you do."

I pressed my lips to his before tearing away and taking off down the hall. Distraction always worked.

CHAPTER
THIRTY

yn

I HAD ALMOST DIED. All-consuming hunger had overtaken me, weakening me to the point of complete and utter collapse. Never before, not even when I was a new Sempiternal, had the longings sucked my life vitality from me. Was it because I'd gone invisible? Used up too much of my energy stores? Gone too long between feedings? Most likely all of the above. All I knew was, if I didn't eat soon, I'd shrivel into a dried-out corn husk.

That was when Canyon had approached me. I remembered smacking my lips together in anticipation of him helping me. I'd fed from him before. The last time at his request. He lifted me into his arms, and I expected salvation. Instead he'd asked me what I'd think if he was the villain. Then everything went black.

Did I pass out? Did Canyon knock me out? I couldn't remember.

My consciousness had swum in and out of a dense fog. I'd waded through, almost breaking free to the other side, but then I'd get sucked back in and have to start all over.

Then something happened. Life flowed through me, reaching my toes, my fingers, my heart, but it wasn't from blood energy I'd consumed. It was different. Filling me, bringing me back from the brink, but different. A sensation I'd never felt before.

Dez.

After her name came to mind, I knew with absolute certainty she was the cause of the energy racing through me now, catapulting me out of the fog with the force of a thousand sisters. Never before had I felt such a connection to her. I reached out with my mind, trying to sense her, but she wasn't anywhere nearby.

But she'd saved me. My sister, my fierce protector, had saved me. Her love warmed my soul. I could feel her concern, her worry, or at least the inkling of it. She was far away, but I wanted to ease her mind, at least a little bit.

Dez. Hey, Sis, can you hear me?

Cynda? she screamed into my subconscious.

I winced, not ready for the intensity of her voice in my head.

The one and only.

Are you okay?

I'm alive. That's something, right?

Oh, thank the goddess," she said with a sigh. *Where are you? I can't sense you on campus.*

I don't know. I just came to. I panted at the effort of telepathy. There was always a cost to magick, and when one's stores of energy were already low, the cost doubled with interest.

Well, assess and get back to me. I can feel you fading. Don't overuse our connection.

Got it. I'll be in touch soon.

Cynda? she whispered in my head, which kinda creeped me out, especially because she sounded hesitant, and that was not an adjective I'd ever use to describe my sister.

Yeah?

I WILL find you. If it's the last thing I do, I WILL find you.

I smiled to myself. The familial connection between us was undeniable. *I know.*

Now, get your ass moving and figure out where the fuck you are.

And that was the sister I knew and loved.

I shut off the connection and came back to full consciousness. I soon realized my situation was much more complicated than last time. The cot in a cell in a professor's office was child's play compared to this. First of all, my arms and legs were strapped down to a bed. The bindings burned, but it wasn't unbearable. Most likely silver chains dipped in wolfsbane. It was a common misconception that silver weakened vampires, but wolfsbane caused a chemical reaction with the silver, making it toxic to many supernaturals. My captors at least knew that much about my true nature, but it was doubtful they knew all of what I was.

I inhaled slowly so as not to hint that I had returned to consciousness. The air smelled musty and damp—an abandoned house perhaps? I pulled back the layers and caught the scent of cedarwood and mint along with a flowery scent. I inhaled more deeply. Definitely a floral aroma, but I hadn't spent enough time in the garden to pick out the nuances. There were also undertones of a sickeningly sweet scent floating about that caused my stomach to roil, triggering a memory of me racing down the dark hallway after Canyon. I hadn't taken note of that sweet smell at the time, but my nose had. It belonged to whoever had met with him. So, at least three guards. But unlike last time, I doubted they'd leave me unsupervised, and with my arms and legs bound, there was little chance of escape.

I closed off my nose and concentrated on my hearing. Two heartbeats, one beating much faster than the other. Canyon maybe? Was he concerned about my welfare.

I could just imagine Dez growling at me, *"Fucking stop, Cyn. He admitted he was the villain."*

And she was right. He did say as much to me, and I couldn't delude myself into thinking he was anything other than the bad guy.

"When do you and I get to have some one-on-one time like you promised?" the female captor asked.

"Quiet," Canyon grunted. "She's waking."

My heart broke. All the times Canyon and I had been together, and he'd made a promise to this chick? She was going to be his side piece?

I sucked in a breath as another thought came to mind.

Or *I* was the side piece.

Or it was a game all along, and I'd played right into it.

None of the options brought particularly warm and fuzzy thoughts to mind. Besides, none of it mattered anyway. And if this was a game, I would play my part beautifully—the damsel in distress who would shove a dagger into Canyon's cold, back-stabbing heart.

I slowly blinked my eyes open as if just coming to. "Canyon?" I whispered.

A chair creaked as someone, Canyon presumably, stood up and walked over.

"Hey there." He smiled down at me, his green eyes bright. Tears pricked the corner of mine. I'd trusted him, and that bastard had kidnapped me and not let me feed from him when it really mattered. When my life depended on it.

"Hi," I whispered, my voice cracking without my even trying. I couldn't remember the last time I'd had anything to drink—blood, water, or otherwise.

He sat down on the bed, causing my body to dip into him and, as a result, my bindings to pull at my wrists and ankles. I quickly took in the side of the room. An end table with a small lamp cast the only light. There was a curtained window less than five feet away and torn wallpaper— classic eighties.

"How you feeling?"

I groaned, which wasn't acting either. "I've been better."

He snorted. "I suspect you have."

I licked my lips, and his eyes tracked the movement. He placed his arm on the other side of my head, leaning closer. Was this part of the act too, or was he naturally drawn to me and merely an unwilling pawn in this game?

Cyn, snap the fuck out of it. It doesn't matter. But you can use any attraction he feels from you to your advantage. You are a Sempiternal. You can compel him if you need to.

"Where am I?"

His eyes darted away from me as if looking at someone on the other side of the bed, then they returned back to me. "You're safe."

I scrunched up my forehead, feigning confusion, which

wasn't far off from my actual feelings. "Safe?" I repeated. "Safe from what?"

"She's not safe from me," the female sneered in such a way that it triggered a memory in me. And then I realized who she was. Azalea. But what was a pixie doing with Canyon? I cringed at the very thought.

"You. Won't. Touch. Her," he growled in his alpha voice. Demand for submission shot across the room at her. I sensed her lower her head, and I realized that I probably should lower mine too and act like he dominated me.

Dez thought he might be part faerie, but he'd never admitted to that. His mom was a turned vampire, though maybe Canyon's father was a wolf or something. But he didn't smell like a shifter . . . at least not one I was familiar with.

"No need to bow, Cynda. That wasn't directed at you," he said in a low, husky voice, as if in confidence to me.

He trailed a finger along the side of my face. Without thinking, I leaned into it as he wound some of my hair around his finger and lifted it to his nose. He inhaled deeply.

"I've never smelled anyone so lovely." He dipped his head toward my ear, his hot breath fanning across my neck. "Someday I will taste you. All of you."

Everything below my belly button tightened at the prospect of Canyon's tongue between my legs. I moaned in pleasure as wetness pooled at my apex.

He inhaled sharply, scenting my arousal. His lips rose into a devilish grin. "Even now, with your arms and legs bound, you still want me."

And to douse myself with a bucket of ice-cold water. What the fuck was wrong with me? And he could freaking smell me, so he was definitely more than human?

But I played the part.

"Yes," I sighed.

"Canyon, you promised once I helped you capture her, you and I would be together," Azalea snapped.

What the . . . ? What the what?

"Quiet," he snarled, his eyes flashing gold, scales shooting up his arms and neck.

Dragon. Canyon was dragon.

And what did dragons cherish most?

Treasure. Did that mean I was part of his hoard?

His eyes shot to mine, realizing that I'd witnessed something I shouldn't have.

"You. Didn't. See. Anything," he said, shooting his alpha power at me.

"I didn't see anything," I parroted. But I totally did.

Three sharp knocks at the door drew his attention away from me.

"Get the door," he barked at Azalea.

I quickly looked over to the other side of the room, and yes, Azalea, the pixie bitch, stood up from her chair, reeking of the promise of delivering violence as soon as she could. She stalked to the door and waved her hand over the knob. A stream of purple magick shot out and sank into the door. The door opened on its own. Before whoever was on the other side walked through, I scanned the rest of the room. One window, three doors—one obviously leading to a hallway or foyer, another to a bathroom if I had to guess, and a third leading to a closet maybe. Sickly yellow wallpaper with blue and orange pineapples and other colonial shapes covered the room. The four-poster mahogany bed sat in the middle of the room. All the decor reminded me of an eighties sitcom of some upper middle class family living in the suburbs. It hadn't been modernized in decades or, based on the dust and cobwebs, lived in since. Where the heck were we?

"Well, well, well. Look who we have here," a woman crowed. My attention snapped to her, and my stomach soured in disgust. Professor Goldwell had kidnapped me. She prowled into the room, ignoring Azalea, who closed the door behind her.

My nose filled, first with the sickeningly sweet scent I now recognized as Goldwell, followed by a delicious metallic scent. My eyes shot to the corner of her mouth, where red blood dripped from it. My mouth watered, and my overwhelming hunger returned.

Her lips curled in delight. "Oh, this?" She swiped it off with the tip of a red-nailed finger and popped it in her mouth. "That was my snack. Too bad she's dead now, or I'd offer you some." She lifted her hand up to the side of her mouth as if conspiring with me. "Actually, no, I wouldn't. You've been a naughty, naughty girl, and I can't wait to reveal to you all the fun we have in store for you."

"Fun?" I squeaked.

She threw back her head and cackled before glaring at me. "By fun, I mean torture. I can't wait to torture you."

Canyon stood up. "Mom, can we talk in my old room?"

Her lips rose into a smile. It seemed genuine. Well, as genuine as a lying bitch could be.

"Of course, darling, whatever you'd like." She spun and stalked over to the door. "Open."

Azalea rushed over and sent her magick across it. Goldwell waltzed through with Canyon close behind. He stopped at the threshold and glared at the pixie.

"You lay a finger on her, and you die. Do you understand?"

She whimpered, dropping her head in submission.

"Excellent. Cynda, baby, I'll see you soon." He winked at me, then closed the door behind him.

Well, I wasn't sure what type of torture Goldwell had in mind, but Canyon might add a fun, spicy component to it.

Goddess, I had been hanging out with my sister too long. But at least I knew where we were. Canyon had dropped that subtle hint for my benefit.

Hey, Dez? I called out in my head.

Where the fuck have you been?

Sorry, bit busy here. Professor Goldwell, Canyon, and Azalea kidnapped me. They're keeping me at Goldwell's old house.

On my way. Cyn, hold on and fight like the fierce warrior you are.

Always, Sister.

Always.

THE END

Preorder VAMP TEMPTED now!

Let's talk about VAMP AWAKENED and other bookish things with Kim at KB Anne's Silver Dagger Readers Facebook Group

Keep reading for a sample of WIDE AWAKE: THE GODDESS CHRONICLES

ABOUT THE AUTHOR

KB Anne is the bestselling author of multiple series including Vamp Revealed: Silver Dagger Sisterhood, Wide Awake: The Goddess Chronicles, and Throne of Silver: Silver Fae series. KB Anne writes urban fantasy and paranormal romance with fierce females, swoon-worthy, irresistible heroes, and explosive action because everyone needs excitement in their lives.

She lives in Northeast PA with 3 goblins, a task master, two hell hound overlords, and 2 unicorns, but they don't fart glitter.

KB Anne loves to hear from readers and can be reached at Kim@kbanne.com or join her Facebook group, KB Anne Silver Dagger Readers, https://www.facebook.com/groups/1029150567998675

Sign up for her monthly newsletter! Get early access to

her books, inside details, and free stuff including VAMP DISCOVERED, about Cyn and Dez's time at Silverwood Prison.

https://mailchi.mp/14f85a3218c6/silverdagger

WANT TO READ ABOUT CYN & DEZ'S TIME IN SILVERWOOD PRISON?
Join KB Anne's Newsletter and get exclusive subscriber only VAMP DISCOVERED for FREE! Plus, be the FIRST to find out about new releases from Best-Selling Author, K.B. Anne. PLUS, receive Newsletter Subscriber Only Bonus Content, insight on Celtic Mythology, Druids, Witches, Werewolves, and Magic, and so much more!

Contact info:

www.KBAnne.com
kim@kbanne.com

facebook.com/KBAnneWrite
twitter.com/KBAnneWrite
instagram.com/KBAnneWrite

ALSO BY KB ANNE

Silver Dagger Sisterhood

Vamp Revealed: Silverwood Academy Book 1

Vamp Awakened: Silverwood Academy Book 2

Vamp Tempted: Silverwood Academy Book 3

Vamp Discovered: Silverwood Prison, A Silver Dagger Sisterhood
Novella (only available to newsletter subscribers)

The Goddess Chronicles (COMPLETE)

Wide Awake: The Goddess Chronicles Book 1

Blood Moon: The Goddess Chronicles Book 2

Dark Moon: The Goddess Chronicles Book 3

Shadow Moon: The Goddess Chronicles Book 4

Oak Moon: The Goddess Chronicles Book 5

Storm Moon: The Goddess Chronicles Book 6

The Goddess Chronicles Books 1-3 Boxset

The Goddess Chronicles Books 4-6 Boxset

The Druid Sisters of the Gallicenial Novella (only available to
newsletter subscribers)

The Silver Fae Series (COMPLETE)

Throne of Silver: Silver Fae 1

Silver Fae Hunter: Silver Fae 2

Heirs of Wings and Shadows: Silver Fae 3

Court of Wings and Shadows: Silver Fae 4

Crown of Flames: Silver Fae 5

Silver Shift Novella (Christian's POV only available to newsletter subscribers)

Silver Fae Games

A Curse of Silver Ruin: Silver Fae Games 1

A Game of Wings & Teeth: Silver Fae Games 2

A Kingdom of Shadows & Blood: Silver Fae Games 3

WIDE AWAKE: THE GODDESS CHRONICLES BOOK ONE

THE PROPHECY

One of love, one of light,
Spring forth from the womb
To guard from the night.

The power to heal. The power of youth.
Their existence to all a living proof.

As immortality weighs,
One shall fall, one shall rise,
To perish from all humankind.

GLITTER-FARTING UNICORNS

I lie. I cheat. I steal.

Parents don't trust me with their daughters or their sons.

That desk shoved next to the teacher's desk? Mine.

The hint of smoke in the bathroom when you apply your lip gloss? That's me.

The "inappropriate" language scrawled across the fifty-seven million posters advertising the pep rally? You're welcome.

Did you find my use of color on the drawing depicting the mating habits of Kensey and her boyfriend particularly intriguing?

Good. I'm glad we agree. But don't get too comfortable with that bony ass of yours, because if I find you in my seat at the principal's office, I'll wrap my black-tipped daggers around your designer-label shirt and make you realize that after-school detention for skipping class is the least of your worries.

"*Freak*," you'll mutter to yourself, and you'll be right.

Oh, and by the way, "Skunk Girl?"

One would think the combined efforts of three-quarters of the junior class could serve as one master brain and come up with a nickname a bit more imaginative than "Skunk Girl." Ever hear of Google?

Honestly.

The torture I'm subjected to on a daily basis is un-freaking-believable.

"Gigi," Mrs. Kelso whispers, pushing her bowl of fall-themed York Peppermint Patties over to me, "he caught you on film."

I shrug with indifference as I unwrap my orange-foiled mint. It's only a matter of time before they kick me out. The school shouldn't spend so much energy disciplining one troubled youth.

Principal Donahue's door swings open.

Make that two troubled youths.

At Donahue's side stands a shiny new plaything.

Black leather jacket.

Black motorcycle boots.

Ripped jeans.

Tall, muscular body wearing his clothing admirably.

Expulsion becomes the last thing on my mind. For once the rumors are true, and I am front and center to the greatest novelty our school has ever witnessed: the foreign exchange student. Three words packed with the promise of awkward fumblings in janitor's closets without all that pesky long-term commitment business getting in the way.

His steely gray eyes pin me in place like the dead swallowtail butterfly I mounted on cardboard when I was seven. Together we fall into a cheesy '80s movie scene with sunshine beaming on the drool-worthy specimen while unicorns fart glitter rainbows out of their asses. In a long, drawn-out moment, I imagine all the legendary things we can do together.

Until he opens his mouth.

"You're mine," he says in a deep, husky Irish accent.

The surprise of his voice combined with his words turns my brain into a useless pile of shit. I have no doubt that an extraterrestrial being is about to rip through my chest full-on *Alien* style.

This boy—no, this man—glides across the room and out the door, leaving Mrs. Kelso and me staring at each other like mind-blown idiots. And the hammering in my chest makes me think I'm having a heart attack.

"Doris!" Principal Donahue bellows from his doorway, jerking us back into the present. "Get Dr. McCleery on the line—"

I reach for a black-foiled mint, hoping to steady my pounding heart. Why would Donahue need to speak to Uncle Mark anyway?

"—And send in The Delinquent."

Ah, yes. That's my other nickname.

Original, I know.

My heart continues to pound against my rib cage, but it has nothing to do with nerves about being called into the principal's office. No, this chest pain is something different. Something life-threatening. I can only hope that Mrs. Kelso's defibrillator certifications are up to date, because if I die on shag carpeting installed by the lowest bidder it would be a travesty. Fitting, but a travesty.

The mountains of reports teetering at the front corner of Donahue's desk beg me to knock into them. I find nothing more beautiful than sending reams of paper spiraling in a chaotic rhythm to the floor. Well, except for maybe watching the giant of a man pick it all up.

But not today.

Today, foreign encounters of the bizarre kind have thrown off my thirst for small acts of violence and disruption.

"Cigarettes, Gigi?" he says, followed by an exasperated sigh. "You don't even smoke."

I choose not to disagree with him. When I lie my throat burns like the hot coals I almost swallowed at the Fourth of July barbecue involving intoxication, a dare, and a poorly executed circus trick. The cameras in the school don't lie either. And the pack of cigarettes on his desk along with the zebra-print lighter carved with "Gigi" sitting on top of the green folder? Cold, hard evidence.

I shrug. "I like the smell."

His eyebrows melt into his protruding forehead. Small children have gone lost in there, never to return.

"You like the smell of cigarettes?"

And so, begins our daily staring contest. Each of us searching for the missing plate in the other's armor before loosing the final black iron arrow. These battles have gone on for hours. Sometimes days. Often weeks. Neither one of us willing to admit defeat. Neither one of us willing to yield.

That is until today.

The intercom squawks during a particularly intense clash. Donahue narrows his eyes, still glaring at me as he presses the button.

"Yes, Doris?"

"Dr. Donahue, Dr. McCleery is on the line."

The bulging vein in his forehead thrums into action. "Miss Brennan, you and I aren't through with this conversation. Tell Mrs. Kelso to add another ten days of after-school detention to your sentence."

"So, that puts me at five years past my graduation date?"

He ignores my smart retort, more interested in speaking with Uncle Mark instead.

"Hello, Dr. McCleery. Yes, I wanted to talk to you about Breas, your foreign exchange student?"

That's the hunky Irishman's name. Figures.

"He and I have had several differences in opinion. I would appreciate it if you could come in to discuss the matter further."

Stunned into silence, I sit as a delinquent-in-waiting.

Fire alarms have gone off. Food fights have broken out. Angry parents have banged on his door, and still, after one of us claims victory, he always, I mean *always*, begins with his "Make Good Choices" lecture and leads into "This is the last time, young lady. Next stop, Juvie."

But he skips the lecture and doesn't even dismiss me with his trademark off-you-go wave, because he's completely absorbed in his conversation with Uncle Mark.

And speaking of Uncle Mark, why did he fail to mention Breas's arrival last night at dinner or the half dozen other nights last week? Having some stranger live with you seems a pretty important event in one's life, but no. He said nothing. He acted as Principal Donahue is acting now. As if I am invisible. As if Breas's housing situation has nothing to do with me.

And as for that initial attraction I felt?

It vanished the moment he claimed me as his.

I, Gigi Brennan, belong to no one.

Keep reading WIDE AWAKE: THE GODDESS CHRONICLES
BOOK ONE

www.ingramcontent.com/pod-product-compliance
Lightning Source LLC
Chambersburg PA
CBHW030117180626
46812CB00002B/454